Mrs Reinhardt 🌿

and other stories

Edna O'Brien

Mrs Reinhardt

and other stories

Weidenfeld and Nicolson
London

For Sonia Melchett

Contents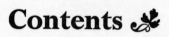

You who by love brought into being delirium in my heart,
O Dion.

Plato

Number Ten 🍂

Everything began to be better for Mrs Reinhardt from the moment she started to sleepwalk. Every night her journey yielded a fresh surprise. First it was that she saw sheep – not sheep as one sees them in life, a bit sooty and bleating away, but sheep as one sees them in a dream. She saw myriads of white fleece on a hilltop, surrounded by little lambs frisking and suckling to their hearts' content.

Then she saw pictures such as she had not seen in life. Her husband owned an art gallery and Mrs Reinhardt had the opportunity to see many pictures, yet the ones she saw at night were much more satisfying. For one thing she was inside them. She was not an outsider looking in, making idiotic remarks, she was part of the picture: an arm or a lily or the grey mane of a horse. She did not have to compete, did not have to say anything. All her movements were preordained. She was simply aware of her own breath, a soft steady, sustaining breath.

In the mornings her husband would say she looked a bit frayed or a bit intense, and she would say, 'Nonsense,' because in fifteen years of marriage she had never felt better. Her sleeping life suited her and, of course, she never knew what to expect. Her daily life had a pattern to it. Weekday mornings she spent at home, helping or supervising Fatima, the Spanish maid. She gave two afternoons a week to teaching autistic children, two afternoons were devoted to an exercise class, and on Fridays she shopped in Harrods and got all the groceries for the weekend. Mr Reinhardt had bought a farm two years before, and weekends they spent in the country, in their newly renovated cottage. In the country she did not sleepwalk, and Mrs Reinhardt wondered if it might be that she was inhibited by the barbed-wire fence that skirted their garden. But there are gates, she thought, and I should open them. She was a little vexed with herself for not being more venturesome.

Then one May night, in her house in London, she had an incredible dream. She walked over a field with her youngest son – in real life he was at university – and all of a sudden, and in unison, the two of them knelt down and began scraping the earth up with their bare hands. It was a rich red earth and easy to crumble. They were so eager because they knew that treasure was about to be theirs. Sure enough, they found bits of gold, tiny specks of it, which they put in a handkerchief, and then to crown her happiness Mrs Reinhardt found the loveliest little gold key, and held it up to the light while her son laughed and in a baby voice said, 'Mama.'

Soon after this dream Mrs Reinhardt embarked on a bit of spring cleaning. Curtains and carpets for the dry cleaners, drawers depleted of all the old useless odds and ends that had been piling up. Her husband's clothing, too, she must put in order. A little rift had sprung up between them and was widening day by day. He was moody. He got home later than usual and, though he did not say so, she knew that he had stopped at the corner and had a few drinks. Once of late he had pulled her down beside him on the living-room sofa and stroked her thighs and started to undress her within hearing distance of Fatima, who was in the kitchen chopping and singing. Always chopping and singing or humming. For the most part, though, Mr Reinhardt went straight to the liquor cabinet and gave them both a gin, pouring himself a bigger one because, as he said, all her bloody fasting made Mrs Reinhardt light-headed.

She was sorting Mr Reinhardt's shirts – tee shirts, summer sweaters, thick crew-neck sweaters – and putting them each in a neat pile, when out of his seersucker jacket there tumbled a little gold key that caused her to let out a cry. The first thing she felt was a jet of fear. Then she bent down and picked it up. It was exactly like the one in her sleepwalk. She held it in her hand, promising herself never to let it go. What fools we are to pursue in daylight what we should leave for night-time.

Her next sleepwalking brought Mrs Reinhardt out of her house into a waiting taxi and, some distance away, to a mews house. Outside the mews house was a black and white tub filled with pretty flowers. She simply put her hand under a bit of foliage and there was the latchkey. Inside was a little nest. The wallpaper in the hall was the very one she had always wanted for their house, a pale gold with the tiniest white flowers – mere suggestions of flowers, like those of the wild strawberry. The kitchen was immaculate. On the landing upstairs was a little fretwork bench. The cushions in the sitting room were stiff and stately, and so was the upholstery, but the bedroom – ah, the bedroom.

It was everything she had ever wanted their own to be. In fact, the bedroom *was* the very room she had envisaged over and over again and had described to her husband down to the last detail. Here it was – a brass bed with a little lace canopy above it, the entire opposite wall a dark metallic mirror in which dark shadows seemed to swim around; a light-blue velvet chaise longue, a hanging plant with shining leaves and a floor lamp with a brown-fringed shade that gave off the softest of light.

She sat on the edge of the bed, marvelling, and saw the other things that she had always wanted. She saw, for instance, the photo of a little girl in First Communion attire; she saw the paperweight that when shaken yielded a miniature snowstorm; she saw the mother-of-pearl tray with the two champagne glasses – and all of a sudden she began to cry because her happiness was so immense. Perhaps, she thought, he will come to me here, he will visit, and it will be like the old days and he won't be irritable and he won't be tapping with his fingers or fiddling with the lever of his fountain pen. He will smother me with hugs and kisses and we will tumble about on the big foamy bed.

She sat there in the bedroom and she touched nothing, not

even the two white irises in the tall glass vase. The little key was
in her hand and she knew it was for the wardrobe and that she
had only to open it to find there a nightdress with a pleated top,
a voile dance dress, a silver fox cape, and a pair of sling-back
shoes. But she did not open it. She wanted to leave something a
secret. She crept away and was home in her own bed without her
husband being aware of her absence. He had complained on
other occasions about her cold feet as she got back into bed,
and asked in Christ's name what was she doing – making tea or
what? That morning her happiness was so great that she leaned
over, unknotted his pyjamas, and made love to him very sweetly,
very slowly and to his apparent delight. Yet when he wakened
he was angry, as if a wrong had been done him.

Naturally, Mrs Reinhardt now went to the mews house night
after night, and her heart would light up as she saw the pillar
of the house with its number, ten, lettered in gold edged with
black. The nought was a little slanted. Sometimes she got into
the brass bed and she knew it was only a question of time
before Mr Reinhardt followed her there.

One night as she lay in the bed, a little breathless, he came in
very softly, closed the door, removed his dressing gown, and
took possession of her with such a force that afterward she
suspected she had a broken rib. They used words that they had
not used for years. She was young and wild. A lovely fever took
hold of her. She was saucy while he kept imploring her to please
marry him, to please give up her independence, to please be
his – adding that even if she said no he was going to whisk her
off. Then to prove his point he took possession of her again. She
almost died, so deep and so thorough was her pleasure, and
each time as she came back to her senses she saw some little
object or trinket that was intended to add to her pleasure – once
it was a mobile in which silver horses chased one another
around, once it was a sound as of a running stream. He gave her
some champagne and they drank in utter silence.

But when she wakened from this idyll she was in fact in her
own bed and so was he. She felt mortified. Had she cried out in
her sleep? Had she moaned? There was no rib broken. She
reached for the hand mirror and saw no sign of wantonness on

her face, no tossed hair, and the buttons of her nightdress were neatly done up to the throat.

He was a solid mass of sleep. He opened his eyes. She said something to him, something anxious, but he did not reply. She got out of bed and went down to the sitting room to think. Where would it all lead to? Should she tell him? She thought not. All morning she tried the key in different locks, but it was too small. In fact, once she nearly lost it because it slipped into a lock and she had to tease it out with the prong of a fork. Of course she did not let Fatima, the maid, see what she was doing.

It was Friday, their day to go to the country, and she was feeling reluctant about it. She knew that when they arrived they would rush around their garden and look at their plants to see if they'd grown a bit, and look at the rose leaves to make sure there were no greenfly. Then, staring out across the fields to where the cows were, they would tell each other how lucky they were to have such a nice place, and how clever. The magnolia flowers would be fully out and she would stand and stare at the tree as if by staring at it she could imbue her body with something of its whiteness.

The magnolia was out when they arrived – like little white china eggcups, each bloom with its leaves lifted to the heavens. Two of the elms definitely had the blight, Mr Reinhardt said, as the leaves were withering away. The elms would have to be chopped, and Mr Reinhardt estimated that there would be enough firewood for two winters. He would speak to the farm manager, who lived down the road, about this. They carried in the shopping, raised the blinds, and switched on the central heating. The little kitchen was just as they had left it, except that the primroses in the jar had faded and were like bits of yellow skin. She unpacked the food they had brought, put some things in the fridge, and began to peel the carrots and potatoes for the evening meal. Mr Reinhardt hammered four picture hooks into the wall for the new prints that he had brought down. From time to time he would call her to ask what order he should put them in, and she would go in, her hands covered with flour and rather absently suggest a grouping.

She had the little key with her in her purse and would open the purse from time to time to make sure that it was there. Then she would blush.

At dusk she went out to get a branch of apple wood for the fire, in order to engender a lovely smell. A bird chirped from a tree. It was more sound than song. She could not tell what bird it was. The magnolia tree was a mass of white in the surrounding darkness. The dew was falling and she bent for a moment to touch the wet grass. She wished it were Sunday, so that they could be going home. In London the evenings seemed to pass more quickly and they each had more chores to do. She felt in some way she was deceiving him.

They drank some red wine as they sat by the fire. Mr Reinhardt was fidgety but at the very same time accused her of being fidgety. He was being adamant about the Common Market. Why did he expound on the logistics of it when she was not even contradicting him? He got carried away, made gestures, said he loved England, loved it passionately, that England was going to the dogs. When she got up to push in a log that had fallen from the grate, he asked her for God's sake to pay attention.

She sat down at once, and hoped that there was not going to be one of those terrible, unexpected, meaningless rows. But blessedly they were distracted. She heard him say, 'Crikey!' and then she looked up and saw what he had just seen. There was a herd of cattle staring in at them. She jumped up. Mr Reinhardt rushed to the phone to call the farm manager, since he himself knew nothing about country life, certainly not how to drive away cattle.

She grabbed a walking stick and went outside to prevent the cows from falling in the swimming pool. It was cold out of doors and the wind rustled in all the trees. The cows looked at her, suspicious. Their ears pricked. She made tentative movements with the stick, and at that moment four of them leaped over the barbed wire and back into the adjoining field. The remaining cow began to race around. From the field the four cows began to bawl. The fifth cow was butting against the paling. Mrs Reinhardt thought, I know what you are feeling – you are feeling lost and muddled and you have gone astray.

Her husband came out in a frenzy because when he rang the farm manager no one was there.

'Bloody never there!' he said. His loud voice so frightened the fifth cow that she made a leap for it and got stuck in the barbed wire. Mrs Reinhardt could see the barb in her huge udder and thought what a place for it to have landed. They must rescue her. Very cautiously they both approached the animal, and the intention was that Mr Reinhardt would hold the cow while Mrs Reinhardt freed the flesh. She tried to be gentle. The cow's smell was milky, and soft compared with her roar, which was beseeching. Mr Reinhardt caught hold of the hindquarters and told his wife to hurry up. The cow was obstreperous. As Mrs Reinhardt lifted the bleeding flesh away, the cow took a huge jump and was over the fence and down the field, where she hurried to the river to drink.

The others followed her and suddenly the whole meadow was the scene of bawling and mad commotion. Mr Reinhardt rubbed his hands and let out a sigh of relief. He suggested that they open a bottle of champagne. Mrs Reinhardt was delighted. Of late he had become very thrifty and did not permit her any extravagances. In fact he had been saying that they would soon have to give up wine because of the state of the country. As they went indoors he put an arm around her. And back in the room she sat and felt like a mistress as she drank the champagne, smiled at him and felt the stuff coursing through her body. The champagne put them in a nice mood and they linked as they went up the narrow stairs to bed. Nevertheless, Mrs Reinhardt did not feel like any intimacy; she wanted it reserved for the hidden room.

They returned to London on Sunday evening, and that night Mrs Reinhardt did not sleep. Consequently she walked nowhere in her dreams. In the morning she felt fidgety. She looked in the mirror. She was getting old. After breakfast, as Mr Reinhardt was hurrying out of the house, she held up the little key.

'What is it?' she said.

'How would I know,' he said. He looked livid.

She called and made an appointment at the hairdresser's. She looked in the mirror. She must not get old. Later, when her hair was set she would surprise him – she would drop in at his gallery and ask him to take her to a nice pub. On the way she would buy a new scarf and knot it at the neck and she would be youthful.

When she got to the gallery, Mr Reinhardt was not there. Hans, his assistant, was busy with a client from the Middle East. She said she would wait. The new secretary went off to make some tea. Mrs Reinhardt sat at her husband's desk brooding, and then idly she began to flick through his desk diary, just to pass the time. Lunch with this one and that one. A reminder to buy her a present for their anniversary – which he had done. He had brought her a beautiful ring with a sphinx on it.

Then she saw it – the address that she went to night after night. Number ten. The digits danced before her eyes as they had danced when she drove up in the taxi the very first time. All her movements became hurried and mechanical. She gulped her tea, she gave a distracted handshake to the Arab gentleman, she ate the ginger biscuit and gnashed her teeth, so violently did she chew. She paced the floor, she went back to the diary. The same address – three, four, or five times a week. She flicked back to see how long it had been going on. It was no use. She simply had to go there.

At the mews, she found the key in the flower tub. In the kitchen were eggshells and a pan in which an omelette had been cooked. There were two brown eggshells and one white. She dipped her finger in the fat; it was still warm. Her heart went ahead of her up the stairs. It was like a pellet in her body. She had her hand on the doorknob, when all of a sudden she stopped in her tracks and became motionless. She crept away from the door and went back to the landing seat.

She would not intrude, no. It was perfectly clear why Mr Reinhardt went there. He went by day to keep his tryst with her, be unfaithful with her, just as she went by night. One day or one night, if they were very lucky, they might meet and share their secret, but until then Mrs Reinhardt was content to leave everything just as it was. She tiptoed down the stairs and was pleased that she had not acted rashly, that she had not lost her head.

Baby Blue 🌿

Three short quick death knocks resounded in her bedroom the night before they met. He said not to give it a thought, not to fret. He asked if she would like a kiss later on and she nodded. They were alike in everything and they talked with their heads lolled against the back of the armchairs so that to any spectators it was their throats that would be readily visible. The others had gone. He had been brought in unexpectedly by a friend and as she said somewhat frankly it wasn't every day that one met an eligible man. He for his part said that if he had seen her in a restaurant he would have knocked over tables to get to her. Her hand was on the serge of his knee, his hand on the velvet of hers and they were telling each other that there was no hurry at all, that their bodies were as perfectly placed as neighbouring plants.

She escorted him to the corner to get a taxi and on the way they found a pack of cards on the wet road, cut them there and then, and cut identically. Next day he would be making the short flight across the channel to his home which sounded stately with its beech trees, its peach houses, its asparagus bed and corinthian pillars supporting the front porch. In time she would be acquainted with the rooms, she would ask him to describe them one by one – library, kitchen, drawing room, and last but very last of all, bedroom. It was his wife's house. His wife was her colouring and also five foot seven and somewhat assertive. His children were adorable. He had thought of suicide the previous summer but that was over, meeting her had changed all that. It was like Aladdin, magical; his hair would begin to grow again and he would trim his black beard so that by the next weekend his lips would feel and imprint hers. He worked as a designer and had to come back each week to continue plans for a little theatre that was being built as part of a modern complex. It was the first thing he had done in years.

The card he sent her was of an historic building going up in flames and she thought 'ominous' but because of the greetings on it she was in an ecstasy.

He would arrive on Fridays, telephone from the airport, and in the hallway with his black mohair bag still in his hand, he would kiss her while she bit as his beard and got to the flesh of his lips. Then he would hold her at a distance from him and tilt her head until she became flawless. There she would be, white skinned, agog, and all of a blush, and there he would be trying not to palpitate so hard. His smell was dearer to her than any she could remember and yet it was redolent of some deep buried memory. Her mother she feared. Something of the same creaminess and the same mildness united them as if poised for life's knife. He plaited her hair around his finger, they constantly swopped plates, glasses, knives, forks and were unable to eat what with all the jumping up and down and swopping of these things. He took her hands to his face and she said all the little pouches of tension would get pressed away and not long after this, and during one of those infinite infinities he cried and she drank in two huge drops of very salty tears. He confessed to her that when he was little and got his first bicycle he had to ride round and round the same bit of safe suburban street so that his mother would not worry about his getting run over on a main road. She said that fused them together, that made him known to her throughout and again she thought of slaughter and of some lamb waiting for life's knife.

'Will it last, Eleanor?' he said.

'It will last,' she said.

She never was so sure of anything in her life. In the bedroom she drew the pink curtains and he peeled the layers of her clothing off, and talked to her skin, then the bones beneath it, then to her blood, then their bloods raced together.

'I can't stop my wife coming to London to shop,' he said, getting out of bed, dressing, and then undressing again. He scarcely knew what he wanted to do. He had a migraine and asked if she ever suffered from that. She said go, please go. They had known each other for six weekends and he intended to get her a ring. Her mascara was badly crusted on her lashes and had smeared onto her lids.

This was no way to be. She had left her earrings on and knew that the crystal would have made a semblance of a gash on each side of her neck. They had gone to bed drunk, and were drunk oftener than they need be. He used to intend to go early to the family he was supposed to be staying with but always his resolution broke and he stayed with her until breakfast time, or later.

'Go, please go,' she said it again.

His smile was like a cowl placed over a very wretched face.

The next weekend it didn't work out too badly. It was a question of him running back and forth to her, and from her, helping his wife with shopping, getting his daughter a diary, getting his son some toy motors, once having to fail her by not showing up at all, and then in a panic ringing her from the flat in the middle of the night – presumably his wife was asleep – saying, 'I have to talk to you, I will see you tomorrow at ten, if you are not there I will wait, I will see you tomorrow at ten, I have to talk to you, if you are not there I will wait . . .'

At ten he arrived and his complexion was that of an old grey sock.

'What is it?' she said, sympathetic, and still relatively in control of herself. If only she had crystal gazed.

'I dread looking into my wife's eyes and telling her that I am in love with another woman.'

'Then don't,' she said.

'Do you love me any more?' he asked.

'Yes,' she said, and they sat in the dining room, on a carving chair, looking out at the winter trees in the winter sky, feeling sad for each other, and for themselves and remembering to the future when the trees would be in leaf, and they would walk in the gardens together and there and then, a bit teary, unslept, and grave beyond belief, they started to build.

* * *

Christmas comes but once a year and when it does it brings families together. He went home and, as the friend who had introduced them said, was probably busy, dressing the tree, going to parties, pulling crackers, and, as she silently added, looking into his wife's eyes, or his cat's eyes, putting drops into his cat's eyes, doing his duty. He used to tell her how he sat on the stairs, talking to his cat as if it were her and then biting one of his whiskers. No letter. She didn't know it but the huge gilt mirror in their hall fell, broke and just missed his wife by inches and she did not know it then but that miss was relevant. New Year's Eve saw her drunk again and maudlinly recalling dead friends, those in the grave and those who were still walking around. She would not leave the restaurant but sat all night at the corner table until the waiter brought her coffee and a little jug of warm milk in the morning. He found her curled up in her fox cape.

'Gigo, am I old . . .?' she said.

'No . . . not old, well-looking,' he said.

He knew her well and had often helped her out with her parties. He knew her as a woman who worked for a public relations firm, and brought them nice customers and did lots of entertaining. They sat and talked of towns in Italy – Siena, Pisa, Padua, Fuerti di Marmi, Spoleto. At the mention of each town he kissed the air. On the twelfth day – little Christmas – her man wrote to say, 'Only that I love you more and miss you desperately, I am in a spruce wood and it is growing dark.' It was. She saw that but she refused to comprehend.

When she saw his wife she thought that yes she would have known her and felt that the scalded expression and marmalade hair would make a niche inside her brain.

'I will dream of this person,' she said warningly to herself as they shook hands. Then she handed him the bottle of white wine but kept the little parcel of quails' eggs because they looked too intimate and would be a revelation in their little nest of chaff, speckled, freshly boiled an hour before, blue-green with spots of brown, eggs as fresh as their sex. It was at his hospital bedside and there beside him were these two women and above him a little screen denoting the waver of his heart. It was all a bit unreal to Eleanor. No two people looked more unsuited what with his shyness and his wife's blatancy, his dark colouring and hers which had the ire of desert sand. For a moment she felt there was some mistake, it was perhaps his wife's sister, but no she was busying herself doing a wife's things, touching the lapel of his pyjamas, putting a saucer over the jug of water, acknowledging the flowers. The lily of the valley that Eleanor had sent him were in a tumbler, the twenty sprays despatched from Ascot. Asked by his wife where they had come from he said an 'admirer' and smiled. He smiled quite a lot as he nestled back against the pillows seeming like a man with nothing on his mind except the happy guarantee that there would be hot milk at ten, two sleeping pills and oblivion. She kept eyeing his wife, and the feeling she got was of a body, tank-like, filled with some kind of explosive. His wife suddenly told them that she was something of a seer and he asked politely if he would recover. The wine she brought they drank from cups. Exquisite, chilled white wine, such as she and he had often drank, and such as he had drank with his wife in the very first stages of their courtship. He was a man to whom the same thing was happening twice. The nurses were beginning to busy themselves and bade goodnight over-loudly to one lame visitor who was getting up to leave. The man in the next bed begged if he could have his clothes in order to go home to his own house whereupon the night sister gave him a little peck on the cheek.

'I must go,' Eleanor said, and looked at him as if there was some means of becoming invisible and staying.

'So must I,' his wife said and it was apparent that she wanted them to go together to have a chinwag perhaps. Eleanor touched the counterpane, and beneath it his feet, and left hurriedly as if she were walking on springs instead of high-heeled patent shoes. No chinwag, no nothing with this self-claimed seer. Yet something in her wanted to tell it, to have it known there and then, to have each person speak their minds. She ran down the stairs, crossed the road and stood trembling in the porchway of the pub, dividing her glance between the darkness of the hospital doorway and the welcoming soft pink light inside the pub itself. When she saw the woman, the wife, emerge in a black coat with a little travel bag she felt momentarily sorry for her, felt her defeat or perhaps her intuition in the way she walked down the street. She watched her and thought that if they had been at school together or were not torn between the same unsure man they might have some crumb of friendship to toss at one another.

Back at his bedside making the most of the two minutes the sister had allowed her she looked at him and said, 'Well?'

'What did you think?' he said.

'She talks a lot,' she said.

'Now you see,' he said and then he held her and she knew that there was something that she did not see, something that existed but was hidden from her. Some deposit of pain that would one day come out.

'I am not jealous,' she said.

'How could you be,' he said, and they sobbed and kissed and rocked back and forth, as if they were in their own room.

'I would like you to have a baby,' he said.

'I'll have twins,' she said.

'My wife says if it was anyone but you.'

'But me,' she said, and she could feel herself boiling.

His wife had gone on a short holiday in order to recoup her strength so that they could finalise the marriage. Eleanor had flown over to see him and was staying in an hotel a few miles from where he lived.

'She won't let me see the children,' he said.

'That's what everyone says, that's standard.'

'I had to lie about your key.'

'How did she find it?'

'In my pocket,' he said then and asked if he might show her.

'No,' she said. 'Don't.'

The question escaped out of her.

'Do you sleep together?'

'Once . . .' he said. 'I thought it was honourable.'

'Don't,' she said.

'It's a big bed, it's almost as big as this room.'

Although meaning to hold her tears at all costs, they accrued, dropped onto the toasted sandwich and into the champagne that he had bought her and onto the orange-coloured napkin. They were like rain softening the paper napkin. He squeezed her hand and led her back to the hotel room; there he undressed her, washed her, powdered her, and put her to dry in a big towel, then told her he loved her, that he would always love her, and she lay inside the towel listening to the crows cawing, then the rain pelting off the roof, and the old trees with their old branches groaning, then the spatters against the windowpane, and she thought of the daffodils getting soaked, as he clasped her through the warm towel and begged of her to let him in, always to let him in. Later that evening when she caught the plane back he simply said, 'Soon, soon.' All through the journey talking to a juggernaut who sat next to her she kept thinking, 'Soon,' and yet there was one little niggle that bothered her, his saying that he would have to tax the car next day, because his wife liked everything to be kept in order.

The night his wife returned he phoned her from a booth and said he was never in all his life so incensed. He said he had no idea what he might do next. She did not know it then but he had a black eye caused by a punch of a ringed finger, and wounds around the thighs where he was ridiculed for being a cunt. She said he ought to leave at once but he was too drunk to understand. The next day when he phoned he said everything was going to be more protracted but that he would phone when he could, and that she was to be well, be well. He was with her within twenty-four hours, sitting on the swivel chair, pale, bruised, and so dishevelled that she realised he had known more ordeal in a day than in the previous sum of his life. He kissed her, asked her to please, please, never pull his hair by the roots, because he minded that more than anything. They made love, and on and off throughout the day and in his short sleeps he kept threshing about and muttering things. He dreamt of a dog, a dog at their gate lodge and when he told her she felt inadequate. She would have to replace wife, children, animals, a sixteen-roomed house, the garden, cloches, the river and the countryside with its ranges of august mountains. As if he guessed her thoughts he said sadly that he owned nothing, and the little stone he once gave her would be the only gift he could afford for a while. The theatre design was complete but no other offers of work loomed. That was the other thing that galled – he had busied himself in craven domesticity and let his work slide. He had beggared himself.

He would telephone her when he was out and say he was on his way 'home, so to speak'. He was seeing various friends and though she did not know it, getting communiqués from his wife to come back, to come back. The evening he told her he asked if she had seen a rainbow in the sky and described how he saw it when standing in a bus shelter. Then he coughed and said, 'I rang my wife,' and she gulped.

'My wife isn't like you, she never cries but she cried, she sounded ill, very ill,' he said.

'She's a manœuvring liar,' she said.

'I have to be there,' he said.

'Go now,' she said, not wanting the ritual of a wake and in fact he had forestalled her in that, because his wife was flying at the very moment and they had arranged to meet in a friend's house, empty as it happened.

Then followed their first dirty quarrel, because he had told her so many hideous things that his wife had said about her, so many slanders.

'She's mad,' she said. 'It's a madhouse.'

'I'll tell you what a madhouse it is,' he said and proceeded to describe how as a farewell barter his wife had induced him to make love to her and was now in the process of looking for an abortionist.

'You mean you did,' she said.

'In the morning I'm always, a man is always . . .'

'You went in?'

'I didn't ejaculate.'

'She stinks.'

'It stinks,' he said, and as he left she held onto his sleeve, that must have been held onto a few mornings earlier, and she saw his hair so soft, so jet, his eyes bright hazel and over-alive and then she let go without as much as a murmur.

'I'll always love you,' he said.

She walked with him in imagination up the road, to the house where he had once brought her, and then to the doorway, his wife waiting, their embrace or their quarrel or their whatever, and all night she kept vigil expecting one or other of them to come back to her to consult her, to include her, to console her, but no-one came.

The Sunday he was due to arrive back she went into the country both to escape the dread of waiting and to pick flowers. She picked the loveliest wild flowers, put them all around the house, then put the side of salmon in a copper pan, peeled cucumber, sliced it thin as wafer, proceeded to make a sauce and was whipping, stopping every other minute for the sound of the telephone when in fact the doorbell rang. He was in a sweat carrying a bag of hers that he had once borrowed. Yes his wife had insisted on coming with him, and was in the friend's house a mile away, making the same threats about writs, about custody, about children, about his whoring. They drank, and kissed, and ate dinner and it was the very same as in the first wayward weeks when he kept kneeling by her, asking for special favours, telling her how much more he loved her. Around midnight he said he had no intention of going back to the house where his wife was, and falling half asleep, and still engaged in the tangle of love he thanked her from the bottom of his heart and said this was only the beginning.

Next day when he telephoned, his wife demanded to see him within the hour but he decided not to go, said 'let it stew'.

They were invited by friends of Eleanor's to the country, and he chose what she should wear, he himself having only the clothes that were on his back, his suitcase being in his wife's possession. It was a beautiful house and he already knew it in imagination by the way she had described it.

'Look, black swans,' she said, pointing to the artificial lake as they drove up to the beautiful house and stepped out onto the very white gravel, her shoes making a grating sound. The butler took their bags and straight away, with their hostess, they set out for a walk. The lawn was scattered with duck droppings and swan droppings and the fallen acacia petals. It was a soft misty day and the black swans were as co-ordinated and elegant as if they were performing a pageant. It was perfect. A few last acacia flowers still clung to the bushes and made a little show of pink. In the grotto one of the guests was identifying the hundreds of varieties of rock there. Had they stayed outside they could have watched a plane go by. He loved planes and for some reason to do with portent, she kept count of them for him. When she entered the dark and caught him by surprise their two faces rubbed together and their breaths met. That night in a different bed, a four-poster, they made love differently, and he told her as he tore at the beautiful lingerie that she had bought for the occasion, that never had he loved her so much as earlier in the dark grotto, with her big eyes and her winged nose looming over him. The torn silk garments fell away from her and she felt at last that they had truly met, they had truly come into their own.

He went back home but in his own time. Each night when he phoned he said there was no question now of their losing each other, because he was recovering his self-esteem. Then he returned sooner than she expected, in fact unannounced. She was hemming curtains, lovely cream lace curtains that she had bought with him in mind. They went to the kitchen and he said yes, that his wife had come again and was making the same contradictory threats, one minute telling him to get out, the next minute begging him to stay, showing him her scarred stomach, scars incurred from all her operations. He was wearing a striped seersucker jacket, and it was the first time that she saw him as his wife's property, dressed expensively but without finesse. He was restless and without knowing it she kept waiting for the crisis.

'I can't phone you in the future,' he said.

'You can,' she said.

'They listen at the exchange,' he said.

'I insist,' she said and began in jest to hit him. All of a sudden he told her how he had thrown his wife out of a room the night before, and how he realised he had wanted to kill her.

'And?' she said.

'She came back to say she was bleeding from the inner ear.'

'And?' she said.

'Good, I said.'

There was a dreadful silence. They sat down to eat a bit of bread and cheese but the jesting was over. Next day he went to enquire about work and when he came home in the evening everything was friendly but something needed to be said. He was going to be incommunicado he said, thus making it impossible for his wife to find him. Next night they went to a party and she made certain not to cling to him, not to make him feel hemmed in. Yet they had to rush to the little cloakroom to kiss. He lifted her dress and touched her lingeringly and she said wasn't he the rascal then. On the way home she expressed the wish to be in Paris, so they could have breakfast and dawdle all day. What she really wished was not Paris but a place where they could be free. It was midsummer night, and they decided to go into the square and sit under a tree where the pigeons were mildly cogitating. He gave her a borough council rose and said would she keep it for ever, crumpled. He said there was no doubt about it but that she was psychic, that his wife who always wore girdles was now buying the same knickers as her. He had seen them in a case – a white, brown and cream with the maker's name and the little borders of lace. She asked a question. He said no, there had not been a reunion, but that he went into the bedroom to get his book from the bedside table and there they were on the top of the opened suitcase.

'I would like to be there, just once, invisible,' she said.

He shook his head and said all she would see would be himself at a table trying to draw something, his wife in her cashmere dressing gown, coming in, snatching it out of his hand saying, 'You cunt, no forget that, you vagina,' then going on about her worth, her intelligence, the sacrifice she had made for him, leaving the room to down another glass of wine, coming back to start all over again with fresh reinforcements, to get into her stride.

'Are you hiding something, Jay?' she said.

'Only that I love you passionately,' he said, and together they held the rose, that was as red, as vibrant as blood.

A few days later he was remote, refused to eat or drink and was always just short of frowning when she entered the room. He sat and watched cricket on television, and sometimes would get up and mime the movement of the batsman, or would point to one of the fielders who were running and say how miraculous it was. A few times he went upstairs to kiss her, kisses of reassurance, but each time when she commenced to talk he was gone again. Young love, outings to the country, a holiday, all those things seemed improbable, a figment. They were too worn by everything. She was glad that there was a guest for dinner, because he became his old self again, warm and friendly, then he sang and in the course of singing put one lock of her hair behind his ear, which made him look like a girl. They met each other's glance and smiled and it was all like before. The friend said no two people were so well matched and they drank to it. In bed he tossed and turned, said it would have been better if he stayed in an hotel, so as not to disturb her sleep, said all in all he was a very spoilt person and that he would have to get a steady job. He said he had to admit that his wife was now nothing, no-one, although he had dreamt of her the previous night, and that he was hoping that she would go far away and, like a Santa Claus, send back some of her money. Yes, it was like that. All his past life was over, finished, then he doubled over with pain and she massaged him gently, but it gave no relief and he said the pain went right through to the fillings of his teeth.

'You have something to tell me,' she asked.

'Yes.' He said it so quietly that the whole room was taut with expectation. The room where eight months previously she had heard the unfathomable death knocks, the room to which they climbed at all hours, drinking one another in, the room where the sun coming through the gauze curtains played on the brass rungs of the bed, seemed to reveal and scatter imaginary petals, the room where he gave her one drop of his precious blood instead of a gold wedding ring. What he had to tell her was that he was giving it all up, her, his wife, his family, his beautiful house, the huge spider's web that he had got himself into. For a moment she panicked. He once told her that he would like to go to a hotel room and write to the people concerned – herself, his children, his wife – and, as he implied, put an end to himself. She thought not that, not that, no matter what, and for a second rehearsed a conciliatory conversation with his wife where they both did everything to help him. He could not be allowed to.

'I'll leave tomorrow,' he said.

'Where will you go?' she asked.

'I'll go home to say goodbye.' And in those few words she knew that he would go home not to say goodbye but to say 'Hello, I'm back.' She prayed that by the morrow he would change his mind and feel less conclusive about things.

'I am not dead,' she thought and clutched at objects as if they could assure her of the fact. Then she did rash things, went outdoors, but had to be indoors at once, and barely inside was she, than suffocation strangled her again and yet out in the street the concrete slabs were marshy and the spiked railings threatening to brain her. It was the very same sadness as if someone had died and she could see, without looking, his returned latchkey, its yellow-green metal reflected in the co-green of her ring stone. The ring she had taken off the previous night in order for her fingers to be completely at one with his fingers. It was not long after, that he said it, and it seemed to her that she must have precipitated it in some mysterious way, and that maybe she had made him feel lacking in something and that it need never have happened but that it had happened and he had suddenly announced that there was no room for her in his life, that she was not someone he wished to spend his life with, that it was over, that she was off the cliff again. The night and the morning were getting crushed together, the night when he told her and the morning when he had packed every stitch while she was having a shower and had his bag down in the hall and was whistling like a merry traveller.

'I can't,' she kept saying. 'Can't, can't,' and then she would refer to his hair, his brown tweed jacket and the beautiful sombreness of him, and then again she would remember the words, the fatal words, his adam's apple moving, juggling, and the way she bit at it out of love, out of need and in the morning – yes it was morning – when she folded his two legs together and kissed as much of him as protruded, and he asked would she do that when he was very old and very infirm and in an institution and for a moment they both cried. He left. She knew in her bones that it was final, that he had deceived her, that all those promises, the reams of love letter, the daily pledge, 'You, I hold fast,' were no longer true, and she thought with wizard hatred that perhaps they never had been true, and she thought uselessly but continuously of his house with the fawn blinds drawn down, his getting home after dark, putting his bag on a chair, throwing down the gauntlet at last, saying he was back for good and all, had sown his wild oats. That would not be for a few hours yet, because he was still travelling but that is what would happen. To get through until dark, she asked of God, as if dark itself had some sort of solution to the problem. Two women held her pressed to a chair, and said commiseratingly to each other that it was impossible to help someone. Judging by their startled faces and by the words that flowed out of her mouth she knew that she was experiencing the real madness that follows upon loss.

'We're here, we're here, pet,' her friend would say.

'Where is he, where is he?' she said, rising, stampeding. The swivel chair was like a corpse in the room and she threw the paper weight at it. What had once been a dandelion clock inside pale green glass, was now pale green splinters and smithereens. If he had had a garden, or rather if he had tended their own garden, he would only cultivate green and white flowers, such things as snowdrops and Christmas roses. Between her tears she tried to tell them that, so as they would have some inkling of what he was like, and what had gone on between them and for a moment she saw those Christmas roses, a sea of them, pale and unassuming in a damp incline from the opposite side, and he eerily still.

She went to a friend's house to write it, being too afraid to do it in her own house, in case that he might telephone. She used a friend's foolscap paper and over that hour filled three full pages. It was the most furious letter she had ever written, and she wished that she had a black-edged envelope in which to post it. There was no tab on the post box telling the time of the next collection, so she went into a nearby shop beside it to ask if it was reliable. It was a lighting shop. Long glass shades hung down like crystals, like domes, like translucent mushrooms reminding her of some non-existent time in the future, when she would entertain him. After posting the letter she went back to the friend's house, to finish her tea, and as she was being conveyed up the street they saw an elderly woman with a big sheepdog in her arms, holding it upright, like a baby, and she wanted to run across and embrace both of them.

'That woman saw her father being run over when she was fourteen and hasn't been the same since,' her friend said.

'And we think we're badly off,' she said.

She felt curiously elated and began to count, first in hours, then in minutes, then in seconds, the length of time before he received the epistle.

He was sleeping in his wife's bedroom again. That was part of the pact, that, and a vow that he would never travel abroad without her, that he would pay attention to her at parties, appreciate her more than he had been doing. He said yes to all her demands and thought that somehow they would not be exacted once she was over her spleen. He slept badly. He talked, shouted in his sleep and in the morning while being rebuked about it, he never enquired in case he might have said the other woman's name. Her photo, the small snapshot of her, that he had kissed and licked so many times was in the woodshed along with the one letter that he had brought away out of the pile that he had left in her study for safety. It was the night of his thirty-fifth birthday, and they had parted but a week. He stood over his son's bed telling himself that what he had done was the right thing. The little boy had one finger in his mouth and the other hand was splayed out like a doll's.

'It's the hands that kill you, isn't it?' said his wife who had crept in to enjoy the moment of domesticity.

He kept going to the front door long before the visitors were
due to arrive, and he was even in two minds about nipping the
lead off to the master telephone because he was in dread of its
ringing. At the party he sang the same songs as he had sung to
her, in fact his repertoire. His wife drank his health, and the old
nanny who had been in the habit of hearing and seeing the most
frightful things and had seen bottles flying, thought how changeable a thing human nature can be. Even staggering to bed he
thought he heard footsteps. His wife dared him to fuck her, but
it was a drunken dare and drunkenly dismissed, in fact it made
him laugh. She didn't sleep well what with her thirst, his tossing
and turning, and those son-of-a-bitch snores. She was downstairs sipping black coffee, putting a touch of pink on her nails
when the footsteps came over the gravel.

'Early Monday,' she thought, and went out to open the door
for the postman who always said the same dumb thing – 'Fine
day, ma'am,' regardless of the weather. Now more than ever his
letters concerned her, and her own letter from her sister in
Florida took mere second place as she looked at the two business envelopes and then the large envelope with its deceiving
blue-ribboned type. She decided to read it out of doors.

'Drivel,' she said, starting in on the first stupid nostalgic bits,
and then in her element as she saw words she knew, words that
could have been her own, the accusation of his being a crooked
cunt, the reference to his wife's dandruffy womb, to his own idle,
truthless, working-class stinking heart, and she knew that she
had won. She re-sealed it and brought it to him.

'What's that?' she said, and snatched the letter from him.
She read it with a speed that made him think for a minute she
had written it herself. He saw her eyes get narrower and
narrower and she was as compressed now as a peach stone. She
pursed her lips the way she did when entering a party. She got
to the bits referring to herself, read them aloud, cursed, and then
jubilantly tore it up and tossed the pieces in the air as if they
were raffle tickets. She danced, and said what whoopee and said
'kiss-kiss' and said he'd be a good boy now. He got out of bed
and said he had to go to the hotel, he had to have a drink. She
said go to the hotel, have a drink, and not forget that they were

going to a party that night and not to get 'drunkies' early in the day as there were plenty of parties for the summer vacation. As he left she was phoning to ask the girl in the boutique to send up some dresses, a few, and then she started discussing colours.

'Wait a minute ... hey ...' He turned round in order to be asked if pale blue and baby blue was one and the same thing.

'Just asking my beau,' she said to the girl on the telephone, but he was unable to give any reply.

In the driveway he tried to remember the letter from start to finish, tried to remember how the sentences led from one to another but all that he could remember were single vicious words, that flew up into the air and it was the very same as if the black crows had turned into great black razors and were inside his head, cutting, cutting away. He would stay in the hotel for as long as possible, all day, all night maybe, and he would go back tomorrow and the next day and maybe one day he would take a room and do the thing he wanted to do, maybe one day?

They were simply little slabs of stone laid into and just beneath the level of the grass, about a hundred of them almost begging for feet to dance, or play hopscotch. Here and there was a vase or mug filled with flowers, mostly roses. She asked one of the gardeners what the slabs signified and he said each one covered someone's ashes. 'There's two boxes in somewhere was a husband and wife, but most of 'em there's one,' he said. The words went straight to her heart. Not long after she found a tomb with Jay's name on it and nearby was his daughter's name. These names swam before her eyes. She wished that her name were there too and began to search. She went round and round the main graveyard, then to that part where the meadowsweet was so high, the tomb and the stone effigies were all covered over and she could not read a thing. Some French children on a conducted tour, were running back and forth amused at what they saw and even more amused when they went in under the red stone ruin that had a big sign saying 'dangerous structure'. A few hundred yards away they were setting up wagons for the weekend's amusement fair and men in vests with big muscles were laying aluminium slabs for the dodgem cars. Graveyard and pleasure-green were side by side with a tennis court and miniature golf course at the northern end. The caravans had arrived, the women were getting out their artificial flowers, their china plates and their bits of net curtain, to set up yet again their temporary dwellings. She tried to hold onto life, to see what she was seeing, these people setting up house for a day or two or three, muscles, burial places, schoolchildren with no thought of death. It was a windy day, and the roses in the containers kept falling over and girls kept bullying each other to come on or not come on. In the church of St Nicholas she looked at the altar, at the one little slit of light from the aperture above and the window beneath, half of which was stained and half clear. Then she looked at oddments in a glass case, bits of tiling, and one tiny bit of bone as perfect as a pillar that had been found by a schoolchild whose statement it bore.

Outside the lawn-mowers were full on, and those plus the shrieks of the visiting children tried to claim her head, and she hoped that they would, therefore banishing forever the thought of all that had gone before. The sun came in fits and starts, the tiers of yellow bulbs were all bunched up waiting to be lit, the haunted caravan with its black skull and its blooded talons looked a little ridiculous since no wicked ogre lurked within. She had come on a train journey to consult a faith healer but was much too early. All was still and only the bright garish daubs of paint suggested that by Saturday all would be in motion and for better or worse people would go and get on the dodgems and the mad merry-go-round.

What would she have not given to see him for a moment, to clasp him, utterly silent, no longer trusting to speech.

'It will pass,' she thought, going from grave to grave and unconsciously and almost mundanely she prayed for the living, prayed for the dead, then prayed for the living again, went back to find the tomb where was his name, and prayed for all those who were in boxes alone or together above or below ground, all those unable to escape from themselves.

The Small Town Lovers 🌿

It is a narrow country road in Ireland, tarred very blue and hedged in by ditches on either side. Growing along the ditches and fighting for place are hawthorns, fuchsias, elderberry trees, nettles, honeysuckle, and foxgloves, so that there is almost always a smell of flowers carried by the breeze from the water – the Shannon is only two fields away from the road. In the mild summer evenings, lovers cross the fields down to the water to lie or sit among the lush bamboos. In the morning, the priest reads his prayers there, and when tinkers come round to these parts they park a caravan in a disused gateway leading off that road.

It was not the road I travelled to school, but I often went out there to convey a friend or collect day-old chicks from the Protestant woman who had the incubator. Always, either coming or going, I encountered the Donnellys – Jack and Hilda, the town lovers. They had met in America twenty or thirty years before, two lonely immigrants working in an asylum, and they had married and returned to Ireland, where they opened a little grocery and pub. They lived in the back of the shop, surrounded with bottles and barrels. It amazed me how anyone could love Hilda. She was fat, stolid, uninspiring. They passed me on the road but did not salute me, being too busy with one another.

'Hilda, love, are we walking too fast?' Jack would say.

'No, darling Jack.'

'Just say so if we're going too fast,' he would say, speaking lovingly to her powdered gooseflesh neck.

'I'll be all right.'

Puffing, she would link him, and it seemed as if her entire weight rested on his arm. He was an insignificant little man in a grey flannel suit and black patent-leather shoes.

When they reached that part of the road where there was a gap in the ditch, Hilda carefully edged sidewise through the gap and Jack held briars aloft so that she did not scratch herself. Then he stepped in after her and they crossed the potato field towards the lake, hands joined, looking into one another's faces.

It astonished everyone how they had not got bored with one another, especially as they had had no children. They were the laugh of the village – Hilda Love and Jack Darling. Each afternoon, they drew down the patched blue blind over the shop window, bolted the shop door, and set out for their walk. Their 'bye-byes', Hilda called it. Winter and summer, she wore a blue silk dress that had a flared skirt and a discreet v-neck. It must have been the style of dress that was in fashion the year she fell in love, or else she thought it disguised her fat. In the v of the neck she had insertions of lace that she crocheted herself as she sat behind the counter waiting for customers. Waiting for customers that never came, that is, except for the few children who wanted a penn'orth of liquorice sweets, or some old woman who would pretend that she was going in to buy groceries and so linger just to have a chat with Hilda. The local fellows did not drink there, because there was no comfort in it – no fire in the big black grate, no free drinks at Christmastime, no cups of tea on a winter's night, no generosity. Visitors to the house were never offered more than a drink of water, and that is why I felt privileged to have been given tea in the kitchen.

It was all due to my father. Once, when he was on the batter, Hilda let him have half a bottle of whiskey. Mama had hidden his wallet and he was so desperate for drink that he promised Hilda free grazing for her cow in exchange for the whiskey. He was true to his word, and the cow was driven over to our front field the next afternoon.

On the following Sunday, Hilda rushed to greet my mother as we came out from Mass. Hilda beamed behind her gold-rimmed spectacles, but Mama looked away towards the horizon and said to us children that it looked like rain. Hilda was hurt. After all, Jack and herself were a model couple, known to love one another, not to eat meat on Friday, to pay more than enough for their church dues, and, in fact, to be so generous as once to have gone bail for a local insurance collector who was in jail for embezzling money – though, of course, they got the insurance man to paint their house during the period of the bail and did not pay him for it.

'How dare she, and only th'other day I read in the paper that they got another legacy!' Mama said as we walked home over the weary dusty road.

Two mornings later, along with the ordinary mail, the post-man brought a letter marked 'By Hand'. It was from Hilda. The letter was an invitation for my sister, my brother, and myself to come to tea the following Sunday. Cunningly, she had not invited Mama, knowing I suppose, that Mama was likely to get confidential and tell her that we could not really afford the free grass, what with our own debts and everything.

'They better go, Mam,' my father said, thinking it a great compliment that we were asked at all.

Sunday came, and we set out in our best clothes and with clean hankies. It was exciting to go around to the hall door at the side of the house, tap the rusty knocker, and in a moment be greeted by Hilda, who was smelling of lavender water as she kissed us. She wore a clean brown dress and a lovely gold pendant, and I envied her the circumstances of her life – mistress of that large house, with money and perfume, and a piano at her convenience. On Sunday evenings, the thin sound of piano music had wandered out into the street as we passed down the chapel road to devotions. Jack was the one who played, usually 'Yankee Doodle Dandy'.

Hilda led us across the tiled hallway and into the front parlour, where it was shaded, as the blind was drawn. She let it up halfway and we saw a large room with several armchairs, which were covered with loose pieces of frayed linen sheets. She lifted off one piece and a cloud of dust rose up and swirled gently in the air as it approached the yellowed ceiling. The room smelled stale, and there was about the place a lingering whiff of whiskey or porter.

'Do any of you children play?' she asked, and very courteously my brother, who was thirteen, said that he played a little. She drew out the piano stool, and ceremoniously he sat down. We sat on high-backed chairs round the big mahogany table, and with my index finger I made mere patterns on the dusty surface. The table was old and stained, and it was also covered with circles of brown directly at the place where I sat – hundreds of circles running into one another. Being bored with the piano music, I put my hand underneath the table to see if there was anything hidden on the shelf there that supported the top. Mama kept bars of chocolate hidden under our dining-room table. I felt dust, cobwebs, then something cold made of metal. It felt like – I almost screamed. It was a gun. At that instant, my brother began to play loudly, and in keeping with the sentiments of the song (it was 'Clare's Dragoons') he moved his head about frantically so that his red hair fell down onto his forehead and he looked like a genius.

None of us saw or heard the movement of the doorknob as it was turned; when we saw Jack, he was already standing in the room, in his shirtsleeves, livid.

'Hilda!' he said in a cross voice.

My brother stopped playing and I took my arms off the table where they had left a crescent on the dusty surface.

Jack stared at us but never said, 'You're welcome,' or 'Hello,' or anything. Hilda pushed him out of the room and went with him, closing the door behind her. We could not hear what they were saying, but we could feel the anger and tension in the hallway. We all felt it.

'They're having a row,' my sister said. We were used to rows. My mother and father had plenty.

'Sh-h-h, sh-h-h,' my brother said. 'That's no thing to say,' and he made us talk about something else.

Within a few minutes, Hilda came back, smiling, but her ears and neck were blazing.

'Poor Jack is trying to get a snooze, the creature. We mustn't make a noise,' she said in a whisper and wagged her finger at each of us in turn.

'Poor Jack, he was awake all night attending to me because I had a dose of heartburn,' and with her white, fat hand she touched her chest round about where her heart must have been beating. Then she suggested that we go down to the kitchen, as the bedroom was directly over the parlour and Jack was likely to be disturbed further if we stayed there.

Very quietly, my brother let down the top of the piano; Hilda drew the blind, and we left the room as ghastly as we had found it, with dust on everything and dead moths clinging to the globe of the brass lamp that stood on the sideboard.

In the kitchen, the table was already laid for tea – white china cups with a thin gold scroll on them, two plates of sandwiches, rock buns, and marietta biscuits.

'She didn't break her heart with preparations,' my sister said to me when Hilda was out in the scullery filling the kettle.

We all sat around, and Hilda said, 'Have a tomato sandwich, children.'

We did. They were not real tomato sandwiches at all. Hilda had just smeared the slices of bread with tomato ketchup. I laughed, but was nudged by my brother, who began talking to Hilda about the distillation of alcohol. He always talked about dull things.

'Have one of these,' my sister said as she passed me the second plate of sandwiches.

The filling was a curious red-brown colour; I took a bite and for a minute could not identify the flavour. And then it came to me. Rhubarb sandwiches! I was choking with laughter by now, and my brother said, 'Perhaps you'd like to share the joke.' However, he ate nothing himself except one rock bun and he left the shreds of lemon peel on his plate. My sister ate like a horse; she was eleven at that time and reckoned that she had to eat a lot so that she would grow very tall. She longed to be a policewoman and had heard that one had to be tall for that.

Hilda was uneasy – you could see by the way she sat on the edge of the chair with her ear cocked – and she asked us no questions. Normally, she tapped the window with her knitting needle and called us in on the way from school to ask about my mother and father and if there were any parcels from America and if Mama had got anything new. But that evening she said very little, and we left immediately after we had done the washing-up.

At home, we kept our parents laughing for an hour as we told them about the house and the food. Mama was very inquisitive to know what the furniture was like and if there were pretty knick-knacks in the parlour. 'Not as nice as ours?' she said, pleased that at least we had a large house furnished in the style and period of the twenties.

After our visit, Hilda began to call on us when Jack and herself came each evening to milk the cow. Tina No-Nose milked in the mornings. (Tina was a flat-nosed girl, who got fits.) While Jack was milking Hilda came round to the back door to have a chat with Mama. 'Am I making a nuisance of myself?' she asked the first evening, and Mama was very cold with her. But after some weeks Mama accepted the fact that the cow was there to stay and she talked to Hilda as she would to a friend. She may even have been glad of Hilda's company, because our house was in the middle of a field and our nearest neighbours were a mile away.

It was summertime when Hilda first came, and I recall them as they sat on the stone step of the back kitchen, Hilda with a glass of milk or homemade wine in her hand and Mama's cheeks flushed with the excitement of talking about their gay days in America, because she also had worked there when she was young. They talked of Coney Island on Sundays, of a boy they had both known in Brooklyn – the lost curly-headed phantoms of their girlhood. And sooner or later Hilda would mention the terrible thunderstorms in New York. I can see her as she sipped the wine greedily – a clean, fat, pampered woman in a blue silk dress, with thick ankles that were brimming over the edges of her black leather shoes.

It was my job to watch for Jack as he came out of the cowshed and went down the avenue towards the road. One evening, I missed him as I was gargling my throat around the side of the house near the rain barrel.

'Your husband is gone, Mrs Donnelly,' I said.

'Oh, I'll be killed!' she said, and she ran after him, her great body flopping in her blue flared dress.

'Darling huh-huh!' she called as she ran, but he did not wait for her.

I grew up and went to boarding school with my sister; still Hilda came. I would see her at holiday time and note that she was getting breathless and grey. Each Christmas, she gave Mama a bottle of cooking sherry; they had become closer, and Mama was heard to say, 'Hilda isn't the worst, you know.' With the annual bottle of sherry, Hilda had found a way to Mama's heart – not that Mama drank, but she liked getting something.

'Darling huh-huh!' Hilda always seemed to be calling when I was home on holiday.

'I don't know what she sees in him; he's a dry fish,' Mama said as we watched the two of them go out the gate one evening.

'She hasn't it all sunshine, either,' Mama remarked, showing a sly pleasure at the fact that someone else's marriage was unhappy also.

Not that Hilda ever said anything openly. But once she hinted that she hoped life would be better in the next world, and quite often her eyelids were swollen as if from crying. When she sent to Dublin for her special corsets, she had to have them posted to our house and later she collected them there.

'What they don't know doesn't trouble them,' she said to Mama in her slow, false voice. Her voice is the thing I remember best – slow, unctuous; oversweet, like golden syrup.

The years passed. One Christmas morning, Hickey, our hired help, said to my mother, 'D'you hear the news, Missis?'

'No,' she said in a piercing voice. She was angry with Hickey, because he had come home drunk on Christmas Eve and had wakened us trying to get in through the back kitchen window, being too drunk to find the door-key, in its usual place under the soap dish on the window ledge.

'Hilda Donnelly is dead,' he said.

'Dead!' my mother said.

'Dead,' he repeated.

'My God!' Mama exclaimed and let the straining cloth fall into the can of milk.

'How could she be dead?' Mama said.

Hilda had been over the previous evening with the bottle of sherry. We had all had tea together in our breakfast room, and Mama had given Hilda a little tray cloth.

'She's dead, that's all I know,' Hickey said. 'Found her dead when he came down this morning. I heard it over at the creamery.'

'Who found her dead?'

Hickey raised his eyes to the ceiling to indicate to me that Mama was stupid.

'Jack Darlin'', of course – who else? She was dead for hours.'

She was found at the foot of the stairs, her face gashed and the lamp in pieces beside her. The thought of a dead woman, a broken globe, a lamp in smithereens and a face running with blood was riveting and just like a scene from a melodrama. My mother said it was lucky the house hadn't burnt down and where was Jack Darling.

'Blankets town tram,' Hickey said, and imitated being asleep.

'And how did he sleep through the night and not miss her out of the bed – was he blind or something?' Mama said.

'You're asking me?' Hickey shrugged. He was a workman, and as a workman he never said anything disrespectful about his superiors. 'She was at the foot of the stairs, stone dead, and the lamp in pieces beside her.'

'Lucky she wasn't burned,' Mama said, again.

'It wouldn't have mattered once she was dead,' Hickey said, quite without pity.

My father came in from feeding the calves and Mama said to him, 'Did you hear that, Father?'

'Hear what?'

She told him word for word, as Hickey had told it to her.

'Poor aul' creature, I always liked her,' my father said proudly, as if his affection could bring Hilda back to life.

Our Christmas dinner was spoiled, because Mama talked of Hilda all the time.

'Well, for all we know now, this could be our last meal on earth. Little did Hilda think, this time yesterday,' she said in a voice that was close to crying. Eventually, my father asked her to shut up moaning and let us enjoy our turkey. When we were tidying up, she said to me, 'You never know the hour nor the minute. You always want to be prepared, because when the Lord wants us He just calls us . . .' And we both looked through the misted window at the rain and the desolate black winter branches outside.

'And my little tray cloth,' Mama said regretfully.

After tea, we went to Hilda's wake. As we set out, it was a bright frosty night with a vast tranquil sky made silver by so many stars – a beautiful, hushed night with white frost on the holly leaves and the ground frozen under our feet. I would rather have sat at home with my brother and sister and listened to the wireless, but Mama said, 'You must come; Hilda was always fond of you.' To be honest, I hadn't noticed that Hilda was fond of any children.

When we got there, the side door was held open with the back of a chair, and we went in the hallway and up the stairs, towards a room where voices murmured softly. The dead room. People, women mostly, sat on chairs, whispering, and two or three knelt beside the bed on which Hilda was laid out – Hilda, solemn and immaculate in a brown habit, younger looking than when I had ever known her, with an amber rosary twined between her fingers. The flame of the candle threw crocus shadows on her face, and she looked almost beautiful. There was no gash to be seen on her face unless it was near the temple. Her snow-white hair was draped in curls all around her. It was odd hair, almost like angora. People remarked on her youthfulness. After we had prayed for her soul, we got up and looked around to sympathise with Jack, but he was not there. Dada concluded that he was downstairs, giving the men drinks in the kitchen, so he went down, and I shared the chair with my mother.

'Was it a stroke, or what?' I heard one woman say.

'She always had an unhealthy flush,' another woman said and then a third asked, 'Where is himself tonight?'

'Uncle Jack is having to lie down because of the shock,' said Hilda's niece, a flashy girl who was passing around glasses of port wine. She was a buttermaker in the next town.

'Oh,' somebody said knowingly.

The room smelled of damp, cold clothes, candle grease, and port wine. It was bitterly cold, as there was no fire at all, and you could see by the stains on the wallpaper that it had been a damp room all winter. Mama leaned over and whispered to me that I ought to go downstairs and see if Dada was all right. Then, out loud, she said to me, 'You could make a cup of tea for the ladies.'

The niece told me where to get the cups and things, and I set off on tiptoe. Down in the kitchen, the men helped themselves to pints of porter, which they filled from the big barrel that rested on a stool. There was a cheerful fire, and they sat around talking. By mistake, Jim Tuohey began to sing. He was nick-named the Ferret, because he kept a ferret and hunted with it for foxes on Sundays. He sang, 'If I were a blackbird I'd whistle and sing and I'd follow the ship that my true love sails in,' and my father shut him up with, 'Bloody fool, have you no respect for the dead?' The Ferret got very embarrassed and went out in the yard and was sick.

'I'm making a cup of tea,' I said to my father.

'Good girl,' he said. I was thankful to him because he hadn't touched a drink; I could tell by his eyes. Always when he drank his eyes got wild.

I carried a candle up to the parlour to get cups out of the sideboard. It was the room where we had sat so many years before. I could see Hilda as she was then, breathing heavily under her clean dress, and I was suddenly nervous in case she should appear to me. Quickly I opened the door of the side-board to get the good cups. As I piled them on the tray, a thought came to me, but I put it aside. It went on bothering me like a stone in the shoe, and finally I could not stop myself. I put my hand under the table to see if the gun was there. I could not find it, so I shone the candlelight under the table and saw nothing but dust and a green bankbook. I felt certain that Jack had shot his wife and had hidden the gun somewhere. Should I run and tell my mother or someone? I ran out of the room with the tray in my hands and almost crashed into Hickey, who was in the hallway.

'God's sake, will you look where you're going!' he said angrily.

'What are you up to?' I asked.

'Mind your own business.' He was stealing a bottle of whiskey from the crate of drink under the stairs. 'Jack Darlin' won't want it all,' he said, as he wrapped a piece of sacking round it.

I couldn't tell Hickey; he would only laugh. He laughed at most things except riddles.

'Where is Jack?' I asked.

'Blotto,' Hickey said.

'Does he drink?' I asked. I had never seen him drunk.

'Can a duck swim?' Hickey said. He tiptoed up the hallway and went outside to hide the whiskey in some convenient spot where he could collect it when he was going home. I made the tea, gave my father a cup, and carried a tray upstairs.

'What time is High Mass in the morning?' I heard Mama ask.

'There isn't a High Mass,' said the niece. 'We couldn't arrange it in time,' she added hurriedly.

'Not High Mass!' A sigh of indignation travelled round the room, and we looked at Hilda's calm face as if to apologise to her.

On the way home, Mama said to my father, 'Not a very nice house, John.'

'Oh, I was very disappointed in it,' he said.

'Not as nice as ours,' she said, knowing what his answer would be.

'Not a patch on ours,' he said proudly, and sniffed.

I could not tell them now about the gun, but in the clean air my suspicions seemed foolish and sordid.

'Poor man was drunk, it seems.'

'What did I always tell you? He never came to milk but there was a smell of whiskey off him.'

Mama sighed and said that Hilda ought to go straight to Heaven, because she had earned it.

* * *

Next morning, we went over to the ordinary Mass. The remains had been brought from the house to the church, and Mass was offered for Hilda's soul. As we knelt down, I nudged Mama and whispered, 'There's Jack up front there.' He was kneeling, with his head lowered and a black diamond of cloth stitched onto the arm of his raincoat, which the niece must have seen to. We were relieved to see him, because there was a lot of gossip about why he hadn't appeared at the wake.

After Mass, while we waited for the coffin to be put in the hearse and for people to get into their cars and pony traps, we went to sympathise with Jack. He looked stupefied and his nose was more purple than ever. Other people came and shook his hand, but he wore the same baffled expression and simply thanked them for coming.

Then the funeral procession began to move. The car following the hearse was the family car, in which sat the niece and her parents. There was a place for Jack, but he didn't get in. He walked beside the hearse, and we all said, 'Ah, the poor man,' thinking that he wanted to be close to her by walking the whole three-mile journey to the graveyard – the same road they had traversed each afternoon. My parents thought it a lovely sentiment and accused themselves for having misjudged him the previous evening.

When the hearse drove by the shop, Jack stepped out of line and went indoors. We gaped through the car window, and someone said that he must have felt faint and gone in for a drink or something. We were sure he would follow in another car.

At the graveside, we looked for him; we could see the niece looking around anxiously, but, like us, she did not find him. The coffin was lowered and we heard the eerie thud of the first sods as they were thrown in, but Jack had not come. He did not come at all.

The mystery was solved, or partly solved, the following week, when the parish priest called on Jack. 'I had enough of her,' Jack said. Or so the priest's housekeeper told us.

My father and the men in the village said it was a scandal, and that they'd give Jack a good hammering to teach him a lesson. They were waiting for him to come out.

A week passed, and still the blinds were drawn and the shutters remained on the shop window. The can of milk left by Tina No-Nose each morning had not been collected. People got worried and said that he must be dead. Tim Hayes decided to break in the side door one Monday morning. He burst it in with the aid of a sledgehammer and went in the hallway, shouting Jack's name. He opened the various doors, and found Jack asleep in an armchair in the parlour. There were rum bottles all round him and he had a rug over his shoulders.

'What has got into you?' Hayes asked.

Jack poured himself a tumbler of rum from the half-full bottle on the mantelshelf and then looked at Hayes and began to laugh.

'The whole town is talking about you. Pull yourself together man,' Hayes said. 'The way your missis died and you didn't even go to her funeral . . .'

Jack stopped laughing quite suddenly, and he rummaged behind the cushion of his chair to look for something. His gun. He held it in his hand, showing it to Hayes, and Hayes, who had deserted from the army for cowardice, ran for his life, up the hallway and into the street, telling everyone that Jack was 'blind drunk'.

After that, children and mongrel dogs came to look in at the mysterious hallway, where Hilda's grey coat and walking stick hung on the dusty old-fashioned hallstand. Hearing them, Jack staggered to the doorway and shouted, 'Be off!' whereupon they scattered like mice down the street. One day, he propped the door back in place and from the inside he put furniture against it, to keep it from falling down.

There were no more callers, except the niece, who cycled over on her half-day to do some cleaning and to buy tea and sugar and things. Her visit coincided with the delivery day of the brewery people and she opened one half of the shop door and took in whatever drink Jack had ordered her to. That was the time when Mama asked the niece if there was any chance of recovering the little tray cloth she had given Hilda; just for sentiment's sake, Mama said, she would like to have it back. The niece gave it to us, along with a few dresses and some table linen. Herself, she took Hilda's jewellery, as Jack had told her that he was going to burn 'the whole damn lot'. True enough we saw a bonfire in their garden one spring night, and the fire smouldered for close on two days.

Gradually, the house came to look deserted; the paintwork peeled on the outside window frames, and the gutters leaked. A statue that stood on the landing upstairs got knocked down and remained in broken pieces behind the lace curtain. The curtain itself was grey and fraying. Some days the can of milk left by Tina No-Nose would be taken in; other times it stayed, for the dogs and the flies. She swears he came to the door once and invited her inside, and that he hadn't a stitch on. She ran down the street, yelling and telling of the incident but people thought she was having one of her fits, and disregarded it.

I was waiting very early one morning for a lift on a creamery car to take me to some cousins. There was not a soul about. Suddenly Jack called from the upstairs window, said 'Missie, Missie'. I could not tell if he knew me but I suppose to him I was a young girl, just waiting there, a little on the plump side, but ripe, and ready for entanglement. Indeed the visit I was taking was primarily to see a young man whom I did not know but whose looks – black hair and very dark sallow skin – lured me. Soon indeed I was startled because a tennis ball fell at my feet. It was grazed and somewhat greenish. I looked to the doorway and saw that Jack was beckoning me urgently. I went across thinking he might want the priest or the doctor and already I was afraid. That fear that makes the whole body shake, like a wind conductor. He was quite drunk and his eyes were vacant. He asked if I was yet clicking, and I said no, a rapid prudish no.

'Can't you come in,' he said.

'I'm in a hurry,' I said, and took a few steps backwards.

'I have nice wine,' he said.

'I have the pledge,' I said and he sniggered at that.

'C'mon, can't you,' he said, and he grasped my arm.

It was summer and I was wearing a flowery dress that I was

most proud of. It had elasticised sleeves and he let his finger go under the elastic, then let it snap, then repeated it. I said that I was waiting for a lift, on the creamery car, and he said the driver was notorious and that I would not be safe in the lorry with him. That did not cheer me one bit.

'He's a prime boy,' he said and his face came very close to mine. His chin was full of grey bristling old-age stubble. A beard would have been better. The thought that I might have to kiss him made me inwardly curdle.

'I'll give you a half a crown,' he said.

'For what,' I rashly asked.

'Just lift your dress,' he said, and a small trickle of spittle flowed from the corner of his lip. His nose and lips were full of cold sores. I thought of saints being boiled in oil, of other saints enduring all sorts of beatings and lacerations and I would have swapped any of these punishments for the ordeal that I felt was imminent.

'Just a sensation,' he said, and he was dragging me in despite my hefty screams. I was stronger than he but it was not put to the test because at that moment, and without yet seeing it we could hear the sound of the lorry. The tankards on the back always made a terrible din. I ran to the driver in a gasp and asked him to take me in. It was high and he had to haul me up. He said had I seen a ghost or what, but I said no, that I was anaemic. I dared not tell him lest the same urge occur to him and in truth I was quivering. It struck me as odd and not uncomical that I was yet going forty miles to meet a man and risk the very proceedings that I was dreading with any other. I told the driver nothing but dreary stories so that his hand would not come onto my knee. The dress was short and I kept pulling it down, down, down so that he did not see flesh. I discussed my mother's corns, my father's lumbago and a workman who had shingles. Halfway up the mountain he stopped the lorry and asked me did I want to get out and cuffuffle. That was a dreadful moment but I bluffed and said I wasn't well. 'Flag day,' he said, and I nodded, giving him the impression that I had my period and was undesirable and untouchable.

*   *   *

Jack died in December, alone in the downstairs room, with only dust and shadows to succour him. The niece found him beside the dead ashes, in the armchair with his clothes on. Nearby on the table was an unfinished game of patience, and, of course, the rum bottles were all around. She found a letter he had scrawled, requesting that his body be cremated. But the parish priest and the locals said that the man was mad and not aware of what he was saying, so they ignored his wishes and buried him alongside Hilda.

I still believe he killed her just as I believe it was clear what he wanted from me that dewy morning, but not being certain of these things I told no one, and yet as the years go by, the certainty dogs me. Indeed it has become a ghost and the trouble with ghosts is that no-one but oneself knows how zealously they inhabit the everyday air.

Christmas Roses 🌿

Miss Hawkins had seen it all. At least she told people that she
had seen it all. She told her few friends about her cabaret life
when she had toured all Europe and was the toast of the richest
man in Baghdad. According to herself she had had lovers of all
nationalities, endless proposals of marriage, champagne in
every known vessel, not forgetting the slipper. Yet Miss
Hawkins had always had a soft spot for gardening and in
Beirut she had planted roses, hers becoming the first English
rose garden in that far-off spicy land. She told how she watered
them at dawn as she returned accompanied, or unaccompanied,
from one of her sallies.

But time passes and when Miss Hawkins was fifty-five she
was no longer in gold meshed suits dashing from one capital
to the next. She taught private dancing to supplement her
income and eventually she worked in a municipal garden. As
time went by, the gardening was more dear to her than ever her
cabaret had been. How she fretted over it, over the health of
the soil, over the flowers and the plants, over the overall design
and what the residents thought of it. Her success with it became
more and more engrossing. She introduced things that had not
been there before and her greatest pride was that the silly old
black railing was now smothered with sweet-smelling honeysuckle and other climbing things. She kept busy in all of the
four seasons, busy and bright. In the autumn she not only
raked all the leaves, but she got down on her knees and picked
every stray fallen leaf out of the flower beds where they tended
to lodge under rose bushes. She burnt them then. Indeed there

was not a day throughout all of autumn when there was not a bonfire in Mis Hawkins' municipal garden. And not a month without some blooms. At Christmas was she not proud of her Christmas roses and the Mexican firebush with berries as bright as the decoration on a felt hat.

In her spare time she visited other municipal gardens and found to her satisfaction that hers was far better, far brighter, more daring while also well-kempt and cheerful. Her pruning was better, her beds were tidier, her peat was darker, her shrubs sturdier and the very branches of her rose bushes were red with a sort of inner energy. Of course the short winter days drove Miss Hawkins into her flat and there she became churlish. She did have her little dog, Clara, but understandably Clara too preferred the outdoors. How they barked at each other and squabbled, one blaming the other for being bad tempered, for baring teeth. The dog was white with a little crown of orange at the top of her head and Miss Hawkins favoured orange too when she tinted her hair. Her hair was long and she dried it by laying it along the length of an ironing board and pressing it with a warm iron.

The flat was a nest of souvenirs, souvenirs from her dancing days – a gauze fan, several pairs of ballet shoes, gloves, photographs, a magnifying glass, programmes. All of these items were arranged carefully along the bureau and were reflected in the long mirror which Miss Hawkins had acquired, so that she could continue to do her exercising. Miss Hawkins danced every night for thirty minutes. That was before she had her Ovaltine. Her figure was still trim, and on the odd occasion when Miss Hawkins got into her black costume and her stiff-necked white blouse, rouged her cheeks, pointed her insteps and donned her black patent court shoes, Miss Hawkins knew that she could pass for forty.

She dressed up when going to see the town councillor about the budget and plans for the garden, and she dressed in her lamé when one of her ex-dancing pupils invited her to a cocktail party. She dressed up no more than three times a year. But Miss Hawkins herself said that she did not need outings. She was quite content to go into her room at nightfall, heat up the previous day's dinner, or else poach eggs, get into bed, cuddle her little dog, look at television and drop off to sleep. She retired early so that she could be in her garden while the rest of London was surfacing. Her boast was that she was often up starting her day while the stars were still in the heavens and that she moved about like a spirit so as not to disturb neighbours.

It was on such a morning and at such an unearthly hour that Miss Hawkins got a terrible shock concerning her garden. She looked through her window and saw a blue tent, a triangle of utter impertinence in her terrain. She stormed out vowing to her little dog and to herself that within minutes it would be a thing of the past. In fact she found herself closing and reclosing her right fist as if squashing an egg. She was livid.

As she came up to it Miss Hawkins was expecting to find a truant schoolchild. But not at all. There was a grown boy of twenty or perhaps twenty-one on a mattress. Miss Hawkins was livid. She noticed at once that he had soft brown hair, white angelic skin and thick sensual lips. To make matters worse he was asleep and as she wakened him he threw his hands up and remonstrated like a child. Then he blinked, and as soon as he got his bearings he smiled at her. Miss Hawkins had to tell him that he was breaking the law. He was the soul of obligingness. He said, 'Oh sorry,' and explained how he had come from Kenya, how he had arrived late at night, had not been able to find a hostel, had walked around London and eventually had climbed in over her railings. Miss Hawkins was unable to say the furious things that she had intended to say, indeed his good manners had made her almost speechless. He asked her what time it was. She could see that he wanted a conversation but she realised that it was out of keeping with her original mission, and so she turned away.

Miss Hawkins was beneath a tree putting some crocus bulbs in, when the young visitor left. She merely knew it by the clang of the gate. She had left the gate on its latch so that he could go out without having to be conducted by her. As she patted the earth around the little wan crocuses she thought, 'What a pity that there could not be laws for some and not for others!'

His smile, his enthusiasm and his good manners had stirred her. And after all what harm was he doing. Yet, thought Miss Hawkins, bye-laws are bye-laws and she hit the ground with her trowel.

As with most winter days there were scarcely any visitors to the square and the time dragged. There were the few residents who brought their dogs in, there was the lady who knitted and there were the lunchtime stragglers who had keys although Miss Hawkins knew that they were not residents in the square. Interlopers. All in all she was dispirited. She even reverted to a bit of debating. What harm had he been doing? Why had she sent him away? Why had she not discussed Africa and the game preserves, and the wilds. Oh how Miss Hawkins wished she had known those legendary spaces.

That evening, as she crossed the road to her house she stood under the lamp light and looked up the street to where there was the red neon glow from the public house. She had a very definite and foolish longing to be going into the lounge bar with a young escort and demurring as to whether to have a gin and tonic, or a gin and pink. Presently she found that she had slapped herself. The rule was never to go into public houses since it was vulgar and never to drink since it was the road that led to ruin. She ran in home. Her little dog Clara and herself had an argument, bared their teeth at each other, turned away from each other, and flounced off. The upshot was Miss Hawkins nicked her thumb with the jagged metal of a tin she was opening, and in a moment of uncustomary self-pity rang one of her dancing pupils and launched into a tirade about hawkers, circulars, and the appalling state of the country. This was unusual for Miss Hawkins, as she had vowed never to submit to self-pity and as she had pinned to her very wall a philosophy that she had meant to adhere to. She read it but it seemed pretty absurd:

> *I will know who I am*
> *I will keep my mouth shut*
> *I will learn from everything*
> *I will train every day.*

She would have ripped it off except that the effort was too much. Yet as she was able to say next day, the darkest hours are before the dawn.

As she stepped out of her house in her warm trouser suit, with the brown muffler around her neck, she found herself raising her hand in an airy, almost coquettish hello. There he was. He was actually waiting for her by the garden gate and he was as solemn as a fledgling altar boy. He said that he had come to apologise, that after twenty-four hours in England he was a little more cognisant of rules and regulations and that he had come to ask her to forgive him. She said certainly. She said he could come in if he wished, and when she walked towards the tool shed, he followed and helped her out with the implements. Miss Hawkins instructed him what to do, he was to dig a patch into which she would put her summer blooms. She told him the Latin name of all these flowers, their appearance and their characteristics. He was amazed at the way she could rattle off all these items while digging or pruning or even over-seeing what he was doing. And so it went on. He would work for an hour or so and then tootle off and once when it was very cold and they had to fetch watering cans of warm water to thaw out a certain flower bed, she weakened and offered him a coffee. The result was that he arrived the next day with biscuits. He said that he had been given a present of two tickets for the theatre and was she by the merest tiniest chance free and would she be so kind as to come with him. Miss Hawkins hesitated but of course her heart had yielded. She frowned and said could he not ask someone younger, someone in his own age group, to which he said no. Dash it, she thought, theatre was theatre and her very first calling and without doubt she would go. The play was *Othello*. Oh how she loved it, under-stood it and was above it all! The jealous Moor, the tell-tale handkerchief, confessions, counter-confessions, the poor sweet wretched Desdemona. Miss Hawkins raised her hands, acted for a moment and said, 'The poor dear girl caught in a jealous web.'

As an escort he was utter perfection. When she arrived breathlessly into the foyer, he was there, beaming. He admired how she looked, he helped remove her shawl, he had already bought a box of truffles, and was discreetly steering her to the bar to have a drink. It was while she was in the bar savouring the glass of gin-and-It that Miss Hawkins conceded what a beauty he was. She called his name, and said what a pretty name it was, what an awfully pretty name. His hands caught her attention. Hands, lovely shining nails, a gleam of health on them and his face framed by the stiff white old-fashioned collar, held in place with a gold stud. His hair was like a girl's. He radiated happiness. Miss Hawkins pinched herself three times in order not to give in to any sentiment. Yet all through the play – riveted though she was – she would glance from the side of her eye at his lovely untroubled and perfect profile. In fact the socket of that eye hurt so frequently and so lengthily did Miss Hawkins glance. Miss Hawkins took issue with the costumes and said it should be period and who wanted to see those drab everyday brown things. She also thought poorly of Iago's enunciation. She almost made a scene, so positive was she in her criticism. But of course the play itself was divine, simply divine.

At the supper afterwards they discussed jealousy, and Miss Hawkins was able to assure him that she no longer suffered from that ghastly complaint. He did. He was a positive pickle of jealousy. 'Teach me not to be,' he said. He almost touched her when she drew back alarmed and offended, apparently, by the indiscretion, He retrieved things by offering to pick up her plastic lighter and light her cigarette. Miss Hawkins was enjoying herself. She ate a lot, smoked a lot, drank a lot, but at no time did she lose her composure. In fact she was mirth personified, and after he had dropped her at her front door she sauntered down the steps to her basement, then waved her beaded purse at him and said as English workmen say, 'Mind how you go.'

But indoors Miss Hawkins dropped her mask. She waltzed about her room, using her shawl as partner, did ooh-la-la's and oh-lay-lays such as she had not done since she hit the boards at twenty.

'Sweet boy, utterly sweet, utterly well bred,' Miss Hawkins

assured herself and Clara, who was peeved from neglect but
eventually had to succumb to this carnival and had to dance
and lap in accordance with Miss Hawkins' ribald humour.
God knows what time they retired.

Naturally things took a turn for the better. She and he now had
a topic to discuss and it was theatre. It too was his ambition
and he had come to England to study theatre. So, in between
pruning or digging or manuring, Miss Hawkins was giving her
sage opinion of things, or endeavouring to improve his pro-
jection by making him say certain key sentences. She even
made him sing. She begged him to concentrate on his alto notes
and to do it comfortably and in utter freedom. Miss Hawkins
made 'no no no' sounds when he slipped into tenor or, as she
put it, sank totally into his chest. He was told to pull his voice
up again. 'Up, up up, from the chest,' Miss Hawkins would
say, conducting him with her thin wrist and dangling hand,
and it is true that the lunchtime strollers in the garden came to
the conclusion that Miss Hawkins had lost her head. No thank
you very much was her unvoiced reply to these snooping
people, these spinsters, these divorcees etcetera. She had not
lost her head nor any other part of her anatomy either, and
what is more, she was not going to. The only concession she
made to him was that she rouged her cheeks since she herself
admitted that her skin was a trifle yellow. All that sunshine in
Baghdad long ago and the hepatitis that she had had.
  As time went by she did a bit of mending for him, put leather
patches on his sleeves, and tried unsuccessfully to interest him
in a macrobiotic diet. About this he teased her and as he dug
up a worm or came across a snail in its slow dewy mysterious
course he would ask Miss Hawkins if that were a ying or yang
item and she would do one of her little involuntary shrugs,
toss her hair, and say, 'D'you mind!' He seemed to like that
and would provoke her into situations where she would have to
do these little haughty tosses and ask, 'D'you mind!'

It was on St Valentine's Day that he told Miss Hawkins he had
to quit the flat he was lodging in.

'I'm not surprised,' she said, evincing great relief and then she went a step further and muttered something about those sort of people. He was staying with some young people in Notting Hill Gate and from what Miss Hawkins could gather they hadn't got a clue! They slept all hours, they ate at all hours, they drew national assistance and spent their time – the country's time – strumming music on their various hideous tom-toms and broken guitars. Miss Hawkins had been against his staying there from the start and indeed had fretted about their influence over him. He defended them as best he could, said they were idealists and that one did the crossword puzzles and the other worked in a health juice bar but Miss Hawkins just tipped something off the end of the shovel the very same as if she was tipping them off her consciousness. She deliberated then said he must move in with her. He was aghast with relief. He asked did she mean it. He stressed what a quiet lodger he would be, and how it would only be a matter of weeks until he found another place.

'Stay as long as you like,' Miss Hawkins said, and all through this encounter she was brusque in order not to let things slide into a bath of sentiment. But inside Miss Hawkins was rippling.

That evening she went to a supermarket so as to stock up with things. She now took her rightful place alongside other housewives, alongside women who shopped and cared for their men. She would pick up a tin, muse over it, look at the price, and then drop it with a certain disdain. He would have ying and yang, he would have brown rice, and he would have curry dishes. Some confusion had entered Miss Hawkins' mind regarding this and rather than confining it to Indian cuisine she felt that all foreigners liked it. She did however choose a mild curry. The colour was so pretty being ochre, that she thought it would be very becoming on the eyelids, that is if it were not stinging. Miss Hawkins was becoming more beauty conscious and plucked her eyebrows again. At the cash register she asked for free recipes and made a somewhat idiotic to-do when they said they were out of them. In fact she flounced off murmuring, about people's bad manners, bad tempers and abominable breeding.

* * *

That night Miss Hawkins got tipsy. She danced as she might dance for him one night. It was all being exquisitely planned. He was arriving on the morrow at five. It would not be quite dark but it would be dusk, and therefore things dim, so that he need not be daunted by her little room. His new nest. Before he arrived she would have switched on the lamps, put a scarf over one; she would have a nice display of forsythia in the tall china jug, she would have table laid for supper and she would announce that since it was his first night they would have a bit of a celebration.

She ferreted through her six cookery books (those from her married days) before deciding on the recipe she wanted. Naturally she could not afford anything too extravagant and yet she would not want it to be miserly. It must, it simply must, have 'bouquet'. She had definitely decided on baked eggs with a sprinkling of cheese and kidneys cooked in red wine and button mushrooms. In fact the wine had been bought for the recipe and Miss Hawkins was busily chiding herself for having drunk too much of it. It was a Spanish wine and rather heady. Then after dinner as she envisaged it, she would toss a salad. There and then Miss Hawkins picked up her wooden spoon and fork and began to wave them in the air and thought how nice it was to feel jolly and thought ahead to the attention that awaited him. He would be in a comfortable room, he would be the recipient of intelligent theatrical conversation, he could loll in an armchair and think rather than be subjected to the strumming of some stupid guitar.

He had suggested that he would bring some wine and she had already got out the cut glasses, washed them and shone them so that their little wedges were a sea of instant and changeable rainbows. He had not been told the sleeping arrangements but the plan was that he would sleep on a divan and that the Victorian folding screen would be placed the length of the room when either of them wished to retire. Unfortunately Miss Hawkins would have to pass through his half of the room to get to the bathroom but as she said a woman who has danced naked in Baghdad has no repression passing through a gentleman's room in her robe. She realised that there would be little débâcles, perhaps misunderstandings but the difficulties could be worked out. She had no doubt but that they would achieve a harmony. She sat at the little round supper table and passed things politely. She was practising. Miss Hawkins had not passed an entrée dish for years. She decided to use the linen napkins and got out two of her mother's bone napkin holders. They smelt of vanilla. 'Nice man coming,' she would tell her little dog, as she tripped about tidying her drawers, dusting her dressing-table, and debating the most subtle position for a photograph of her, from her cabaret days.

At length and without fully undressing Miss Hawkins flopped onto her bed with her little dog beside her. Miss Hawkins had such dratted nightmares, stupid rigmaroles in which she was incarcerated, or ones in which she had to carry furniture or cater on nothing for a marquee of people. Indeed an unsavoury one, in which a cowpat became confused with a fried egg. Oh was she vexed! She blamed the wine and she thanked the gods that she had not touched the little plum pudding which she had bought as a surprise for the Sunday meal. Her hands trembled and she was definitely on edge.

In the garden Miss Hawkins kept looking towards her own door lest he arrive early, lest she miss him. Her heart was in a dither. She thought, 'Supposing he changes his mind, or supposing he brings his horrid friends, or supposing he stays out all night,' and each new crop of supposing made Miss Hawkins more badtempered. Supposing he did not arrive. Unfortunately it brought to mind those earlier occasions in Miss Hawkins' life when she had been disappointed, nay jilted. The day when she had packed to go abroad with her diamond-smuggling lover who never came, and when somehow out of shock, she had remained fully dressed even with her lace gloves on, in her rocking chair for two days until her cleaning woman came. She also remembered that a man proposed to her, gave her an engagement ring and was in fact already married. A bigamist. But, as he had the gall to tell her, he did not feel emotionally married, and then to make matters worse took photos of his children, twins, out of his wallet. Other losses came back to her and she remembered bitterly her last tour in the provinces when people laughed and guffawed at her and even threw eggs.

By lunchtime Miss Hawkins was quite distraught, and she wished that she had had a best friend. She even wished that there was some telephone service by which she could ring up an intelligent person, preferably a woman and tell her the whole saga and have her fears dismissed.

By three o'clock Miss Hawkins was pacing her floor. The real trouble had been admitted. She was afraid. Afraid of the obvious. She might become attached, she might fall a fraction in love, she might cross the room, or shyly, he might cross the room and a wonderful surprise embrace might ensue and Then. It was that then, that horrified her. She shuddered, she let out an involuntary no. She could not bear to see him leave, even leave amicably. She dreaded suitcases, packing, goodbyes, stoicism, chin-up, her empty beseeching hand, the whole unbearable lodestone of it. She could not have him there. Quickly she penned the note then she got her coat, her handbag, and her little dog in its basket and flounced out.

The note was on the top step under a milk bottle. It was addressed to him. The message said: 'YOU MUST NEVER EVER UNDER ANY CIRCUMSTANCES COME HERE AGAIN.'

Miss Hawkins took a taxi to Victoria and thence a train to Brighton. She had an invalid friend there to whom she owed a visit. In the train, as she looked out at the sooty suburbs Miss Hawkins was willing to concede that she had done a very stupid thing indeed, but that it had to be admitted that it was not the most stupid thing she could have done. The most stupid thing would have been to welcome him in.

Ways ❧

A narrow road and the first tentative fall of snow. A light fall that is merely preparatory and does not as yet make life cumbersome for the people or the herds. Around each clapboard house a belt of trees, and around the younger trees wooden Vs to protect the boughs from the heavier snow. The air is crisp and it is as if the countryside is suddenly miraculously revealed – each hill, each hedgerow, each tiny declivity more pronounced in the mantle of snow. Autumn dreaminess is over and winter is being ushered in.

The road could be anywhere. The little birches, the sound of a river, the humped steel bridge, the herds of cattle, the silo sheds, and the little ill-defined tracks suggest the backwardness of Ireland or Scotland or Wales. But in fact it is Vermont. Together they are braving the elements – two women in their thirties who have met for a day. Jane has lent Nell, her visitor, a cape, snow boots, and fuzzy socks. They pass a house where three chained guard dogs rear up in the air and bark so fiercely it seems as if they might break their fetters and come and devour the passers-by. Jane is a little ashamed; it is, after all, her neighbourhood, her Vermont, and she wants things to be perfect for Nell. She is glad of the snow and points proudly to the little pouches of it, like doves' feathers, on a tree. She apologises for the dogs by saying that the poor man has a wife who has been mentally ill for twenty years and has no help in the house.

'In there?' Nell says.

'Yes, she's in there somewhere,' Jane says, and together they look at a little turret window with its second frame of fresh snow and a plate glass with a tint of blue in it. Together they say, 'Jane Eyre,' and think how odd to be telepathic, having only just met.

'You were wonderful last night,' Jane says.

'I was nervous,' Nell says.

'Ironing your dress, I guess I was, too. It was so delicate, I was so afraid.'

'Afraid?'

'That it might just disappear.'

Nell remembers the evening before – arriving from New York, going up to a cold bedroom and taking out a sheaf of poems she was going to read to the English Department of the university where Jane and her husband teach. Scrambling through her notes in the guest bedroom, searching anxiously for a spare refill for her pen, she was once again envisaging a terrible scene in which her head would be hacked off and would go rolling down the aisle between rows of patient people, while her obedient mouth would go on uttering the lines she had prepared. Always, before she appeared in public, these nervous fits assailed her, and more than anything she longed for a kind hand on her brow, a voice saying, 'There, there.'

Jane had ironed the dress Nell had chosen to wear and brought it up, moving on tiptoe. She asked if Nell wanted to wash and had given her a towel that was halfway between a hand towel and a bath towel. Nell said that she might like a drink to steady her nerves – only one – and shortly afterwards, on a tiny little gallery tray, there was a glass of sweet sherry and some oatmeal biscuits. As she changed into the dress, taking her time to fasten the little buttons along the cuffs, the bells from three different churches pealed out, and she said an impromptu prayer and felt dismally alone. As if guessing, her hostess re-entered carrying an electric heater and a patchwork bedcover.

They stood listening to the last peal of the last bell, and Nell thought how Jane was kindness itself in opening her house to a stranger. Not only that, but Jane had gone to the trouble of typing out a list of people at the university whom Nell would meet, adding little dossiers as to their function and what they were like.

'And what do you do apart from teaching?' Nell asked.

'I like to give my time to my family,' Jane said.

'Social life?'

'No, we keep to ourselves,' Jane said, following this with a little smile, a smile with which she punctuated most of her remarks.

Jane took her on a tour of the house then, and Nell saw it all – the three bedrooms besides the guest room with the patchwork quilt, the series of identical shells on the little girl's bureau, the Teddy bear with most of its fur sucked bare, four easy chairs in the living room, and the seven new kittens around the kitchen stove, curled up and as motionless as muffs in a shop window. Jane explained how two kittens were already booked, three would be taken on loan, and the remaining two would stay with the mother and be part of their family. Pinned to the wall in the kitchen was a list of possible Christmas gifts, and when Nell read them she felt some sort of twinge:

> Make shirt for Sarah
> Grape jelly for Anne
> Secondhand book for Josh
> Little bottles of bath essence

The house and its order made such an impression on her that she thought she would like to live in it and be part of its solidity. Then two things happened. A kitten detached itself from the fur mass, stood on its hind legs, and nibbled one of Jane's slippers that was lying there. Then it shadow-boxed, expecting the slipper also to move. Next thing, the hall door opened, someone came in, went through to the parlour, another door was heard to bang, and almost at once Mozart was being played on a fiddle. It was Jane's husband. Jane went to see him, to enquire if he wanted anything, and to tell him that the new guest had come and was very content and had brought a wonderful present – a cut-glass decanter, no less. He seemed not to reply. The fiddle playing went on, and to Nell there was something desperate in it.

Soon after, the two women left for the reading and Jane kept a beautiful silence in the car, allowing Nell to do her deep breathing and memorise her poems. Afterward, they went to a party, and during the party Nell went into the bathroom, watched herself in someone's cracked mirror, and asked herself why it was that everyone was married, or coupled – that everyone had a husband to go home to, a husband to get a drink for, a husband to humour, a husband to deceive – but not she. She wondered if there was some basic attribute missing in her that made her unwifely, or unlovable, and concluded that it must be so. She then had an unbearable longing to be at home in her own house in Ireland, having a solitary drink before bed as she looked out at the River Blackwater.

'What does your husband look like?' she asks of Jane now as they trudge along the road. It is colder than when they set out, and the snow is pelting against their faces. They have to step aside to let a snow plough pass them on the road, and Jane is smiling as she envisages her answer. It is as if she enjoys the prospect of describing her husband, of doing him justice.

'You two girls in trouble?' asks the driver of the snow plough, and they both say that they are simply taking a walk. He shakes his head and seems to think that they are a little mad, then he smiles. His smile reaches them in a haze of snow. They wave him on.

The branches of the birches teeter like swaying children. The icicles are just formed and wet; they look edible and as if they might melt. With her thumbnail Jane flicks open a round locket that hangs from a fine chain about her neck, and there in cameo is a man – gaunt and pensive, very much the type that Nell is drawn towards. At once she feels in herself some premonition of a betrayal.

'He's lovely,' she says, but off-handedly.

' "I don't want you lovely" was what he told me,' Jane says.

'Not one of King Arthur's knights,' Nell says, sampling a few flakes of snow.

'It wasn't a romantic thing,' Jane says.

'What was it?' Nell says, nettled.

'It was me very adoring,' Jane says. 'I have a theory it's better that way.'

'I don't believe you,' Nell says, and stands still, causing Jane to stand also, so that she can look into Jane's eyes. They are grey and not particularly fetching, but they are without guile.

'You're prying,' Jane says.

'You're hiding,' Nell says, and they laugh. They are bickering now. They look again at his likeness. The snow has smeared the features, and with her gloved thumb Jane wipes them. Then she snaps the locket closed and drops it down inside her turtleneck sweater – to warm him, she says.

'How did you catch him?' Nell says, putting her arm around Jane and tickling her lightly below her ribs.

'Unfortunately, I was one of those exceptional women who get pregnant even when they take precautions,' Jane says, shaking her head.

'Was he livid?' Nell says, putting herself in the man's shoes.

'No, he said, "I guess I'll have to marry you, Sarah Jane," and we did.'

It is the 'we' that Nell envies. It has assurance, despite the other woman's non-assertiveness.

'I was married in grey,' Jane says. 'I simply had a prayer book and spring flowers. Dan's mother was so upset about it all that she left during the breakfast. Then we went back to the college, and he read a paper to the students on Mary Shelley.'

'Poor Mary Shelley,' Nell says, feeling a chill all of a sudden, a knife-edged chill that she cannot account for.

'You'd like him,' Jane says, worried by the sudden silence.

'Why would I like him?' Nell says, picturing the face of the man that stared out of the locket. All of a sudden, Nell has a longing not to leave, as planned at six o'clock, for New York, but to stay and meet him.

'Why don't I stay till tomorrow?' she says as casually as she can.

'But that would be wonderful,' Jane says, and without hesitation turns sharply round so that they can hurry home to get the Jerusalem artichokes out of the pit before it has snowed over. She discusses a menu, says Dan will play his favourite pieces for them on the phonograph – adding that he never lets anybody else touch the machine, only himself.

Nell's thought is 'a prison' – a prison such as she had once been in, where the precious objects belonged to the man, and the dusters and brooms belonged to her, the woman.

'He's good to you?' Nell says.

'He's quite good to me,' Jane says.

Men are hunting deer up in the hills, and the noise of the shots volleys across the field with far greater clarity because of the soundlessness created by the snow. Again, on their way back, they pass the snarling dogs and they literally run down a hill and across a stubbled field to take a short cut home. The menu is decided – artichoke soup, roast pork, fried potatoes, and pecan pie. They both profess to be starving.

They pass through a village on the way home and Nell stays behind to buy wine and other treats. She lingers outside the one general store, imagining what it would be like to live in such a place – to be wife, widow, or spinster. She thinks again of her own stone house, the scene of occasional parties and gatherings, when her friends come and she and Biddy, a helper from the village, cook for days; then the aftermath, when they clean up.

The three village churches are white and enveloped in snow; the garage is offering a discount on snow tyres, and an elderly woman is pushing open the door to the general store, bringing back three circulating-library novels. In the shop window are two hand-printed signs:

> We are a family of three sisters looking for a
> house to rent.
> We can afford up to $300.

> LOST: Harvest table, weathered.

She goes inside and buys rashly. Yes, she is curious. Something in Dan's expression makes her tremble with pleasure. Already she has decided on her wardrobe for tonight, and resolves to be timid, in her best sky-blue georgette dress. She buys a gourd filled with sweets for the little girl, and a storm lamp for the little boy.

The children are in the kitchen when she gets back, and how excited they are at receiving these presents. They gabble outrageously about their school lunch, and how gooey it was; then they sing a carol out of harmony; then the little girl admits in a whisper that she loves Nell and gives her a present of a composition she has just written about King Arthur. Nell reads it aloud, and it is about King Arthur looking for a magic harp for his bride, Guinevere. The little boy says it is soppy and his sister whacks him with his new lamp. What can she do to help, Nell asks. Jane says she can do nothing. After the ordeal of the night before, and the fitful sleep because of the boiler going on and off, she must be tired and should nap. Jane tells the children that they must be like little mice and do their homework and not squabble.

There is a harness bell attached to the back door, and it trembles a second before it actually rings and by then he is in. He is like someone out of Nell's childhood – an ascetic man in a long leather coat turned up about the neck, and he wears gauntlet gloves, which he immediately begins to remove. His children run to him; he kisses his wife; and, upon being introduced to Nell, he nods. There is something in that nod that is significant. It is too off-hand. Nell sees him look at her with his lids lowered, and she sees him stiffen when his wife says that their guest will stay overnight and then points to the wine. He says, 'Fancy,' as he looks at the labels with approval, and the children ask if they can make butter sauce for the pecan pie.

Nell is having to tell them, the children, the size of her house in Ireland, the kind of ceiling, the cornices, the different wallpapers in the bedrooms, the orchard, the long tree-lined drive, the white gate, the lych gate, the supposed ghost, and everything else pertaining to the place. They say they will visit her when they come to Europe. He does not comment but keeps moving about the kitchen. He looks at the thermometer, pushes the kittens to one side with the toe of his shoe, rakes the stove, and then very slowly begins to open the wine. He smells the corks and very carefully attaches them to the sides of the bottles, using the metallic paper as a cord.

Jane is recalling London – springtime there, a hotel in Bayswater, a trip she had made as a girl with a blind aunt – and remarking to Nell how she saw everything so much more clearly simply by having had to describe it to her aunt. She speaks of the picture galleries, the parks, the little squares, the muffins they were served for breakfast, and the high anthracite-coloured wire meshing around the London Zoo.

'I like being an escort,' she says shyly.

Suddenly Nell has to excuse herself, saying that she must take a last-minute nap, that her eyes feel scorched.

'I can't,' she says later as she lies coiled on her bed, trying to eat back her own tears. All she wants is for the man to come up and nuzzle her and hold her and temporarily squeeze all the solitude out of her. All she wants is a kiss. But that is vicious. She foresees the evening, a replica of other evenings – a look, then ignoring him, then a longer look, a signal, an intuition, a hand maybe, pouring wine, brushing lightly against a wrist, the hair on his knuckles, her chaste cuffs, innocent chatter stoked with something else. She imagines the night – lying awake, creaks, desire fulfilled or unfulfilled. She sees it all. She bites the bedcover; she makes a face. Every tiny eye muscle is squeezed together. The chill that she felt up on the road is upon her again. She might clench the bedpost, but it is made of brass and is unwelcoming.

'I'm afraid I can't,' she says, bursting into the bathroom where Jane has taken a shower. She knows it is Jane because of the shadow through the glass-panelled door.

'Oh, my dear,' Jane says, pushing the door open and stepping out.

'I just realised it isn't possible,' Nell says, not able to make any excuse except that she has packed and that she must make her plane for New York. Jane says she understands and reaches for a towel to dry herself. Nell begins to help.

'I'm tiny up top,' Jane says, apologising for her little nipples and flat chest. She drags on a thick sweater, slacks, her husband's socks, and then she reaches to a china soap dish and picks up a cluster of hairpins, putting them quickly in her long damp hair.

Dan is in the toolshed, and the two women holler goodbye. The children say, 'No, no, no,' and to make up for this sudden disappointment, Jane and Nell carry them to the car in their slippers and put them under a blanket on the back seat. They will come for the drive. In the car, Jane says that maybe next year, when the attic room is ready, Nell will come back and stay up there and write her poetry. Jane's face is faintly techni-colour because of the lights from the dashboard, and her hair is gradually starting to fall down because of the careless way she has put in the hairpins. She looks almost rakish. She says what a shame that Nell has not seen one maple tree in full leaf, to which Nell says yes, that she might come back one day – but she knows that she is just saying this.

Does Jane know, Nell wonders. Does Jane guess? Behind that lovely exterior is Jane a woman who knows all the ways, all the wiles, all the heart's crooked actions?

'Are you jealous, or do you ever have occasion?' Nell asks.

'I have had occasion,' Jane says.

'And what did you do?' Nell asks.

'Well, the first time I made a scene – a bad scene. I threw dishes,' she says, lowering her voice.

'Christ,' Nell says, but is unable to visualise it, is unable to connect the violence with Jane's restraint.

'The second time, I started to teach. I kept busy,' Jane says.

They are driving very slowly, and Nell wonders if, in the back, the children are listening as they pretend to sleep under the blanket. Nell looks out of the window at rows of tombstones covered in snow and evenly spaced. The cemetery is on a hill, and, being just on the outskirts of the town, seems to command it. It seems integral to the town as if the living and the dead are wedded to one another.

'And now?' Nell says.

'I guess Dan and I have had to do some growing up,' Jane says.

'Who's growing up – Daddy?' asks the little girl from under the blanket.

Her mother says, 'Yes, Daddy,' and then adds that his feet are getting bigger.

All four of them laugh.

'He liked you,' Jane says, and gives Nell a little glance.

'I doubt it,' Nell says.

'He sure did,' Jane tells her, convinced.

Nell knows then that Jane has perceived it all and has been willing to let the night and its drama occur. She feels such a tenderness, a current not unlike love, but she does not say a word.

In the airport, they have only minutes to check in the luggage and have Nell's ticket endorsed. The children become exhilarated and pretend to want to place their slippered feet on the conveyor belt so as to get whisked away. The flight is called.

'I think you're very fine,' Nell says at the turnstile by the passenger area.

'Not as fine as you,' Jane says.

Something is waiting to get said. It hangs in the air and Nell recalls the newly formed icicles that they had seen on their walk the day before. More than anything she wants to turn back, to sit in that house, beside the stove, to exchange stories and become a friend of this woman. Politeness drives her forward. Her sleeve catches in the metal pike of the turnstile and Jane picks it out, in the nick of time.

'Clumsy,' Nell says, holding up a cuff with one thread ravelled.

'We're all clumsy,' Jane says.

They exchange a look and, realising that they are on the point of either laughing or crying, they say goodbye hurriedly. Ahead of her Nell sees a long slope of linoleum floor and for a minute she's afraid that her legs will not see her safely along it, but they do. Walking down, she smiles and thanks the small voice of instinct that has sent her away without doing the slightest damage to one who met life's vicissitudes with an unquenchable smile.

A Woman by the Seaside 🍂

MORNING

They had been there now four days and each morning she got up early and went for a walk along the promenade. At the end of the promenade there was a golf links and she walked over the grass towards the empty, treeless plain that revealed nothing except an old, grey ruin. On the fourth morning a man who was searching for golf balls warned her not to walk in high heels over the putting greens, though he could see perfectly well that she wore flat shoes. He told her the other grass, the sturdy yellow stuff, had been imported from New Zealand because the Irish grass could not stand up to the flaying seawind. As he talked he twitched and jerked. She recognised him as the 'Clock' so nicknamed because of the regularity of his twitching.

'Have a sweet,' he said, taking a bundle of toffees from his overall pocket. She declined and moved on. She walked about a mile and sat on a hillock – the same one each day – and looked out at the sea and thought more or less the same thoughts. Would one see him today? Would he renew it? Give her back her youth, her pre-life, the thing everyone craved, except children. And when they met and he said 'How are you?' what was she to say? Tell him that she was a doctor's wife, that she had a daily woman who polished knockers and wrote calls into an elaborately designed daybook which had a special prayer printed for each day of the year. They were good Catholics. Some days they had mashed potatoes, some days boiled, on Fridays they had chips; it was important to vary life. And she could tell him that she spent her spare time up-stairs – they had converted a bedroom into a sitting room – where she read and did her nails and listened to sad music. On the evenings her husband did not come home she sat at the window hawing on it, wiping it clear, thinking of the other courses her life might have taken, thinking of her childhood and of the children she would never have. She had had an operation for an inner ailment and they took too much away. A friend of her husband's did the job, for free. In bitter moments she thought her husband had fixed it so that she would be childless and could go on indulging him. The operation had cut into her.

When they married seven years before she loved him, the way people do; then she began not to love him and now she disliked him so much she could not believe that she had ever loved him at all. He was weak, forgetful, happy when he got a new shirt, scared to go out in the garden after dark to get coal, mean about food bills, extravagant in pubs, a bully, a charmer. That was why she came back to find the other man, her old sweetheart, the sandy-haired boy whom she knew for a few nights and had danced with, and had kissed under a hollowed poplar outside her lodgings in Dublin. They were both students at the time, though he never qualified. He became a folk singer and was famous in America. She engineered it that she and her husband would come for a holiday to this place where her sweetheart was born. It was easy to achieve. They needed a holiday. She was sick, she said, of telephones and doorbells and the budgie they kept in a cage and the meat bills regularly once a month.

'Book somewhere,' her husband said. 'We have money, we can afford it.'

So, she booked at this seaside town in the west of Ireland hoping that since it was summer he might be on holiday. Her hope was realised. The first evening they arrived she heard from the hotel owner that he was home but she hadn't seen him yet. Perhaps today? At least, she looked pretty. Her dark hair being long made her seem a lot less than thirty and from the wind and breeze her eyes glowed the way they used to, when she was a girl and eager to fall in love.

Walking back she faced the town and the hill of houses that rose towards the new, pebble-dashed chapel which overlooked the sea. One house, painted a peacock blue, stood out above all the others, which were white. Even the white ones had a suggestion of blue because she'd been told that their owners dipped a blue-bag in the limewash and the blue tinge came faintly into the white like the curlew's distant whimper underneath the shriek of the gulls. The gulls cried like old women, the curlews mourned like sad ones and the human voices were quelled by the noise of the birds and the roar of the wind. It would rain. Shop owners were taking in the coloured balls and home-knit jerseys which they had hung outside, on display. A few visiting children played on the beach, a few adults leaned over the railings watching and warning the children. She smiled. They were the starchy ones whom the hotel owner did not care for – English people who gorged big breakfasts, big lunches, big suppers and pale ales. No profit.

She changed into high heels and then went towards the hotel bar to look for her husband whom she knew was certain to be there.

'Mrs Mullally come in!'

'Ellen.' Her husband had that happy faraway smile which enveloped him whenever he held a glass containing alcohol.

'She'll be a cross-country walker yet.'

'Fine colour she has.'

She crossed the polished stone floor to join them – her husband Dr Mullally, Mr Carmody a bank manager from the next county, James the hotel owner in his black, clerical-like suit, the 'Clock', who was trying to cadge a drink in exchange for clay-covered golf balls, and a man called Tim who kept a puck goat and was complaining about the lack of business in his line.

'Take my problem,' he was saying. 'The noble goat is extinct, materialism and dialectism is in danger of . . .'

'Yeh,' the returned American kept saying. He was not a member of any party really but moved on the fringes trying to engage people. Also he hoped to wean customers away and James eyed him with due suspicion. He had come home from America and bought a big mansion which he had converted into a hotel and decorated with green carpets and green drapes. Visitors seemed to prefer the smaller hotel with its white-washed walls and floors of blackstone that had been quarried from a mine nearby.

'What will you have?' the doctor asked his wife.

'Anything, sherry . . .' He was drinking whiskey. By lunch-time he would be hanging off that backless stool and James would fetch him soup which he would slobber.

'You met the "Clock",' Mr Carmody said to her. 'Did he molest you?'

The 'Clock' found it so difficult to get a kiss from a girl that he could only get it by force in the dark. I should have kissed him she thought and sighed at her own meanness, the meanness of all women who measure what they'll give by what they know they will get.

'I, I di'id notin' to Mrs Doctor dat I wouldn'ttt do to . . .,' the 'Clock' began but James, who employed him for odd jobs, told him to go in and help in the kitchen. They watched – they were unable not to – as he moved to the door in fitful jerks, parodying his own affliction. Ellen would ask in a moment if her friend had been seen. Too late. The doctor was talking.

'Tell Ellen the story,' he said to Mr Carmody. 'Ellen will appreciate it.'

'Will I?' Bitterness had become a habit between them.

'Oh yes,' said Mr Carmody, licking his lips and preparing. He could not tell a story until he had ruined it first by describing its significance.

'This is a model example of an Irish conversation, an exercise in native deviousness if you like . . .'

'Tell it,' said the doctor who knew better.

Well,' said Mr Carmody, 'there were these two girls and one was inside a wall and the other was going by on a bicycle. For the purpose of the story let us call the one inside the wall Mary, and her friend Martha.'

'The bloody bible,' said the man who kept the goat.

Mr Carmody went on, ' "What time is it?" asked the girl who was going by on her bicycle.

' "Are you off to the village?" said Mary, who was inside the wall.

' "Can I get you something?" said Martha.

' "What are you getting for yourself?" said Mary.

' "I don't know if I'll go at all," said Martha, and Mr Carmody then laughed, giving Ellen her cue to laugh with him. There was no doubt, she wasn't funny. Soulful was probably the word for her, bloody soulful.

James knew what was on her mind. 'We're having company,' he said, and told her that Tom had rung up and booked a table for three.

'We'll get him to sing,' she said, pretending it was the thought of singing which made her happy and so inspired her that she bought a round of drinks. She hummed a little song for her husband:

Oh doctor, dear doctor, dear doctor John,
Your cod liver oil is so pure and so strong,
I'm afraid of my life I'll fall down on my bike,
If I drink any more of your cod liver oil.

'Lovely,' James said. She sang it the day they were married. Her husband was still a student and she taught school. Then he qualified and they got on in the world, and she had to resign because it did not look well for a successful man to have a working wife. However it was all unimportant now because her friend was coming back and they would sit close together and renew their acquaintance.

'By God,' said Mr Carmody, warming his hands on the glow of her happy face. 'There is no understanding women; one minute they cut you with a look, the next minute they shower you with loveliness.'

'I didn't cut you,' Ellen said, flirting with him, 'when did I cut you?'

'My wife,' the doctor proclaimed to the shelf of whiskey bottles, 'is a rare woman and a poet, and is out of her depth in a society like ours.'

'She's out of her mind,' said the man who kept the goat because she was nibbling some of the sweet-peas that were in a vase on the counter, humming different lines from different songs.

'Yeh,' said the returned American.

'I will go,' said James, 'and prepare a feast for our friend,' and going, he smiled.

AFTERNOON

The first thing Ellen noticed was the total abstinence badge in her friend's buttonhole. He'd been a drinker when she knew him and her husband had been temperate. He bowed and smiled across two tables and she fingered her own lapel stupidly to make some reference to the badge in his. He sat with his parents who were so shy that they'd kept their coats on, and talked only in whispers. His hair had darkened, but he had the same face – hacked out of yellow limestone.

She sat with the doctor and Mr Carmody, receiving their jokes and their attentions. They had a bottle of white wine and she drank from a glass with a long, green stem to it.

'I like to see you with a glass in your hand,' the doctor said.

'And turn me into a dipso.,' she said. Already a little drunk she was slurring her words.

'Take the one with the stem,' Mr Carmody said, repeating the story he'd already told about the town's evangelist who drank in secret and had an arrangement to get a glass with a stem whenever a drink was proposed after a church function.

'I love your rag-bag of stories,' she said to him, catching Tom's eye for the fifth time.

'Madam,' he said, using his napkin as a cloak to lay before her eyes. Fool. Tom's parents were getting embarrassed. She began to chew her food and look alert.

'I took a little drink about an hour ago,' said the doctor, yawning, 'and it's gone right through my head.'

'I'll tell you a thing I love,' she said, to try and keep him from dropping off to sleep right there, 'an image.'

'An image,' the doctor said as if she had just undressed.

'There is a glass, which if you hold it hard enough, it crushes in your grip,' and as she was telling it Tom came over and shook hands with them and she was obliged to tell the story a second time. Her old sweetheart smiled and said they must join tables. When they did she found herself sitting next to his father, a thin, grey-haired man with the blue, sea-eyes which he had passed on to his son.

'You must be very proud of him,' she said.

'We are. Very proud of him,' he said, but in an unnatural, learnt-off voice. How could he say, we're not.

Tom's mother on hearing that a doctor had joined the group leant across and said her back was at her.

'You should go to hospital,' the doctor said. His only way of dismissing people.

'The food in hospitals is not good,' she said, although she'd had nothing for her lunch but tea and buns.

'How long have you had it?' Ellen asked, fearing that her husband had been abrupt.

'Ever since Tom was born,' the low-voiced, fat, flushed woman told the gathering. Mr Carmody came to the rescue by suggesting that, as they had a famous singer among them they should have a sing-song, and to strengthen the suggestion James the hotel owner came in with a tray of Gaelic coffees.

'Tuck in,' he said. It had begun to rain so no-one need have any anxiety about saving hay or missing the sunshine. He pulled the cord of the venetian blind until the room became quite dark and then he turned on the various lamps and sat at the head of the two tables which had been drawn together. The 'Clock' slipped in from the kitchen door and a few more locals came to the other doorway to look at the famous singer who was balancing one fork on top of another. He had strikingly thin hands, with blond hairs on the backs of his fingers as far down as his knuckles.

'You remember,' he said to his father, 'you could balance a poker on the floor, you had such delicate hands.'

His father didn't know what to say. He was flushed from the coffee and the friendship, and he would have liked a song.

'You remember,' Ellen said to her friend and as he looked at her everyone seemed to gather interest in their reminiscence.

'What?' Tom said, quite stern now.

'Nothing,' she said and made a little movement by hunching her shoulders and drawing her hands up, fingers splayed outwards as if she was holding off an enemy. It began as an affectation, now she could not stop herself doing it. The 'Clock' thought she was making a friendly gesture towards him and came over and put his hand on her shoulder. She was the only young woman in the room and each of the men deferred to her whenever they spoke. Lucky, lucky her.

'Tis America at home,' James said as he nodded to the waitress for more coffees. Outside they could hear the rain-gutters overflowing, rain as it beat against the stone wall bringing with it the memory of all the nights of rain they had ever known.

'Are you staying here?' Tom asked and also seemed to say, 'How can I see you without all this surveillance?'

'We're here for two weeks,' she said. Her husband looked over.

'Sea air,' said her husband with a sting in his voice, 'makes chaste women pregnant.' As though he and she had never lived together as man and wife. Although in the last few years they scarcely did. She lived more to herself, undressed in the bathroom, crept in to bed fortified by her wool, ankle-length nightgown.

'My husband is always teasing me,' she said to cover up her embarrassment. More people pressed around the doorway and she was grateful that she could draw attention to them.

'There's the "tank", now, Tom,' Mr Carmody said, pointing to a brassy woman in curling pins. She was the mother of four children and had never been married, hence her nickname. James hushed them off as he didn't like that sort of thing in his hotel.

'Although,' he said, 'I get many a laugh here,' and he took the postcard from his pocket which had a brown picture of a church and printed underneath was 'Bird's Eye View of St

Patrick's Purgatory'. He asked Mr Carmody to read it to Tom and Mr Carmody did, in his eager, plum voice:

Dear Sir,
I Bridie Donoghue of Mill Road, Carrick on Suir, Co. Tipperary was on Mr. Dunne's pilgrimage and fear that I have left a corset in a toilet of yours or elsewhere. I guarantee return postage if you send it to me.
I, Bridie Donoghue of Mill Road, Carrick-on-Suir, Co. Tipperary.

It was the first time Ellen saw him laugh. His whole face broke up and split with laughter and his blue eyes were merry again the way she remembered them.

'The poor girl,' he said, laughing for her.

'You see,' said Mr Carmody, 'after the trials of penance, prayer and fasting the new corset became too much for her. She had to divest.'

'I often meant to do that pilgrimage,' said Tom's mother, 'for the sake of my back.' She meant the remark for her son but he was busy laughing.

'I'll go when the pleasures of the body have deserted me,' said Mr Carmody, taking the second Gaelic coffee that had been appointed to Tom. The doctor took the previous one, fair was fair. Tom drank tea. Soon he would get impatient, the way people do when they are outside the mood of false hilarity created by drink.

'You should show Tom your goat,' she said to the man who kept the puck. She'd had a brainwave, 'Maybe he'll buy it from you and bring it back to America.'

'A noble thought,' said the goat owner and without any trouble or explanation she and Tom got up on the excuse that they must look at the puck which was kept in an outhouse down the street.

'So,' he said, once they'd escaped. She had her head back, her mouth fully open to catch the rain. She wanted to have a breath of rain for him.

'So,' she said on the same note, but first they had to look at the animal because Tim was waiting to convey them. They saw a white, sulky goat chained to the back door with a small

radius of garden to move on. Some rhubarb had been put there
but it was untouched.

'What does he eat?' Tom asked.

'Anything,' its owner began. 'Now take a piece of a palm
tree, at least we call it a palm tree, it's a dupress really . . .'

Would they ever get away? Would they merely learn about
that boring goat and waste seconds?

'Of course, he'll eat skins,' the owner was saying. 'If you're
hungry you'll eat anything.'

'I like him,' Tom said. 'He's surly and I like that.'

'Will you buy him?' asked the loyal owner who had sworn two
minutes before that he would not be separated from his puck.

'What would I do with him?' Tom asked. She could see that
he wanted to escape but first he wanted to leave a pound note
somewhere for Tim.

'Put him on television,' said the owner.

'He might make a show of me.'

'He might, and then again he might not.'

'Buy him a tree,' said Tom, handing out some money.

'Oh God I couldn't take it,' said the owner closing his
fingers on it and smiling – secure in porter for three nights
now. They got away.

They walked out of the town towards the golf links.

'I dream about you,' Tom said when they had gone down the
street and past the row of silent, inquisitive, censuring houses.

'And I,' Ellen said, 'I think of your purple eyes.'

'They're not purple, they're blue.'

'They're sea eyes,' she said, 'they're changeable.'

'And how are you?'

'I'm well, marvellous.' They were climbing the first grass
hillock, unaware of rain or damp because their hands were now
joined.

'You're like a little child,' he said. They were both the same
age, but he had grown up and gone out in the world and fought
for auditions, fame, money, recognition; fought to get up the
ladder.

'Talk,' he told her.

'Why cloud it with words?' she asked.

'Because you want to talk, you're restless.'

'Have I aged?' she asked him. He said no, that her face was the same sorrowful, lovely face and her neck the neck of a young swan.That undone her. He could be dour and stern for hours scorning her girlish sentiments and then he could make her dizzy with his own tenderness.

The rain had lightened so they sat in the shelter of a grass cliff in order to look at one another. He took a cellophane packet from his pocket and broke off two squares which contained white lozenges.

'Have you a pain?' she asked.

'No, it's to stop me having a pain.' He chewed them quite openly and without shame.

'You remember the night we were nearly thrown out of a pub in Dublin because you said the word "maidenhead"?'

He remembered everything, the pub, the sawdust floor, the black-labelled whiskey and the crystal earrings which made long shadows on her neck. And he kissed her now as he had kissed her then. Her body flooded open. She lay on the wet, imported grass while he entwined her with arms and legs saying that if she got pneumonia her husband would have to take over.

'The courtesy of your mouth,' she said. He kissed her from the widow's peak of her high, serene brow down the length of her sorrowing face.

'If it was fine there would be golfers here,' she said, a little overcome.

'To hell with them,' he said.

By some connection of ideas they both thought of the crushable glasses and he held her tighter, mashing her bones.

'You can make love to me if you want to,' she said.

'I want to,' he said.

'Well then you can.' She had sunk very low, she was almost asking the man.

'You'd get pregnant,' he said, 'and I wouldn't want that.'

'I wouldn't get pregnant,' she said. She could not tell him her secret because it was sordid and had nothing to do with the soft rain and sough of his mauve tongue saying prayers to hers.

'I wouldn't, honest, not now.'

'You're sure?'

'I'm sure and I'm sure that I love you and that I saved myself up for you,' she said, not speaking the truth but not lying either. Hadn't she said this to the doctor, once, too?

'Ellen,' he said, picking up her name from when he had whispered it years ago, 'there's just one thing.'

'What?'

'I'm getting married in a couple of months.'

'Oh.' That changed the complexion of everything. 'Why didn't you tell me first?'

'Because I didn't want to hurt you.'

'But you are hurting me.'

'I know. Does it make any difference? Can we still?'

'You'd like a last fling,' she said, hating her own voice that had become pinched in a matter of seconds. God knows how her face looked. Someone said that when she heard disappointing news the light went out of her as if a lamp had been quenched from inside. She stirred underneath him and he sat up and took out a pocket comb to comb his hair although it was not ruffled. She watched intently, waiting for the reconciliation.

'Is she Irish?' she asked at length, because he'd keep up the silence for the whole evening.

'No, she's American.'

'Oh lovely,' she said, the falsely confident voice taking over. 'They're great at hygiene, and togetherness and snacks, good old American snacks.'

'You know nothing about her,' he said.

'You're absolutely right,' she said, and looked out at the sea and planned how she would stand up decorously without letting her knees creak or her age show. As she brooded, the old everyday ache took charge of her again and she regretted having said that bit about the snacks and the togetherness.

They turned and walked back facing the town now, and the peacock house, and the white ones darkening because of the vicious sky.

'Where would we have made love?' she asked.

'In the ruin,' he said. They were walking away from it.

'You mean the old, grey ruin?'

'The very one.'

'Where eagle and cuckoo live gay?'

'You're gay again,' he said.

'Of course,' she said, 'I'm gay because I'm virtuous.' It was important to seem happy. She talked about her life, her gleaming door-knockers, the books she read, the patients her husband saw, and the music she listened to. He told her about America and Greenwich Village where he lived, and pumpkins he ate, and concerts he gave and how he sweated in television studios.

'To sweat is good,' she said, and they instantly laughed at her pomposity. He asked if she ever heard a good folk song would she send it to him and he wrote his address on a cigarette carton balancing it against the end wall of the first house in the town. The address he gave was of a record company for whom he did recordings. He did not trust her with his private one. She said she might go to New York sometime and he said he thought she'd like it. As they got near the hotel she turned to him.

'We should go back I think, to our ruin.'

'You'd hate me,' he said.

'I could never do that.'

'They can spot us now through the window,' he said. 'And anyhow my poor mother and father will think I've eloped with you.'

'How long more are you home for?'

'Two days.'

'I might see you.'

'You might.'

'When?'

'We'll leave it to chance,' he said, 'I hate planned action.'

'Except for marriage,' she said, but he was lifting the door latch of the hotel bar and may not have heard her. On the threshold, he turned and gave her the semblance of a kiss by arching his lips, 'When I said I dreamt about you it was true, it was all true,' he said. They went in looking innocent and the people inside merely looked at them as if they'd been absent for a few minutes. Time had got muffed in the dining room, smoke settled above the tables, and the steam of hot coffee and warm breath had fogged the windows and the mirrors, and fogged the company who were at loggerheads about something they could not quite articulate.

'You're wrong, wrong, wrong,' she heard Tom's father say.

Tom had a job getting his parents out, and all the while as he bullied them, he held Ellen's hand, because he had begun to say goodbye to her, and could not conclude it until he was actually leaving.

NIGHT

Ellen stayed downstairs with her party – other people joined them – and they ate around nine. Because it was such a lost day her husband drank more than usual and before eleven he was escorted to bed by two of the men. She was staying, she said, for a little while to digest her duck. She was frightened out of her wits. He'd timed the length she'd been away with Tom – one hour and twenty-seven minutes. He said next time she ought to repair her face before she came back in. She had to say that Tom got very swellheaded and had insisted on kissing her just to prove his attractiveness.

'You saw his pimples,' she said to humour her husband.

'I didn't have my face that close to his, thank God.' It was all he had the chance to say. Other people's arrival rescued them from going over every second of it, from his interrogations, from her having to reply where her hands were when she walked beside the singer and where her desires? Mr Carmody and James came in from the Gents with a new opinion as to why the writing in Ladies' lavatories was more dignified than that in Gents. Lovely, old fuddy-duddy Mr Carmody had saved her.

There was nobody else in the dining room at this hour except two priests who eyed her with pity, curiosity, disapproval. Their white priest's collars were almost obscured by black polo-neck sweaters. They drank brandy and talked to each other about golf. She was sober now, her mind ticking over the pleasures and disappointments of the day, her body tired the way it suddenly tires out of defeat. He had not come back although she divined that he would. She wound her watch, counted the number of roses in each of the rose-patterned curtains, practised some deep breathing and reluctantly left the table when a girl came to lay the breakfast things.

Up in her bedroom she had just taken off her necklace when she heard the scream. One, piercing scream. She gasped but of course her husband was sound asleep and could not ask what was wrong. She laid the necklace on the bureau and hurried downstairs to tell someone. James and Mr Carmody were in the hall tapping the weather glass.

'There's something wrong,' she said. 'I heard a woman scream.'

'In the hotel?' James asked. He dreaded a scandal ever since the time a priest had fallen down the stairs, coshed his head on the grandfather clock at the bottom and died. Without absolution either.

'No, outside,' she told him. 'It was a scream for help.'

'From what direction?' Mr Carmody looked red in the face, the look he might have if his bank was raided at midday and the chief hold-up man had evidence of Mr Carmody's infidelity with two different cinema usherettes. He looked to James. They must do something gallant. They must go out and defend women.

'What sort of scream?' Mr Carmody asked.

'For help,' Ellen said. 'That sort of scream.'

Without another word they set off. Ellen walked in the middle between the two of them, their steps rang out on the near-empty street with determination. They went down the promenade in the direction of the golf links because she said that was where the scream seemed to have come from.

'It could be anyone,' Mr Carmody said.

'Tons of women live alone, could be one of them,' James said. They had to slow down a little because they did not know, quite, where they were going.

'We'll search houses,' Carmody said.

'We can't gain entry without a warrant,' James said, changing his voice to match the seriousness of his mood. After a short discussion it was decided to waken up Guard Donaghy who lived nearby, the barracks being half a mile away. Guard Donaghy was not pleased.

'I'm married only six weeks, have you no nature in you?' he asked the two men. Then he noticed Ellen who had stood farther out at the gateway and he got very businesslike and said they would need a second guard for such a job. Once again Ellen had to describe the scream, the direction it came from, and the exact time. She said she had looked at her watch going up the stairs and it was about three minutes after that. James thought to himself that the victim would be dead by now.

Ten more minutes elapsed before they had wakened the second guard and were ready to set out armed with batons and flashlamps. They paused at the hill of houses and conjectured where to knock first.

'It might be the "tank",' said James. 'I heard there was trouble brewing there, th'other fellow is home from England.'

They knocked on her green, knockerless door – four stout men with bare knuckles and brave hearts. Ellen stood back and spread the wool scarf over her shoulders to keep warm. She shivered – that they might hear it again. It *was* a woman she said to reassure herself. The 'Clock' stumbled up from nowhere, asked why the commotion and insisted on joining in.

'Did you hear a noise?' James asked while they waited at the entrance to the 'tank's' narrow, crumbling, sinful house.

'I thhh'nk I did,' said the 'Clock', lying. At that instant a light came on inside and within seconds a man opened the door about a foot and put his head out. He was a strange man altogether whom none of them recognised.

'What do you want?' he asked in a Scottish accent.

'We're guards now,' said one of the two policemen about to enter, 'trying to locate a scream.'

'Locate my breeches,' said the strange man, closing the door in the guard's face and turning the key inside.

'It's a great world,' Mr Carmody declared to the full moon. 'There was a different fella in there at lunch time.'

'Full programme, matinee and evening performance,' said the guard.

For a long while they wondered who this man might be? Did he have anything to do with the train robbery? A flagrant train robbery had taken place in England and some of the culprits were said to have escaped to Ireland. Guard Donaghy thought of it first. He smiled, saw himself promoted to superintendent, handing out orders to whole barracks of raw policemen, taking salutes, going home early to sleep with his young wife.

'She bought porter this evening,' said the 'Clock', without a stammer. 'If she had money, she'd have bought the hard stuff.'

That settled it. Guard Donaghy followed the others wearily towards the house of Miss Cooney, the town's Evangelist. For years the prime boys had threatened to terrify the gizzard out of her, because she interrupted their courtships by beating walls with a stick, and flashing a torch light into byways where they were with girls entwined in a trench coat.

They found her front door wide open and they went in stealthily, fearful for what they might see. The older guard climbed the stairs, waving his baton. The others followed step by step. She was in her bed, not murdered, but so inebriated she would not have stirred if they had set fire to the sagging mattress underneath her. A small red, Sacred-Heart lamp cast light on her unlovely face and on the porter bottles strewn around. She had a rosary in her hand and was breathing heavily. Her dreams took her to boways where she beat women away and cuddled close to the men.

'Holy Mary in private life,' the young guard said. His colleagues nudged him. Mr Carmody held the bottles up to the red light, for dregs. They needed to fortify themselves.

'Nothing,' he said. 'Not a bloody drop.' They repaired downstairs and onto the street again. It was so bright Ellen could see their faces – gratified for such a night's adventure. Above them a full moon, like a distant and impassive God, was passing sentence on their gratified faces. They walked in the middle of the street because at that hour no traffic was abroad.

'What is the correct side of the road to walk on?' Mr Carmody asked.

'Strictly speaking there is no correct side,' the older guard said. Mr Carmody welcomed it as invaluable information. He loved anarchy, the world's greatest poets were anarchists he said. He began some story about a sculptor who put a fish into a statue he made for a church, and was still telling it when they reached the third house which was set in its own grounds. The guards were petrified about being bitten by the 'Beware of the Dog' dog, who had a fearful edge about uniforms.

'You go first,' they said to the other men. The lady who lived inside was an English widow who got her wine and foodstuffs sent direct from a wholesalers in Dublin. She would not admit them. She said she'd read plenty of stories where criminals pretend they were policemen. She spoke through the letter box and the huge, fawn animal was snarling beside her.

'You recognise me,' the older guard said. He'd gone there at considerable risk to fix up about the dog licence.

'That is the whole point of you criminals, you sound authentic,' she said.

'Let her go to hell, suspicious aul crow,' James said, she never having given his hotel a shilling's custom. They marched away and walked down another street, listening at doors, put their faces to windows, crossing when they saw a light, disturbing people who were on the point of sleep, or on the lavatory, or in their armchairs planning to stand up and climb the long calvary to their beds. It was past midnight.

'Then it must be someone on the golf links,' a guard said, turning to Ellen in the moon's bright glare.

'It must be,' she said, avoiding his look. She felt guilty for not having led them to the scene of some crime. A girl running up the street crying 'Rape, Rape,' would have been a sweet and welcome sound. The guards watched her and the full moon was passing silver sentence on her guilt. She shivered.

'You're cold,' James said and put his jacket over her.

They walked over the golf links, training the lamps on the grass cliffs that sloped right down to the putting greens. The small areas of cropped green looked like baize card tables in the moonlight. Someone saw or thought he saw a hare, the 'Clock' insisted that he heard a groan as if a woman was being choked; they lit matches and lit cigarettes and called out 'Anyone there', but heard no reply except the quiet, washing sound of the sea and the melody of a stream as it flowed from isolation towards its sea bed. They walked the eighteen holes and crossed the road to the ruin which stood in a swampy field. She felt relief because they'd come at last.

It was bigger than she had imagined and two intact walls formed a rectangle where the altar had been. Nettles stung her through her stockings and she wobbled fiercely on the uneven soil, having to balance herself on whoever happened to be next to her. Was it too late? Through the stone windows above the altar place she could see part of the sky outside and the fiercely bright stars and the moon slipping by. The same moon shone on him, wherever he was.

'Can I borrow the torch?' she said to Mr Carmody, who was shining it on the stone ceiling, drawing attention to its beauty. It looked like bones, the grey coiled bones of the ancient dead. She took the torch and went outside to look. Perhaps he'd fled when he heard the gang. She whistled. The men wondered what she was up to but thought she was probably relieving herself and whistling to distract them. She whispered his name – Tom, Tom – but no voice came back to her. She had been sure he would be there, waiting. That was why when she heard the scream she ran to the rescue with a twofold purpose.

'It's terrible that we haven't located it,' she said coming back in, not daring to look at any of them but staring through the long window-space at the sky and the lit-up fields. To have made love under the altar place, with his coat over the nettles, beneath the boned roof would have been a sort of sacrament. As if they guessed her thoughts, they began to grouse.

'You're sure you didn't have one too many, Mrs Mullally,' the older guard said to her.

'It's not fools' day, just in case you think it is,' Mr Carmody said, and then in a harsher voice. 'Or are we all playing gooseberry for you?' In other words are we all deprived of our sleep just on the off-chance of your meeting with your pimpled, little non-drinking upstart.

'Well that's a night well wasted,' the young guard said. He'd be on night duty the following week and there was no use begging his wife to go to bed with him in the daytime because she thought it dirty in daylight.

In that humour they set back for home.

Not a light shone from the village, it was the dead hour of night when even the sea seemed to be resting. The 'Clock' was the first to drop off, then the two guards, then the other three approached the hotel.

'Well I have a new anecdote for my rag-bag,' Mr Carmody said as he went indoors without bidding them goodnight.

She stood outside with James, too ashamed to speak, too concerned not to.

'You thought you'd see him again,' James said.

'I did and I didn't,' she said. 'I don't know what I thought.'

'You can't fool me,' he said. 'God damn it I'm a man too and I fell for you the evening you came here, and you weren't in the door but you were asking about him.'

She stood guiltily and watched the moon slip behind an eiderdown of cloud. Had she heard a woman scream, or was it a bird or was it a scream that came out of her own desperateness?

'Say something,' he said.

'I kept you up,' she said.

'I have the winter to sleep,' he said, 'the whole, five bloody months of it.' He thought her the most pure and calm statue of a woman he had ever seen. He would remember and love her for all of next winter. Statues, someone told him, took the sun at midday and gave it back at night. Would she warm him? She was agitated and wanted to say something.

'What is it, pet?' he said. If the lads saw him now, softening his voice they'd say he was a right eejit.

'It was so selfish,' she said and thought, 'Love as we practise it is small, mean and fixated.'

'Stop blaming yourself.' He touched her shoulder and felt how thin she was.

'If only I could love you all,' she said, knowing how his hand shook.

'And the doctor?' James added.

'And the doctor,' she said woefully. He'd got drunk because his pride was hurt. There was always a real reason for everything – why spoons tarnished, and jam furred, and people declined into God or drink, or card games.

'Can I kiss you?' James asked and immediately withdrew the request saying it was no thing to ask a decent woman.

'Kiss me,' she said and submitted to his too-tight, unaccustomed embrace. A statue in his arms. Earlier in the day when Tom had kissed her, her whole body had swooned, now her body was in possession of itself, but her soul fluttered. The first time in her life she had done something that was not exclusively for herself. Her own identity was lost for a minute. She thought of Japanese geisha girls who are trained to please men, she thought of the long winter James had to put in year after year, as long as her own. She thought he should wash his teeth more often.

'Lovely,' he said and drew back for her to scold him. The years had lifted from his withered cleric's face. In the dark she put her fingertips to her cheeks and felt tears of joy. So this was what she wanted for herself – not a fur stole as she had told her husband, not children as she had told the specialist, not her legs prised open and his love secreted as she had told Tom – but this, the generosity to give as effortlessly as flowers give out smell, and red rowan berries their startle of colour.

'Do you want to walk?' she asked, 'or sit in the bar, or lie in the rocks? Do what you want, please, please.'

'You're tired,' he told her, 'You must go to bed and so must I.'

So that was what he wanted really, to retire and tot up the day's takings and the night's kiss at the end of the day.

'Will you sleep?' he asked, taking his tweed jacket softly from her shoulders.

'Of course I'll sleep,' she said, but she was reluctant to go in. Something had happened but she was not sure what. Might she have grown older and a fraction changed? Might her goal in life begin to be different? She felt a strange peace as if she had found a new resource in herself and she prayed to God that it was not a passing thing and that on the morrow it would be there.

In the Hours
of Darkness 🌿

On a stretch of road far from London and not yet in sight of
Cambridge, Lena suddenly remarked that it was like Australia.
There was more than one reason for this: the physical loneliness was exactly like that she had experienced in the countryside above Sydney one warm intoxicating Saturday and the
road itself, devoid of houses or tillage, suggested a depopulated
land. Also the high grass on either side was tawny, bleached no
doubt by the long phenomenal English summer. The bridges
too that flanked the motorways were ugly and graceless and
reminded her of that other time.

Her son Iain said that any minute they would see the spires
of Cambridge and already her mind ran on to her first view of
the old historic town, the various university complexes, the
stout walls, the stained-glass windows and the overall atmosphere of studiousness. She was intrigued. She envisaged going
into the hotel bedroom and drawing curtains – they would be
dark red and once drawn she would click on a light and sit in
an armchair to read some of Jane Austen in order to re-dis-
cover through that woman reserve and perseverance.

Her youngest son was going up to Cambridge and she was
facing the predicament she had read about in novels – that of a
divorced woman, bereft of her children, having to grow old
without these beloved props, having in some indescribable way to
take the first steps into loneliness as if she were a toddler again.

Two signposts read the same mileage for Cambridge even
though they were miles apart and she said that was typical,
then instantly decided that she was becoming a shrew. Soon

maybe she would be questioning bills, talking to herself and finding fault with any services that were to be done to her house. To save face she remarked on the beauty of a fairly ordinary little village in which she noticed a post office, an ale house, whimsy-looking cottages and an antique shop.

The hotel at Cambridge was not what she had imagined. The entrance adjoined the car park and in the too huge lobby there were arrows pointing to several bars. Then hammering to testify that construction work was in progress. Would it stop at night? She was obsessed with noise and could, she believed, be wakened by an air bubble in her water pipes at night. She followed the porter and was dismayed to find that he lost his way. It was a big ramshackle place with various flights of stairs leading to different quarters. Her bedroom was on the first floor and just outside was a child's cot and a single mattress standing on its end. The room was everything she dreaded – a single bed with a stained orange coverlet, matching curtains, plastic lampshade, wardrobe with three empty metal hangers that moved slightly as if propelled by some shiver. The one summoning bell brought no response – no buxom girl, no doddery old man, no housekeeper with motherly smile came in answer to the ringing of the green oblong button. In fact there was no way of telling if it was connected, or if in fact a bell had rung somewhere in the bowels of that place and was being ignored with a shrug. 'Bad place to die', she thought, and as fervently as she had longed for the surprise and repose of that little room, she now longed to be out of it and safely at home.

She wanted tea. Her stockings were wet. She and Iain had had to walk the last bit of the journey carrying baskets, a record player, a drawing board and loose bits of lighting flex. He had parked the car outside the town because it was against university rules to own one. On their walk it had begun to drizzle and by now it was raining heavily. Lifting the curtain she looked at the spatters as they crawled down the window-pane and lodged on the frame beneath. The view was of a football field empty except for its goal posts. She would make the best of it.

In the lobby the guests were being served with tea and everything about them suggested not an academic life but a life of commerce. She had to step over bags bursting with shopping, and at first glance every mouth seemed to be allied to a piece of oily chocolate cake. She sat at one empty table waiting for service, and in her restlessness began to eat the bits of damp ribbony lettuce that served as decoration on the plate of sandwiches that the previous occupant had devoured. The waiter strolled across and caught her in this nonsensical theft. She asked him to bring tea quickly as she was dining at seven. He spurned her to her face, he also spurned the entire human race and did both of these offices in broken English.

Dinner was in one of the most esteemed of the colleges and they foregathered in a small overheated sitting room, that was full of furniture and pieces of china. Her host, a professor, had invited a younger professor and two freshmen. They sat and awkwardly sorted each other out, the young men laughing lightly at everything and constantly interjecting their remarks with bits of French as they bantered with each other about their sleeping habits and their taste for sherry or classical music. It was stiff. Her son should have had a different introduction, something much less formal, a bit of gaiety. The conversation centred for a long time on a professor who had the nickname of a woman and who received students in his long johns and thought nothing of it. Incongruously he was described as a hermit even though he seemed to be receiving students most mornings in his cluttered room. It was stifling hot. To calm herself, Lena thought of the beautiful mist like fine gauze sparkling on the courtyard outside, and above it a sky perfectly pictorial with its new moon and its thrilling stars.

They went down a short flight of stairs and then climbed some other steps to their early dinner. The host had done everything to make it perfect – smoked salmon, grouse, chantilly, different wines for each course and all this printed alongside each person's nameplace. The old servant was so nervous that he trembled as he stood over her and kept debating with his long hands whether to proffer the entrée dish or the gravy jug.

It was touch and go. His master told him for God's sake to put the jug down. A movement that caused his neck to tremble like that of a half-dead cockerel's. Yes, 'It was so' that students were sent down but they had to be awfully bad or else awfully unlucky and of course it was an awfully amusing thing. 'I am in a modern English play,' she thought, the kind of play that portrayed an intelligent man or woman going to seed and making stoical jokes about it. Academic life was not for her. She would rather be a barbarian. She sucked on the word as if it were sherbet. Barbarian.

The grouse was impossible to tackle. Everyone talked too much and tried too eagerly and this all-round determination to be considerate caused them instead to be distracted and noisy. Little bright jets of blood shot up as knives vainly attacked the game. To conceal his embarrassment the young professor said it was too delicious. The host said it was uneatable and if young Freddie's was delicious to give it to Lena since hers was like a brick. She demurred, said it was lovely, while at the same time resolved that she would eat the sprouts and would drink goblets of wine. A toast was raised to her son and he went scarlet as he heard himself being praised. Looking downwards she saw that the various plates contained a heap of little bones, decked with bits of torn pink flesh, and true to her domestic instinct she said they would make good broth, those leavings. A most tactless slip. Everyone raved over the nice raspberry chantilly and quite huge portions of it rested on the young men's dessert plates.

Having dined so early she felt it was appropriate to leave early. Earlier, her host had confessed to being tired and yet in his bedroom where she went to fetch her coat, she felt that he wanted to talk, that he was avid to tell some little thing. He simply said that he had never married because he could not stand the idea of a woman saying 'we', organising his thought, his time, his suits of clothing and his money. It was a small, functional room with a washstand, an iron bed with a frayed paisley robe laid across it. Staring from the wall was a painting of a wolf with a man's eyes and she thought this professor is not as mild as he seems. On an impulse she kissed him and he seemed so childishly glad that she then became awkward and tripped over a footstool.

Out on the street they lingered, admiring the courtyard, the stone archways, and the beautiful formidable entrance. The town itself was just shops, and shut cafés, with cars whizzing up and down as on any high street. At the hotel she bade Iain goodnight and knew that the hour had come when they were parting more or less for ever. They made light of it and said they would cruise Cambridge on the morrow.

As she approached her bedroom she began to remonstrate with herself, began to laugh. The music she heard was surely phantom music because after all she had been insistent about securing a quiet room. But as she proceeded down the corridor the sound increased in volume and pitch and she wondered if anxiety could play such a thorough trick. When she put the key in her own door and entered, the furnishings were shaking from the implosion of the noise and she looked instinctively for men in white coats with hair oil, which was her outdated version of the members of a dance band. Yes, a dance was in progress. The metal hangers which she had forborne to use were almost doing a jig. The hotel telephonist could do nothing, was not even sympathetic.

She took her key and went down the stairs, then crossed the street to the college where her son was. The porter directed her and seemed to sense her dismay because he kept repeating the instructions, kept saying, 'If you walk down now, towards the rectangular buildings, and take the first turning on the left you will find your son will be the fifth staircase along, and you will find him there.' Walking along she thought only of the sleep that would 'knit up the ravelled' day and hoped that in one of those buildings a bed awaited her, a bed, an eiderdown and total silence.

Coming towards her was a young man wearing a motor-cyclist's leather jacket that was too small for him. Something about the way he walked reminded her of restless youths that she had seen in an American film, of gangs who went out at night to have fights with other gangs, and inventing as a reason

for murder their virility or their honour. This boy reminded her
of that group. She wondered who he would be, thought that
probably he had put on the jacket to give himself an image, was
looking for friends. Four or five hundred young men were now
installed in that college and she thought of the friendships that
would ensue, of the indifferent meals they would all eat, the
gowns they would buy, the loves and hatreds that would
flourish as they became involved. She was glad not to be one of
them. Just before the figure came level with her she realised
that it was Iain and that obviously he was going in search of
adventure. She lost heart then and could not tell him of her plan
to find a bed in his house. She joked, pretended not to know
him, walked past with her hips out and then in an affected
voice said, 'Haven't we met somewhere.' Then she asked him
if he was enjoying it and he said yes, but he always said yes at
an awkward moment. They walked towards the gates and he
said that his name was painted at the foot of the landing, his and
three other names and how he had a little kitchen with a fridge
and that there was a note informing him of a maid who would
be at his services on the Monday. How she wanted to be that
maid. They said goodnight again, this time a little more gamely
since there was a mutual suspicion that they might meet a third
time.

In the lobby some people had come out from the dance and
a drunken woman was holding up a broken silver shoe asking if
the heel could be mended. The dance would go on till two.
Lena felt like crying. The manager asked if she would like
another hotel and she said yes then ran to her room and packed
things quickly, viciously. In the lobby yet again she felt herself
to be conspicuous, what with half her belongings falling out of
the bag and a look of madness. In the taxi she thought of warm
milk laced with whisky. Vain thought. The porter in the new
hotel was fast asleep and stirred himself only when the black
Dalmatian dog bared his teeth at her legs which she quickly
shielded with her suede bag. She had to pay there and then, and
had to write the cheque by balancing the book against the wall
as the counter space was taken up with various advertisement
cards. Home, home, her heart begged. The last train for

London had left an hour ago. She followed the porter down the corridor and herself let out a shriek when he admitted her to a room in which a shocked woman sat up in bed-jacket screaming. In fact the two women's screams coincided.

'Sorry about that, Madam.' He had made a mistake. He made a similar mistake three times over, leaving some occupants of that wing in a state of anger and commotion. At last he conducted her to an empty room, that was weirdly identical to the one she had just vacated. He said not to open the window in case of burglary.

Such nights are not remarkable for their sound sleeping, but this one had extra impediments. The single bed was so narrow that each time she tried to turn over she had to stop herself from falling onto the floor. The tap let out involuntary groans and now and then the Dalmatian gave a watchdog's moan. She put her black cardigan over the telephone to blot out its faint luminous glow. She was fighting for sleep. She took two large two-toned capsules that were filled with barbiturate. Her son at that same hour had climbed up by means of scaffolding to the roof of Christ's College and with his friend was debating whether to pee on it or not, and make a statement that might result in their being rusticated. Up there they had brought the wine, the roast fillets of pork and the cheeses that she had given him for his first night's picnic. She could feel the sleeping pills starting to work as she put her hand out to assist herself in turning over. Nevertheless she tumbled, fell and conked her head on the bedside locker. It made her wide awake. The last sure little route to sleep was closed. It was a question of waiting till morning, so she dressed and then grappling with anger paced the room.

A hand-printed sign above the mirror caught her attention. It said, 'In the hours of darkness, if a client has an urgent need will he or she please ring *and wait* because due to security the night porter may be prowling the building and not find himself adjacent to the switchboard.' She took it down, re-read it with amazement, then wrote, 'You must be joking', and signed her name in full. Then she sank into the gaping armchair and waited stoutly for morning.

A Rose in the Heart 🍂

December night. Jack Frost in scales along the outside of the
windows giving to the various rooms a white filtered light. The
ice like bits of mirror bevelling the puddles of the potholes. The
rooms were cold inside, and for the most part identically
furnished. The room with no furniture at all – save for the apples
gathered in the autumn – was called The Vacant Room. The
apples were all over the floor and in rows along the curb of the
tiled fireplace. Their smell was heady, many of them having
begun to rot. Rooms into which no-one had stepped for days
and yet these rooms and their belongings would become part
of the remembered story. A solemn house, set in its own
grounds, away from the lazy bustle of the village. A lonesome
house it would prove to be, and with a strange lifelikeness as if
it was not a house at all but a person observing and breathing,
a presence amid a cluster of trees and sturdy wind-shorn
hedges.

The overweight midwife hurried up the drive, her serge cape
blowing behind her. She was puffing. She carried her barrel-
shaped leather bag in which were disinfectant, forceps, instru-
ments and a small bottle of holy water lest the new child should
prove to be in danger of death. More infants died around
Christmas time than in any other month of the year. When she
passed the little sycamore tree that was halfway up she began to
hear the roaring and beseeching to God. Poor mother, she
thought, poor poor mother. She was not too early, had come
more or less at the correct time, even though she had been
summoned hours before by Donal the serving boy who worked

on the farm. She had brought most of the children of that parish into the world yet had neither kith nor kin of her own. Coming in the back door she took off her bonnet and then attached it to the knob by means of its elastic string.

It was a blue room – walls of dark wet morose blue, furniture made of walnut, including the bed on which the event was taking place. Fronting the fireplace was a huge lid of a chocolate box with the representation of a saucy-looking lady. The tassel of the blind kept bobbing against the frosted windowpane. There was a washstand, a basin and ewer of off-white with big roses splashed throughout the china itself, and a huge lumbering beast of a wardrobe. The midwife recalled once going to a house up the mountain, and finding the child smothered by the time she arrived; the fatherless child had been stuffed in a drawer. The moans filled that room and went beyond the distempered walls out into the cold hall outside, where the black felt doggie with the amber eyes stood sentinel on a tall varnished whatnot. At intervals the woman apologised to the midwife for the untoward commotion, said sorry in a gasping whisper, and then was seized again by a pain, that at different times she described as being a knife, a dagger, a hell on earth. It was her fourth labour. The previous child had died two days after being born. An earlier child, also a daughter, had died of whooping cough. Her womb was sick unto death. Why be a woman. Oh cruel life, oh merciless fate, oh heartless man, she sobbed. Gripping the coverlet and remembering that between those self-same, much-patched sheets, she had been prised apart, again and again, with not a word to her, not a little endearment, only rammed through and told to open up.

When she married she had escaped the life of a serving girl, the possible experience of living in some grim institution but as time went on and the trousseau drawer was emptied of its gifts, she saw that she was made to serve in an altogether other way. When she wasn't screaming she was grinding her head into the pillow, and praying for it to be all over. She dreaded the bloodshed long before they saw any. The midwife made her ease up as she put an old sheet under her and over that a bit of oilcloth.

The midwife said it was no joke and repeated the hypothesis that if men had to give birth there would not be a child born in the whole wide world.

The husband was downstairs getting paralytic. Earlier, when his wife had announced that she would have to go upstairs because of her labour, he said, looking for the slightest pretext for a celebration, that if there was any homemade wine or altar wine stacked away, to get it out, to produce it, and also the cut glasses. She said there was none and well he knew it since they could hardly afford tea and sugar. He started to root and to rummage, to empty cupboards of their contents of rags, garments and provisions, even to put his hand inside the bolster case, to delve into pillows; on he went, rampaging until he found a bottle in the wardrobe, in the very room into which she delivered her moans and exhortations. She begged of him not to, but all he did was to wield the amber-coloured bottle in her direction, and then put it to his head so that the spirit started to go glug-glug. It was intoxicating stuff. By a wicked coincidence a crony of his had come to sell them another stove, most likely another crock, a thing that would have to be coaxed alight with constant attention and puffing, to create a draught. The other child was with a neighbour, the dead ones in a grave-yard six or seven miles away, among strangers and distant relatives, without their names being carved on the crooked rain-soaked tomb.

'Oh Jesus,' she cried out as he came back to ask for the knitting needle to skewer out the bit of broken cork.

'Blazes,' he said to her as she coiled into a knot and felt the big urgent ball – that would be the head – as it pressed on the base of her bowels, and battered at her insides.

Curses and prayers combined to issue out of her mouth, and as time went on, they became most pitiful and were interrupted with screams. The midwife put a facecloth on her forehead and told her to push, in the name of the Lord to push. She said she had no strength left, but the midwife went on enjoining her, and simulating a hefty breath. It took over an hour. The little head showing its tonsure would recoil, would reshow itself, each time a fraction more, although in between it was seeming to shrink from the world that it was hurtling towards. She said to the nurse that she was being burst apart, and that she no longer cared if she died, or if they drank themselves to death. In the kitchen they were sparring over who had the best greyhound, who had the successor to Mick the Miller. The crucifix that had been in her hand had fallen out, and her hands themselves felt bony and skinned because of the way they wrenched one another.

'In the name of God push, Missus.'

She would have pushed everything out of herself, her guts, her womb, her craw, her lights and her liver but the centre of her body was holding on and this centre seemed to be the governor of her. She wished to be nothing, a shell, devoid of everything and everyone and she was announcing that, and roaring and raving when the child came hurtling out, slowly at first as if its neck could not wring its way through, then the shoulder – that was the worst bit – carving a straight course, then the hideous turnabout, and a scream other than her own, and an urgent presage of things, as the great gouts of blood and lymph followed upon the mewling creature itself. Her last bit of easiness was then torn from her, and she was without hope. It had come into the world lopsided and the first announcement from the midwife was a fatality, was that it had clubbed feet. Its little feet she ventured to say, were like two stumps adhering to one another, and the blasted cord was bound around its neck. The result was a mewling piece of screwed-up, inert, dark, purple misery.

The men subsided a little when the announcement was shouted down and they came to say congrats. The father waved a strip of pink flesh on a fork that he was carrying and remarked on its being unappetising. They were cooking a goose down-stairs and he said in future he would insist on turkey as goose was only for gobs and goms. The mother felt green and dis-gusted, asked them to leave her alone. The salesman said was it a boy or a child, although he had just been told that it was a daughter. The mother could feel the blood gushing out of her, like water at a weir. The midwife told them to do down and behave like gentlemen.

Then she got three back numbers of the weekly paper, a shoe box with a lid, and into it she stuffed the mess and the unnecessaries. She hummed as she prepared to do the stitching down the line of torn flesh that was gaping and coated with blood. The mother roared again and said this indeed was her vinegar and gall. She bit into the crucifix, and dented it further. She could feel her mouth and her eyelids being stitched too, she was no longer a lovely body, she was a vehicle for pain and for insult. The child was so quiet it scarcely breathed. The afterbirth was placed on the stove, where the dog Shep sniffed at it through its layers of paper and for his curiosity got a kick in the tail. The stove had quenched and the midwife said to the men that it was a crying shame to leave a good goose like that, neither cooked nor uncooked. The men had torn off bits of the breast so that the goose looked wounded, like the woman upstairs who was then tightening her heart and soul, tightening inside the array of catgut stitches and regarding her whole life as a vast disappointment. The midwife carried the big bundle up to the cellar, put an oil rag to it, set a match to it and knew that she would have to be off soon to do the same task elsewhere. She would have liked to stay and swaddle the infant, and comfort the woman and drink hot sweet tea but there was not enough time. There was never enough time and she hadn't even cleaned out the ashes or the cinders in her grate that morning.

The child was in a corner of the room in a brown cot with the slats that rattled because of the racket they had received from the previous children. The mother was not proud, far from it. She fed the child its first bottle, looked down at its wizened face and thought where have you come from and why. She had no choice of a name. In fact she said to her first visitor, a lieutenant from the army, not to tell her a pack of lies because this child had the ugliest face that had ever seen the light of day. That Christmas the drinking and sparring went on, the odd neighbour called, the mother got up on the third day and staggered down to do something about the unruly kitchen. Each evening at nightfall she got a bit of a candle to have handy and re-oiled the Sacred Heart lamp for when the child cried.

They both contracted bronchitis and the child was impounded in masses of flannel and flannelette.

Things changed. The mother came to idolise the child, because it was so quiet, never bawling, never asking for anything, just covert, in its pram, the dog watching over it, its eyes staring out at whatever happened to loom in. Its very ugliness disappeared. Its feet were all right. It seemed to drink them all in with its huge, contemplating, slightly hazed-over, navy eyes. They shone at whatever they saw. The mother would look in the direction of the pram and say a little prayer for it, or smile, and often at night she held the candle shielded by her hand to see the face, to say pet, or tush, to say nonsenses to it. It ate whatever it was given but as time went on it knew what it liked and had a sweet tooth. The food was what united them, eating off the same plate using the same spoon, watching one another's chews, feeling the food as it went down the other's gullet. The child was slow to crawl and slower still to walk but it knew everything, it perceived everything. When it ate blancmange or junket it was eating part of the lovely substance of its mother.

They were together, always together. If its mother went to the post office the child stood in the middle of the drive praying until its mother returned safely. The child cut the ridges of four fingers, along the edge of a razor blade that had been wedged upright in the wood of the dresser, and seeing these four deep horizontal identical slits the mother took the poor fingers into her own mouth and sucked them, to lessen the pain, and licked them to abolish the blood, and kept saying soft things until the child was stilled again. Her mother's knuckles were her knuckles, her mother's veins were her veins, her mother's lap was a second heaven, her mother's forehead a copybook onto which she traced A B C D, her mother's body was a recess that she would wander inside for ever and ever, a sepulchre growing deeper and deeper. When she saw other people, especially her pretty sister, she would simply wave from that safe place, she would not budge, would not be lured out.

Her father took a hatchet to her mother and threatened that he would split open the head of her. The child watched through the kitchen window because this assault took place out of doors on a hillock under the three beech trees where the clothes line stretched, then sagged. The mother had been hanging out the four sheets washed that morning, the two off each bed. The child was engaged in twisting her hair, looping it around bits of white rag, to form ringlets, decking herself in the kitchen mirror, and then every other minute running across to the window to reconnoitre, wondering what she ought to do, jumping up and down as if she had a pain, not knowing what to do, running back to the mirror, hoping that the terrible scene would pass, that the ground would open up and swallow her father, that the hatchet would turn into a magic wand, that her mother would come through the kitchen door and say, 'Fear Not,' that travail would all be over. Later she heard a verbatim account of what had happened. Her father demanded money, her mother refused same on the grounds that she had none, but added that if she had it she would hang sooner than give it to him. That did it. It was then he really got bucking, gritted his teeth and his muscles, said that he would split the head of her and the mother said that if he did so there was a place for him. That place was the lunatic asylum. It was twenty or thirty miles away, a big grey edifice, men and women lumped in together, some in strait jackets, some in padded cells, some blindfolded because of having sacks thrown over their heads, some strapped across the chest to quell and impede them. Those who did not want to go there were dragged by relatives, or by means of rope, some being tied onto the end of a plough or a harrow and brought in on all fours like beasts of the earth. Then when they were not so mad, not so rampaging, they were let home again where they were very peculiar, and given to smiling and to chattering to themselves and in no time they were ripe to go off again or to be dragged off. March was the worst month, when everything went askew, even the wind, even the March hares.

Her father did not go there. He went off on a batter and then went to a monastery, and then was brought home and shook in the bed chair for five days eating bread and milk, and asking who would convey him over the fields, until he saw his yearlings, and when no one volunteered to, it fell to her because she was the youngest. Over in the fields he patted the yearlings and said soppy things that he'd never say indoors, or to a human, and he cried and said he'd never touch a drop again, and there was a dribble on his pewter-brown moustache, that was the remains of the mush that he had been eating, and the bay yearling herself became fidgety and fretful as if she might bolt or stamp the ground to smithereens. The girl and her mother took walks on Sundays – strolls, picked blackberries, consulted them for worms, made preserve, and slept side by side, entwined like twigs of trees or the ends of the sugar tongs.

When she wakened and found that her mother had got up and was already mixing meal for the hens or stirabout for the young pigs she hurried down carrying her clothes under her arm and dressed in whatever spot that she could feast on the sight of her mother, most. Always an egg for breakfast. An egg a day and she would grow strong. Her mother never ate an egg but topped the girl's egg and fed her it off the tarnished eggy spoon and gave her little sups of tea with which to wash it down. She had her own mug, red enamel and with not a chip. The girl kept looking back as she went down the drive for school, and as time went on she mastered the knack of walking backwards to be able to look all the longer, look at the aproned figure waving or holding up a potato pounder or a colander or whatever happened to be in her hand.

The girl came home once and the mother was missing. Her mother had actually fulfilled her promise of going away one day and going to a spot where she would not be found. That threatened spot was the bottom of the lake. But in fact her mother had gone back to her own family because the father had taken a shotgun to her and had shot her but was not a good aim like William Tell, had missed, had instead made a hole in the Blue Room wall. What were they doing upstairs in the middle of the day, an ascent they never made except the mother alone to dress the two beds. She could guess. She slept in a neighbour's house, slept in a bed with two old people who reeked of eucalyptus. She kept most of her clothes on, and shrivelled into herself, not wanting to touch or be touched by these two old people buried in their various layers of skin and hair and winceyette. Outside the window was a climbing rose with three or four red flowers along the bow of it, and looking at the flowers and thinking of the wormy clay she would try to shut out what these two old people were saying, in order that she could remember the mother whom she despaired of ever seeing again.

Not far away was their own house with the back door wide open so that any stranger or tinker could come in or out. The dog was probably lonely and bloodied from hunting rabbits, the hens were forgotten about, and were probably in their coops, hysterical, and picking at each other's feathers because of their nerves. Eggs would rot. Her father could be anywhere. If she stood on the low whitewashed wall that fronted the cottage she could see over the high limestone wall that bounded their fields and then look to the driveway that led to the abandoned house itself. To her it was like a kind of castle where strange things had happened and would go on happening. She loved it and she feared it. The sky behind and above gave it mystery, sometimes made it broody and gave it a kind of splendour when the red streaks in the heavens were like torches that betokened the performance of a gory play. All of a sudden standing there, with a bit of grass between her front teeth, looking at her home and imagining this future drama she heard the nearby lich gate open, and then shut with a clang, and saw her father appear, and jumped so clumsily she thought she had broken everything, particularly her ribs. She felt she was in pieces. She would be like Humpty Dumpty, and all the king's horses and all the king's men would not be able to put her together again.

Dismemberment did happen, a long time before, the time when her neck swelled out into a big fleshed balloon. She could only move her neck on one side, because the other side was like a ball and full of fluid that made gluggles when touched with the fingers. They were going to lance it. They placed her on a kitchen chair. Her mother boiled a saucepan of water. Her mother stood on another chair and reached far into the rear of a cupboard and hauled out a new towel. Everything was in that cupboard, sugar and tea, and round biscuits and white flour and linen and must and mice. First one man, then another man, then another man, then a last man who was mending the chimney, and then last of all her father, each took a hold of her – an arm, another arm, a shoulder, a waist and her two flying legs that were doing everything possible not to be there. The lady doctor said nice things and cut into the big football of her neck and it was like a pig's bladder bursting all over, the waters flowing out, and then it was not like that at all, it was like a sword on the bone of her neck sawing, cutting into the flesh, deeper and deeper, the men pressing upon her with all their might saying that she was a demon and the knife went into her swallow or where she thought of forever more as her swallow, and the lady doctor said 'drat it', because she had done the wrong thing – had cut too deep and had to start scraping now and her elder sister danced a jig out in the flag, so that neighbours going down the road would not get the impression that someone was being murdered to death. Long afterwards she came back to the world of voices, muffled voices, and their reassurances, and a little something sweet to help her get over it all and the lady doctor putting on her brown fur coat and hurrying to her next important work of mercy.

When she slept with the neighbours the old man asked the old woman were they ever going to be rid of her, were they going to have this dunce off their hands, were they saddled with her for the rest of their blooming lives. She declined the milk they gave her because it was goat's milk and too yellow and there was dust in it. She would answer them in single syllables, just yes or no, mostly no. She was learning to frown so that she too would have ABCs. Her mother's forehead and hers would meet in heaven, salute, and all their lines would coincide. She refused food. She pined. In all it was about a week.

The day her mother returned home – it was still January – the water pipes had burst and when she got to the neighbours, and was told she could go on up home, she ran with all her might and resolution so that her windpipes ached and then

stopped aching when she found her mother down on her knees
dealing with pools of water that had gushed from the red pipes.
The brown rag was wet every other second and had to be
wrung out, and squeezed in the big chapped basin, the one she
was first bathed in. The lodges of water were everywhere,
lapping back and forth, threatening to expand, to discolour
the tiles, and it was of this hazard they talked and fretted over
rather than the mother's disappearance, or the dire cause of it,
or the reason for her return. They went indoors and got the
ingredients and the utensils and the sieve so as to make an
orange cake with orange filling and orange and lemon icing.
She never tasted anything so wonderful in all her life. She ate
three big hunks and her mother put her hand around her
and said if she ate any more she would have a little corpora-
tion.

The father came from the hospital, cried again, said that
sure he wouldn't hurt a fly and predicted that he would never
break his pledge or go outside the gate again, only to Mass,
never leave his own sweet acres.

As before, the girl slept with her mother, recited the rosary
with her, and shared the small cubes of dark raisin-filled chocolate, then trembled while her mother went along to her father's
bedroom, for a tick, to stop him bucking. The consequences of
those visits were deterred by the bits of tissue paper, a protection
between herself and any emission. No other child got conceived
and there was no further use for the baggy napkins, the bottle,
and the dark-brown mottled teat. The cot itself was sawn up
and used to back two chairs, and they constituted something
of the furniture in the big upstairs landing, where the felt dog
still lorded it, but now had an eye missing because a visiting
child had poked wire at it. The chairs were painted ox-blood red
and had the sharp end of a nail dragged along the varnish to
give a wavering effect. Also on the landing there was a bowl
with a bit of wire inside to hold a profusion of artificial tea
roses. These tea roses were a two-toned colour, were red and
yellow plastic and the point of each petal was seared like the
point of a thorn. Cloth flowers were softer. She had seen some
once, very pale pink and purple, tumbling roses made of voile, in

another house, in a big jug, on a lady's bureau. In the landing at home too was the speared head of Christ that assayed on all the proceedings with endless patience, endless commiseration. Underneath Christ was a pussy cat of black papier mâché which originally had sweets stuffed into its middle, sweets the exact image of strawberries and even with a little leaf at the base, a leaf made of green glazed angelica. They liked the same things – apple sauce and beetroot and tomato sausages and angelica. They cleaned the windows, one the inside, the other the outside, they sang duets, they put newspapers over the newly washed dark-red tiles so as to keep them safe from the muck and trampalations of the men. About everything they agreed, or almost everything.

In the dark nights the wind used to sweep through the window and out on the landing and into the other rooms, and into the Blue Room, by now uninhabited. The wardrobe door would open of its own accord, or the ewer would rattle, or the lovely buxom Our Lady of Limerick picture would fall onto the marble washstand and there was a rumpus followed by prognostications of bad luck for seven years.

When the other child came back from secretarial school the girl was at first excited, prepared lovingly for her, made cakes, and soon after, was plunged into a state of wretchedness. Her mother was being taken away from her, or worse was gladly giving her speech, her attention, her hands, and all of her gaze to this intruder. Her mother and her elder sister would go upstairs where her mother would have some little treat for her, a hanky or a hanky sachet, and once a remnant that had been got at the mill at reduced price, due to a fire there. Beautiful, a flecked salmon pink.

Downstairs *she* had to stack dishes onto the tray. She banged the cups, she put a butter knife into the two-pound pot of black-currant jam and hauled out a big helping, then stuck the greasy plates one on top of the other whereas normally she would have put a fork in between to protect the undersides. She dreamt that her mother and her rival sister were going for a walk and she asked to go too but they sneaked off. She followed on a bicycle, but once outside the main gate could not decide whether to go to the left or the right, and then having decided, made the wrong choice and stumbled on a herd of bullocks, all butting one another and endeavouring to get up into one another's backsides. She turned back and there they were strolling up on the drive, like two sedate ladies linking and laughing, and the salmon-flecked remnant was already a garment, a beautiful swagger coat which her sister wore with a dash.

'I wanted to be with you,' she said, and one said to the other, 'She wanted to be with us,' and then no matter what she said, no matter what the appeal, they repeated it as if she wasn't there. In the end she knew that she would have to turn away from them because she was not wanted, she was in their way. As a result of that dream, or rather the commotion that she made in her sleep, it was decided that she had worms and the following morning they gave her a dose of turpentine and castor oil the same as they gave the horses. When her sister went back to the city happiness was restored again. Her mother consulted her about the design on a leather bag which she was making. Her mother wanted a very old design, something concerning the history of their country. She said there would have to be atrocious battles and then peace and wonderful lace-like scenes from nature. Her mother said that there must be a lot of back history to a land and that education was a very fine thing. Finer than the bog her mother said. She said when she grew up that she would get a very good job and bring her mother to America. Her mother mentioned the street in Brooklyn where she had lodged and said that it had adjoined a park. They would go there one day. Her mother said maybe.

The growing girl began to say the word 'backside' to herself and knew that her mother would be appalled. The girl laughed at bullocks and the sport they had. Then she went one further and jumped up and down and said 'Jumping Jack' as if some devil were inside her, touching and tickling the lining of her. It was creepy. It was done out of doors, far from the house, out in the fields, in a grove, or under a canopy of rhododendrons. The buds of the rhododendrons were sticky and oozed with life and everything along with herself was soaking wet and she was given to wandering flushes, and then fits of untoward laughter so that she had to scold herself into some state of normality and this she did by slapping both cheeks vehemently. As a dire punishment she took cups of glauber salts three times a day, choosing to drink it when it was lukewarm and at its most nauseating. She would be told by her father to get out, to stop hatching, to get out from under her mother's apron strings, and he would send her for a spin on the woeful brakeless bicycle. She would go to the chapel finding it empty of all but herself and the lady sacristan who spent her life in there, polishing and rearranging the artificial flowers; or she would go down into a bog and make certain unattainable wishes, but always at the end of every day, and at the end of every thought, and at the beginning of sleep, and the precise moment of wakening it was of her mother and for her mother she existed and her prayers and her good deeds and her ringlets and the ire on her legs – created by the serge of her gym frock – were for her mother's intention, and on and on. Only death could part them and not even that because she resolved that she would take her own life if some disease or some calamity snatched her mother away. Her mother's three-quarter length jacket she would don, sink her hands into the deep pockets and say the name 'Delia,' her mother's, say it in different tones of voice, over and over again, always in a whisper and with a note of conspiracy.

A lovely thing happened. Her mother and father went on a journey by hire car to do a transaction whereby they could get some credit on his lands, and her father did not get drunk but ordered a nice pot of tea, and then sat back gripping his braces and gave her mother a few bob, with which her mother procured a most beautiful lipstick in a ridged gold case. It was like fresh fruit so moist was it, and dark red in colour. Her mother and she tried it on over and over again, were comical with it, trying it on, then wiping it off, trying it on again, making cupids so that her mother expostulated and said what scatterbrains they were, and even the father joined in the hilarity and daubed down the mother's cheek and said Fannie Annie and the mother said that was enough, as the lipstick was liable to get broken. With her thumb nail she pressed on the little catch pushing the lipstick down into its case, into its bed. As the years went on it dried out, and developed a peculiar shape and they read somewhere that a lady's character could be told by that particular shape, and they wished that they could discover whether the mother was the extrovert or the shy violet.

The girl had no friends, she didn't need any. Her cup was full. Her mother was the cup, the cupboard, the press with all the things in it, the tabernacle with God in it, the lake with the legends in it, the bog with the wishing wells in it, the sea with the oyster and the corpses in it, her mother a gigantic sponge, a habitation in which she longed to sink and disappear for ever and ever. Yet she was afraid to sink; caught in that hideous trap between fear of sinking and fear of swimming, she moved like a flounderer through this and that; through school, through inoculation, through a man who put his white handkerchief between naked her and naked him, and against a galvanised boway door came, gruntling and disgruntling like a tethered beast upon her; through a best friend, a girl friend who tried to clip the hairs of her vagina with a shears. The hairs of her vagina were mahogany coloured and her best friend said that that denoted mortal sin. She agonised over it.

Then came a dreadful blow. Two nuns called and her mother and her father said that she was to stay outside in the kitchen and see that the kettle boiled and then lift it off so that the water would not boil over. She went on tiptoe through the hall and listened at the door of the room. She got it in snatches. She was being discussed. She was being sent away to school. A fee was being discussed and her mother was asking if they could make a reduction. She ran out of the house in a dreadful state. She ran to the chicken run and went inside to cry and to go berserk. The floor was full of damp and grey-green mottled droppings. The nests were full of sour sops of hay. She thought she was going out of her mind. When they found her later her father said to cut out the bull but her mother tried to comfort her by saying they had a prospectus and that she would have to get a whole lot of new clothes in navy blue. But where would the money come from?

In the convent to which they sent her she eventually found solace. A nun became her new idol. A nun with a dreadfully pale face, and a Master's Degree in Science. This nun and herself worked out codes with the eyelids, and the flutter of the lashes, so they always knew each other's moods and feelings, so that the slightest hurt imposed by one was spotted by the other and responded to with a cough. The nun gave another girl more marks at the mid-term examination, and did it solely to hurt her, to wound her pride; the nun addressed her briskly in front of the whole class, said her full name and asked her a theological conundrum that was impossible to answer. In turn she let one of the nun's holy pictures fall on the chapel floor where of course it was found by the cleaning nun who gave it back to the nun who gave it to her with a 'This seems to have got mislaid.' They exchanged Christmas presents and notes that contained blissful innuendos. She had given chocolates with a kingfisher on the cover and she had received a prayer book with gilt edging and it was as tiny as her middle finger. She could not read the print but she held it to herself like a talisman, like a secret scroll in which love was mentioned.

Home on holiday it was a different story. Now *she* did the avoiding, the shunning. All the little treats and the carrageen soufflé that her mother had prepared were not gloated over. Then the pink crêpe-de-chine apron that her mother had made from an old dance dress, did not receive the acclamation that the mother expected. It was fitted on and at once taken off, and flung over the back of a chair with no praise except to remark on the braiding which was cleverly done.

'These things are not to be sniffed at,' her mother said, passing the plate of scones for the third or fourth time. The love of the nun dominated all her thoughts and the nun's pale face got between her and the visible world that she was supposed to be seeing. At times she could taste it. It interfered with her studies, her other friendships, it got known about. She was called to see the Reverend Mother. The nun and herself never had a tête-à-tête again and never swapped holy pictures. The day she was leaving for ever they made an illicit date to meet in the summer-house, out in the grounds, but neither of them turned up. They each sent a message with an apology and it was in fact the messengers who met, a junior girl and a postulant carrying the same sentence on separate lips – 'So-and-so is sorry – she wishes to say she can't . . .' They might have broken down or done anything, they might have kissed.

Out of school, away from the spell of nuns and gods and flower gardens and acts of contrition, away from the chapel with its incense and its brimstone sermons, away from surveillance, she met a bakery man who was also a notable hurley player and they started up that kind of courtship common to their sort – a date at the pillar two evenings a week, then to a café to have coffee and cream cakes, to hold hands under the table, to take a bus to her digs, to kiss against a railing and devour each other's faces, as earlier they had devoured the mock cream and the sugar-dusted sponge cakes. But these orgies only increased her hunger, made it into something that could not be appeased. She would recall her mother from the very long ago, in the three-quarter-length jacket of salmon tweed, the brooch on the lapel, the smell of face powder, the lipstick hurriedly put on so that a little of it always smudged on the upper or the lower lip and appeared like some kind of birthmark. Recall that they even had the same mole on the back of the left hand, a mole that did not alter winter or summer and was made to seem paler when the fist was clenched. But she was recalling someone whom she wanted to banish. The bakery man got fed-up, wanted more than a cuddle, hopped it.

Then there was no-one; just a long stretch, doing novenas, working in the library, and her mother's letters arriving, saying the usual things, how life was hard, how inclement the weather, how she'd send a cake that day or the next day as soon as there were enough eggs to make it with. The parcels arrived once a fortnight, bound in layers of newspaper, and then a strong outer layer of brown paper, all held with hideous assortments of twines – binding twine, very white twine, and coloured plastic string from the stools that she had taken to making; then great spatters of sealing wax adorning it. Always a registered parcel, always a cake, a pound of butter, and a chicken that had to be cooked at once, because of its being nearly putrid from the four-day journey. It was not difficult to imagine the kitchen table, the bucket full of feathers, the moled hand picking away at the pin feathers, the other hand plunging in and drawing out all the undesirables, tremulous, making sure not to break a certain little pouch, which if broken its tobacco-coloured contents would taint the flavour of the bird itself. Phow. Always the same implications in each letter, the same cry – 'Who knows what life brings. Your father is not hard-boiled despite his failings. It makes me sad to think of the little things that I used to be able to do for you.' She hated those parcels despite the fact that they were most welcome.

She married. Married in haste. Her mother said from the outset that he was as odd as two left shoes. He worked on an encyclopaedia and was a mine of information on certain subjects. His theme was vegetation in pond life. The family lived to themselves. She learned to do chores, to bottle and preserve, to comply, to be a wife, to undress neatly at night, to fold her clothes, to put them on a cane chair making sure to put her corset and her underthings respectfully under her dress or her skirt. It was like being at school again. The mother did not visit, being at odds with the censuring husband. Mother and daughter would meet in a market town midway between each of their rural homes and when they met they sat in some hotel lounge, ordered tea and discussed things that can easily be discussed – recipes, patterns for knitting, her sister, items of furniture that they envisaged buying.

Her mother was getting older, had developed a slight stoop and held up her hands to show the rheumatism in her joints. Then all of a sudden, as if she had just remembered it, she spoke about the cataracts and her journey to the specialist and how the specialist had asked her if she remembered anything about her eyes and how she had to tell him that she had lost her sight for five or six minutes one morning and that then it came back.

He told her how lucky it was because in some instances it does not come back at all. She said yes that the shades of life were closing in on her.

The daughter knew that her marriage would not last but she dared not say so. Things were happening such as that they had separate meals, that he did not speak for weeks on end, and yet she defended him, talked of the open pine dresser he had made and her mother rued the fact that she never had a handyman to do odd things for her. She said the window had broken in a storm and that there was still a bit of cardboard in it. She said she had her eye on two armchairs with a slight rock. The daughter longed to give them to her and thought that she might steal from her husband when he was asleep, steal the deposit that is, and pay for them on hire purchase. But they said none of the things that they should have said.

'You didn't get any new style,' the mother said, restating her particular dislike for a tweed coat.

'I don't want it,' the girl said tersely.

'You were always a softie,' the mother said, and inherent in this was disapproval for a man who allowed his wife to be dowdy. Perhaps she thought that her daughter's marriage might have amended for her own.

When her marriage did end the girl wrote and said that it was all over and the mother wrote post-haste exacting two dire promises – the girl must write back on her oath and promise her that she would never touch an alcoholic drink as long as she lived and she would never again have to do with any man in body or soul. High commands. At the time the girl was walking the streets in a daze and stopping strangers in her plight. One day in a park she met a man who was very sympathetic, a sort of tramp. She told him her story and then all of a sudden he told her this terrible dream. He had wakened up and he was swimming in water and the water kept changing colour, it was blue and red and green and these changing colours terrified him. She saw that he was not all there and invented an excuse to be somewhere.

In time she sold her bicycle and pawned a gold bracelet and

a gold watch and chain. She fled to England. She wanted to go somewhere where she knew no one. She was trying to start afresh to wipe out the previous life. She was staggered by the assaults of memory – a bowl with her mother's menstrual cloth soaking in it and her sacrilegious idea that if lit it could resemble the heart of Christ, the conical wick of the aladdin lamp being lit too high and disappearing into a jet of black, the roses, the five freakish winter roses that were in bloom when the pipes burst, the mice that came out of the shoes, then out of the shoe closet itself, onto the floor where the newspapers had been laid to prevent the muck and manure of the trampling men, the little box of rouge that almost asked to be licked so dry and rosy was it, the black range whose temperature could be tested by just spitting on it and watching the immediate jig and trepidation of the spit, the pancakes on Shrove Tuesday (if there wasn't a row), the flitches of bacon hanging to smoke, the forgotten jam jars with inevitably the bit of mouldy jam in the bottom, and always, like an overseeing spirit, the figure of the mother who was responsible for each and every one of these facets, and always the pending doom in which the mother would perhaps be struck with the rim of a bucket, or a sledgehammer, or some improvised weapon; struck by the near-crazed father. It would be something as slight as that the mother had a splinter under her nail and the girl felt her own nail being lifted up, felt hurt to the quick, or felt her mother's sputum, could taste it like a dish.

She was possessed by these thoughts, in the library where she worked day in and day out, filing and cataloguing and handing over books. They were more than thoughts, they were the presence of this woman whom she resolved to kill. Yes she would have to kill. She would have to take up arms and commit a murder. She thought of choking or drowning. Certainly the method had to do with suffocation, and she foresaw herself holding big suffocating pillows or a bolster, in the secrecy of the Blue Room where it had all began. Her mother turned into the bursting red pipes, into the brown dishcloths, into swamps of black-brown blooded water. Her mother turned into a streetwalker, and paraded. Her mother was taking down her knickers in public, squatting to do awful things, left little piddles, small as puppies' piddles, her mother was drifting down a well in a big bucket, crying for help but no help was forthcoming. The oddest dream came along. Her mother was on her deathbed, having just given birth to her – the little tonsured head jutted above the sheet – and had a neck rash, and was busy trying to catch a little insect, trying to cup it in the palms of her hands and was saying that in the end 'all there is, is yourself and this little insect that you're trying to kill'. The word kill was everywhere, on the hoardings, in the evening air, on the tip of her thoughts.

But life goes on. She bought a yellow two-piece, worsted, and wrote home and said, 'I must be getting cheerful, I wear less black.' Her mother wrote, 'I have only one wish now and it is that we will be buried together.' The more she tried to kill the more potent the advances became. Her mother was taking out all old souvenirs, the brown scapulars salvaged from the hurtful night in December, a mug, with their similar initials on it, a tablecloth that the girl had sent from her first earnings when she qualified as a librarian. The mother's letters began to show signs of wander. They broke off in mid-sentence, one was written on blotting paper and almost indecipherable, they contained snatches of information such as 'So-and-so died, there was a big turn-out at the funeral', 'I could do with a copper bracelet for rheumatism', 'You know life gets lonelier.'

She dreaded the summer holidays but still she went. The geese and the gander would be trailing by the river bank, the cows would gape at her as if an alien had entered their terrain. It was only the horses she avoided – always on the nervy side as if ready to bolt. The fields themselves as beguiling as ever, fields full of herbage and meadowsweet, fields adorned with spangles of gold as the buttercups caught the shafts of intermittent sunshine. If only she could pick them up and carry them away. They sat indoors. The dog had a deep cut in his paw and it was thought that a fox did it, that the dog and the fox had tussled one night. As a result of this he was admitted to the house. The mother and the dog spoke although not a word passed between them. The father asked pointed questions such as would it rain or was it tea-time. For a pastime they then discussed all the dogs that they had had. The mother especially remembered Monkey and said that he was a queer one, that he'd know what you were thinking of. The father and daughter remembered further back to Shep the big collie who guarded the child's pram and drove thoroughbred horses off the drive, causing risk to his own person. Then there were the several pairs of dogs all of whom sparred and quarrelled throughout their lives, yet all of whom died within a week of one another, the surviving dog dying of grief for his pal. No matter how they avoided it, death crept into the conversation. The mother said unconvincingly how lucky they were never to have been crippled, to have enjoyed good health and enough to eat. The curtains behind her chair were a warm red velveteen and gave a glow to her face. A glow that was reminiscent of her lost beauty.

She decided on a celebration. She owed it to her mother. They would meet somewhere else, away from that house, and its skeletons and its old cunning tug at the heart strings. She planned it a year in advance, a holiday in a hotel, set in beautiful woodland surroundings and on the verge of the Atlantic Ocean. Their first hours were happily and most joyfully passed as they looked at the rooms, the view, the various tapestries, found where things were located, looked at the games room and then at the display cabinets where there was cut glass and marble souvenirs on sale. The mother said that everything was 'Poison, dear.' They took a walk by the seashore and remarked one to the other on the different stripes of colour on the water, how definite they were, each colour claiming its surface of sea, just like oats or grass or a ploughed land. The brown plaits of seaweed slapped and slathered over rocks, long-legged birds let out their lonesome shrieks and the mountains that loomed beyond seemed to hold the spectre of continents inside them so vast were they, so old. They dined early. Afterwards there was a singsong and the mother whispered that money wasn't everything. She said, 'Look at the hard-boiled faces.'

Something snapped inside of the girl and forgetting that this

was her errand of mercy, she thought instead how this mother
had a whole series of grudges, bitter grudges concerning love,
happiness, and her hard inpecunious fate. The angora jumpers,
the court shoes, the brown and the fawn garments, the milk
complexion, the auburn tresses, the little breathlessnesses, the
hands worn by toil, the sore feet, these were but the trimmings
and behind them lay the real person who demanded her pound
of flesh from life. They sat on a sofa. The mother sipped tea and
she her whiskey. They said cheers.

The girl tried to get the conversation back, to before she was
born, or before other children were born, to the dances and the
annual race-day and the courtship that pre-empted the marriage.
The mother refused to speak, baulked, had no story to tell,
said that even if she had a story she would not tell it. Said she
hated raking up the past. The girl tweezed it out of her in
scraps. The mother said yes, that as a young girl she was bold
and obstinate and she did have fancy dreams but soon learnt
to toe the line. Then she burst out laughing and said she climbed
up a ladder once into the chapel, and into the confessional so
as to be the first person there to have her confession heard by
the missioner. The missioner nearly lost his life because he
didn't know how anyone could possibly have got in, since the
door was bolted and he had simply come to sit in the confessional to compose himself, when there she was spouting sins.
What sins? The mother said, 'Oh I forget, love, I forget everything now.'

The girl said, 'No you don't.'

They said good-night and arranged to meet in the dining
room the following morning.

The mother didn't sleep a wink, complained that her eyes and
her nose were itchy, and she feared she was catching a cold.
She drank tea noisily, slugged it down. They walked by the sea
that was now the colour of gun-metal and the mountains were
no longer a talking point. They visited a ruined monastery
where the nettles, the sorrel, the clover and the seedy dock grew
high in a rectangle. Powder shed from walls that were built of
solid stone. The mother said that probably it was a chapel or a

chancery, a seat of sanctity down through the centuries and she genuflected. To the girl it was just a ruin, unhallowed, full of weeds and buzzing with wasps and insects. Outside there was a flock of noisy starlings. She could feel the trouble brewing. She said that there was a lovely smell, that it was most likely some wild herb and she got down on her knees to locate it. Peering with eyes and fingers among the low grass she came upon a nest of ants that were crawling over a tiny bit of ground with an amazing amount of energy and will. She felt barely in control.

They trailed back in time for coffee. The mother said hotel life was demoralising as she bit into an iced biscuit. The porter fetched the paper. Two strange little puppies lapped at the mother's feet, and the porter said they would have to be drowned if they were not claimed before dusk. The mother said what a shame and recalled her own little pups who didn't eat clothes on the line during the day but when night came got down to work on them.

'You'd be fit to kill them, but of course you couldn't,' she said lamely.

She was speaking of puppies from ten or fifteen years back.

He asked if she was enjoying it and the mother said, 'I quote the saying "See Naples and Die", the same applies to this.'

The daughter knew that the mother wanted to go home there and then, but they had booked for four days and it would be an admission of failure to cut it short. She asked the porter to arrange a boat trip to the island inhabited by seabirds, then a car drive to the lakes of Killarney and another to see the home of the liberator, Daniel O'Connell, the man who had asked to have his dead heart sent to Rome, to the Holy See. The porter said certainly and made a great to-do about accepting the tip she gave him. It was he who told them where Daniel O'Connell's heart lay, and the mother said it was the most rending thing she had ever heard, and the most devout. Then she said yes that a holiday was an uplift, but that it came too late as she wasn't used to the spoiling. The girl did not like that. The girl showed the porter a photograph of a gouged torso, said that was how she felt, that was the state of her mind. The mother

said later she didn't think the girl should have said such a thing
and wasn't it a bit extreme. Then the mother wrote a six-page
letter to her friend Molly and the girl conspired to be the one
to post it so that she could read it and find some clue to the
chasm that stretched between them. As it happened she could
not bring herself to read it, because the mother gave it to her
unsealed, as if she had guessed those thoughts and the girl bit
her lower lip and said 'How's Molly doing?'

The mother became very sentimental and said 'Poor creature,
blind as a bat,' but added that people were kind and how when
they saw her with the white cane, they knew. The letter would
be read to her by a daughter who was married and overweight
and who suffered with her nerves. The girl recalled an autograph
book, the mother's, with its confectionery-coloured pages and
its likewise rhymes and ditties. The mother recalled ice creams
that she had eaten in Brooklyn long before. The mother remembered the embroidery she had done, making the statement in
stitches that there was a rose in the heart of New York. The girl
said stitches played such an important role in life and said,
'A stitch in time saves nine.' They tittered. They were getting
nearer.

The girl delicately enquired into the name and occupation of
the mother's previous lover, in short the father's rival. The
mother would not divulge, except to say that he loved his
mother, loved his sister, was most thoughtful, and that was
that. Another long silence. Then the mother stirred in her chair,
coughed, confided, said that in fact she and this thoughtful
man, fearing, somehow sensing that they would not be man and
wife, had made each other a solemn pact one Sunday afternoon
in Coney Island over an ice. They swore that they would get in
touch with each other towards the end of their days. Lo and
behold after fifty-five years the mother wrote that letter!

The girl's heart quickened, and her blood danced to the news
of this tryst, this long sustained clandestine passion. She felt
that something momentous was about to get uttered. They
could be true at last, they need not hide from one another's gaze.
Her mother would own up. Her own life would not be one of
curtained shame. She thought of the married man who was

waiting for her in London, the one who took her for delicious weekends and she shivered. The mother said that her letter had been returned and probably his sister had refused it, always being jealous. The girl begged to know the contents of the letter. The mother said it was harmless. The girl said go on. She tried to revive the spark but the mother's mind was made up. The mother said that there was no such thing as love between the sexes and that it was all bull. She reaffirmed that there was only one kind of love and that was a mother's love for her child.

There passed between them then such a moment, not a moment of sweetness, not a moment of reaffirmation but a moment dense with hate – one hating and the other receiving it like rays, and then it was glossed over by the mother's remark about the grandeur of the ceiling. The girl gritted her teeth and resolved that they would not be buried in the same grave, and vehemently lit a cigarette although they had hardly tasted the first course.

'I think you're very unsettled,' her mother said.

'I didn't get that from the ground,' the daughter said.

The mother bridled, stood up to leave, but was impeded by a waiter who was carrying a big chafing dish, over which a bright blue flame riotously spread. She sat down as if pushed down and said that that remark was the essence of cruelty. The girl said sorry. The mother said she had done all she could and that, without maid, or car or cheque book or any of life's luxuries. Life's dainties had not dropped on her path, she had to knit her own sweaters, cut and sew her own skirts, be her own hairdresser. The girl said for God's sake to let them enjoy it. The mother said that at seventy-eight one had time to think.

'And at thirty-eight,' the girl said.

She wished then that her mother's life had been happier, and had not exacted so much from her and she felt she was being milked emotionally. With all her heart she pitied this woman, pitied her for having her dreams pulped and for betrothing herself to a life of suffering. But also she blamed her. They were both wild with emotion. They were speaking out of turn and eating carelessly, the very food seemed to taunt them. The mother wished that one of those white-coated waiters would tactfully take her plate of dinner away and replace it with a nice warm pot of tea, or better still that she could be home in her own house by her own fireside, and furthermore she wished that her daughter had never grown into the cruel feelingless hussy that she was.

'What else could I have done?' the mother said.

'A lot,' the girl said, and gulped at once.

The mother excused herself. 'When I pass on, I won't be sorry,' she said.

Up in the room she locked and bolted the door, and lay curled up on the bed, knotted as a foetus, with a clump of paper handkerchiefs in front of her mouth. Downstairs she left behind her a grown girl, remembering a woman she most bottomlessly loved, then unloved, and cut off from herself in the middle of a large dining room while confronting a plate of undercooked lamb strewn with mint.

Death in its way comes just as much of a surprise as birth. We know we will die, just as the mother knows that she is primed to deliver around such and such a time, yet there is a fierce inner exclamation from her at the first onset of labour and when the water breaks she is already a shocked woman. So it was. The reconciliation that she had hoped for, and indeed intended to instigate never came. She was abroad at a conference when her mother died and when she arrived through her own front door the phone was ringing with the news of her mother's death. The message though clear to her ears was incredulous to herself. How had her mother died and why? In a hospital, as a result of a heart attack. Straight away she set back for the airport hoping to get a seat on a late-night flight.

The last plane had gone but she decided to sit there until dawn and thought to herself that she might be sitting up at her mother's wake. The tube lighting drained the colour from all the other waiting faces and though she could not cry she longed to tell someone that something incalculable had happened to her. They seemed as tired and as inert as she did. Coffee, bread, whiskey, all tasted the same, tasted of nothing, or at best of blotting paper. There was no man in her life at the moment, no one to ring up and tell the news to. Even if there was, she thought that lovers never know the full story of one another, only know the bit they meet, never know the iceberg of hurts, that have gone before, and therefore are always strangers, or semi-strangers, even in the folds of love. She could not cry. She asked herself if perhaps her heart had turned to lead. Yet she dreaded that on impulse she might break down, and that an attendant might have to lead her away.

When she arrived at the hospital next day the remains had been removed and was now on its way through the centre of Ireland. Through Joyce's Ireland as she always called it, and thought of the great central plain open to the elements, the teeming rain, the drifting snow, the winds that gave chapped faces to farmers and cattle dealers and sometimes croup to the young calves. She passed the big towns and the lesser towns, recited snatches of recitation that she remembered and hoped that no one could consider her disrespectful because the hire car was a bright ketchup red. When she got to her own part of the world the sign of the mountains moved her as they had always done – solemn, beautiful, unchanging except for different streaks of colour. Solid and timeless. She had bought a sandwich at the airport and now removed the glacé paper with her teeth and bit into it. The two days ahead would be awful. There would be her father's wild grief, there would be her aunt's grief, there would be cousins and friends, and strays and workmen, there would be a grave wide open and as they walked to it they would walk over other graves under hawthorn stamping the nettles as they went. She knew the graveyard very well, since childhood. She knew the tombs, the headstones and the hidden vaults. She used to play there alone and both challenge and cower from ghosts. The inside of the grave was always a rich broody brown and the gravedigger would probably lace it with a trellis of ivy or convolvulus leaf.

At that very moment she found that she had just caught up with the funeral cortegé but she could hardly believe that it would be her mother's. Too much of a coincidence. They drove at a great pace and without too much respect for the dead.

She kept up with them. The light was fading, the bushes were like blurs, the air bat-black, the birds had ceased and the mountains were dark bulks. If the file of cars took a right from the main road towards the lake town then it must certainly be her mother's. It did. The thought of catching up with it was what made her cry. She cried with such a delight, cried like a child who has done something good and is being praised for it and yet cannot bear the weight of emotion. She cried the whole way through the lakeside town and sobbed as they crossed the old bridge towards the lovely dark leafy country road that led towards home. She cried like a homing bird. She was therefore seen as a daughter deeply distressed when she walked past the file of mourners outside the chapel gate, and when she shook the hand or touched the sleeves of those who had come forward to meet her. Earlier a friend had left flowers at the car-hire desk and she carried them as if she had specially chosen them. She thought they think it is grief but it is not the grief they think it is. It is emptiness more than grief. It is a grief at not being able to be whole-hearted again. It is not a false grief but it is unyielding, it is blood from a stone.

Inside the chapel she found her father howling, and in the first rows closest to the altar and to the coffin the chief mourners, both men and women, were sobbing, or having just sobbed were drying their eyes. As she shook hands with each one of them she heard the same condolence – 'Sorry for your trouble, sorry for your trouble, sorry for your trouble.'

That night in her father's house, people supped and ate and reminisced. As if in mourning a huge branch of a nearby tree had fallen down. Its roots were like a hand stuck up in the air. The house already reeked of neglect. She kept seeing her mother's figure coming through the door with a large tray, laden down with dainties. The undertaker called her out. He said since she had not seen the remains he would bring her to the chapel and unscrew the lid. She shrank from it but she went because to say no would have wrought her disgrace. The chapel was cold, the wood creaked and even the flowers at night seemed to have departed from themselves, like ghost flowers. Just as he lifted the lid he asked her to please step away and she thought something fateful has happened, the skin has turned black or a finger moves or, the worst or, she is not dead, she has merely visited the other world. Then he called her and she walked solemnly over and she almost screamed. The mouth was trying to speak. She was sure of it. One eyelid was not fully shut. It was unfinished. She kissed the face and felt a terrible pity.

'Oh soul,' she said, 'where are you, on your voyaging and oh soul, are you immortal?'

Suddenly she was afraid for her mother's fate and afraid for the fact that one day she too would have to make it. She longed to hold the face and utter consolations to it but she was unable. She thought of the holiday that had been such a fiasco and the love that she had first so cravenly and so rampantly given and the love that she had so callously and so conclusively taken back. She thought why did she have to withdraw, why do people have to withdraw, why?

After the funeral she went around the house tidying and searching – as if for some secret. In the Blue Room damp had seeped through the walls and there were little burrs of fungus that clung like bobbins on a hat veiling. In the drawers she found bits of her mother's life. Wishes. Dreams contained in such things as a gauze rose of the darkest drenchingest red. Perfume bottles, dance shoes, boxes of handkerchiefs and the returned letter. It was from the man called Vincent, the man her mother had intended to marry but whom she had forsaken when she left New York and came back to Ireland, back to her destiny. For the most part it was a practical letter outlining the size of her farm, the crops they grew, asking about mutual friends, his circumstances and so forth. It seems he worked in a meat factory. There was only one little leak – 'I think of you, you would not believe how often.' The envelope had marked on the outside – 'Return to Sender'. The words seemed brazen as if he himself had written them.

There were so many hats, hats with flowers, hats with veiling, all of pastel colour, hats conceived for summer outings and meant for rainless climes. Ah the garden parties she must have conceived. Never having had the money for real style her mother had invested in imitation things – an imitation crocodile hand-bag and an imitation fur bolero. It felt light as if made of hair. There were, too, pink embroidered corsets, long bloomers and three unworn cardigans.

For some reason she put her hand above the mantelpiece to the place where they hid shillings when she was young. There wrapped in cobweb was an envelope addressed to herself in her mother's handwriting. It sent shivers through her and she prayed that it did not bristle with accusations. Inside there were some trinkets, a gold sovereign and some money. The notes were dirty, crumpled and folded many times. How long had the envelope lain there? How had her mother managed to save? There was no letter, yet in her mind she concocted little tendernesses that her mother might have written – words such as 'Buy yourself a jacket', or 'Have a night out', or 'Don't spend this on masses'. She wanted something, some communi-qué. But there was no such thing.

A new wall had arisen, stronger and sturdier than before. Their life together and all those exchanges were like so many spilt feelings and she looked to see some sign, or hear some murmur. Instead a silence filled the room and there was a vaster silence beyond as if the house itself had died or had been carefully put down to sleep.

Mary 🍂

Dear Sadie

I am in the toilet as it's the only place I get a bit of peace. She is calling me down to do the dinner as I am a good cook and she is not. He raised ructions yesterday about cabbage water and I got red and you won't believe it but he smiled straight into my face. He never smiles at her. If I tell you a secret don't tell anyone. She sees another man. Didn't I walk straight into them the night I was to meet Tom Dooley and he never came. Next day she gave me a frock of hers, I suppose so's I'd keep my mouth shut. And now I am in a fix because she expects me to wear it when I go dancing and I want to wear a frock of my own. It is brushed wool, mine is, and I know it is brushed wool but I am not telling her.

Tom Dooley came the next night. He got the nights mixed up, a good job I was there. We went for a walk in the park opposite this house – there's a park, I told you that, didn't I? It's nice in the summer because there's a pavilion where they sell icecream and stuff but dead boring in the winter. Anyhow we had a walking race through the woods and he beat me blind and I got so winded I had to sit down and he sat next to me and put his arm around me. Then he kissed me and all of a sudden he raised the subject of SEX and I nearly died. I got such a fright that I took one leap off the seat and tore across the field and he tore after me and put his arms around me and then I burst out crying, I don't know why. And I had to come in home and when I did he was here by himself. She's always out. Goes to pubs on her own or wandering around the road gather-

ing bits of branches saying how sad and how beautiful they are.
Did you ever hear such nonsense in all your life. She wouldn't
darn a sock. Anyhow he was here listening to music. He always
is. And he called me in to warm my feet and sat me down and
we hardly said one word except that he asked me was I all
right and I had to say something, so I said I got a smut in my eye.
Didn't he get an eye-glass and was poking away at it with a
little paint brush and didn't she come in real quiet in her crêpe-
soled shoes.

'Oh, togetherness,' she said in her waspy voice and you
wouldn't see me flying up the stairs to bed. Next morning –
and you mustn't breathe this to a soul – she was up at cock-
crow. Said she had heartburn and went out to do some weed-
ing. It's winter and there's nothing in those flower beds only
clay. Guess what, wasn't she waiting for the postman and no
sooner had he come than she was all smiles and making coffee
and asking me what kind of dancing did I like, and didn't the
phone ring and when she tripped off to answer it I had a gawk
at the letter she got. I could only scan it. Real slop. It was from
a man. It said darling be brave. See you a.m. Now I haven't
told you this but I love their child. He has eyelashes as long as
daisies and lovely and black. Like silk. I admired them one day
and he wanted to pull one out for me. I'd do anything for that
kid.

Anyhow I discovered where she keeps the letters – under
the hall carpet. She presses flowers there too. Of course if I
wanted to, I could show them to hubby, find them, pretend I
didn't know what they were. I'm not sure whether I will or not.
I heard him telling her once that he'd take the kid and go to
Australia. I'd love to go. The kid has a pet name – he's called
Buck – and he loves bread and jam and I think he prefers me
to her. I have to go now as she's calling me. Not a word to my
mother about this. I'll let you know developments.
Your fond friend
Mary

PS I am thinking of changing my name. How do you like the
sound of Myrtle?

Forgetting 🍂

Mornings on the Italian Mediterranean after it has rained, are the very best. Then the foliage is still wet, the sun shining on it, while all the umbrellas and parasols are already dry and people hurrying down on their push bicycles or on their pop-pop bicycles or on foot, down to the sea, and women are asking each other if they heard the storm and everyone – or nearly everyone – professes not to have slept a wink but that is merely exaggeration. A woman sits on the wall, lifts her vest up and feeds the baby that has been fretting all along. Six or seven, or maybe more, women utter endearments to the child, tell it how good, how bonny it is, and one supposes that the child takes it all in and will remember these endearments later and will dimly be the result of these words, that breast, when it is sitting in some city with some girl or some group of people.

The road is dusty and there are bits of young pine forest in between, there are wild flowers and the mingled smell of rose-mary and camomile. Alsatians chained to the trees are baying at one another like wolves. One lot of piers are so recently painted, that it looks as if snow-white towels have been spread over them, and on one the various bells and various sets of intercoms suggest that the building is in a capital city but no, the light playing on the trees says it is the countryside, it is the Mediterranean.

Up on the main road the bonnets of the cars are simmering in the sun, but the vegetables underneath the awnings are cool, fresh, vivid and of every variety. Lorries have been delivering since dawn, and already on the counters there are empty beer

bottles and empty mineral water bottles. By evening the yellow
flower of the marrow tops will have wilted to an unrecog-
nisable shred, holiday couples will have quarrelled, will have
made love and half-built castles will be like forlorn forts on the
vistas of dark sand.

They have arrived on the beach and everybody is talking and
changing, tying and untying straps, smearing on oil, and ex-
claiming over the water which is still meltingly cool. There are
several nationalities, but the family we speak of are combined
of English and Italian. The pigment in their skins tells how long
each one has been there, and the newcomers are covetous for
the sun, stretching their arms or their insteps to it, asking it to
tan them 'quick, quick.' A little girl who resembles a china
shepherdess is sifting sand onto her brother's back, and he,
because he is engaged in making a plastic model, is either unaware of, or indifferent to this assault. Their mother, Paula,
remarks how beautiful they are, everyone agrees, and for the
first time in months Julia is aware of a complete absence of
privacy in her life. If she cries it will be noticed, if she goes red
it too will be noticed, and if she peels everyone will suggest
some kind of remedy. She is whiter than the others and constantly she is on the brink of tears, but as Paula says to her,
she has to fight it, she has to completely forget. She strives to
do this first by lying down, and remembering. She lies on a
green bath towel, spread out over the sand, and Paula at once
comes over and whisks the sunglasses from her face so that her
tan will be evenly distributed.

The sand is furrowed under her back and while getting used
to the glare of the sun, she at the same time tries to flatten the
sand by pressing on it with her backbone. She is remembering
everything about him. She is remembering his face, his skin,
and the one black hair that grew between his eyebrows. She is
remembering the ring he wore on his little finger, that had on it
a crest relating to God, she is remembering all the layers of
colours that she saw in him, the indigos and blues in winter,
then an amber when the summer came and they sat in gardens,
and then a beautiful bulrush brown when the autumn came and
the bonfires were lit, when he left. She is remembering his cock,

when it was alive and pearled, then nearly asleep, diminishing, nearly absent. She is trying to sustain her hurt. She plays with these memories, while watching the sun rotate on the various surfaces, making its dappled movements, enhancing something then passing on to some other random object. Just like a lover, she thinks. She remembers a hole in his black, home-knit socks, she remembers a little plastic marker he had in his pocket, a memento from his golfing days, she remembers his having a bath, she starts to cry but no-one sees because she covers her face with a headscarf and also because they are doing the various things that get done on a beach. They are drinking and joking and discussing the next day's shopping expedition. Men are playing a game of improvised bowls and besides the dry clank of the blanks there are voices saying, 'Buon fatto, buon fatto, well done.' She will achieve it, she will give birth to the death in her, the death of him.

A man goes by selling blouses and bits of carpet. He is the darkest person in sight. He is phenomenally tall, walks like a tree trunk. He is Arabic. She buys a blouse, a yellow chiffon with matching colour needlework, then holds it close to her chest as if it were a pet and thinks how Rod will never see her like this in the bright gold enriching light of the Mediterranean. She smells the chiffon, smells the thread with which it is held together, and thinks of the very first dress she had been given as a child, and the dressmaker who took ages before sewing it. The material had lain beside the foot machine for a whole week and she used to be afraid that it would slip down and get soiled or lost. It was yellow seersucker, that bright yellow of butter-cups.

Newcomers join their group. A beautiful girl, in black chiffon, with great crescents of green waterproof eyeshadow, is suddenly queen. Upon coming out of the water she disports herself like a nymph. Her voice, though, is wrong for her looks, and her eyes, which are soft as scorched almonds, have nothing behind them only brittleness. She is rattling on and on about the *only* place that one must eat or dance, or shop or whatever. She herself goes to the stables each afternoon to pat the horses' noses, has a nap at six, goes out in the evening to the *only* place where a dozen or more of her friends are to be found. She is called Jocasta and makes 'peck-peck' noises at her boyfriend who is myopic. Julia thinks yes, that Rod would admire this girl's smouldering looks, would momentarily seduce her, remark on something, perhaps the little coral insect that she wore on a chain around her neck, be flirtatious for a moment, and then he would come back to her and kneel by her and say, 'Where are you, now, my love, my love,' and all would be forgiven.

Thinking of him again. It was forbidden. She ran towards the sea, the sand was scorching under her feet. The only way to combat it was to run, run, go so fast that it barely touched the soles of her feet and did not burn her brain. She put her head under the water, and prayed that she would come up with a new head, and a whole new God-given complex of thoughts and vigorous grey matter.

One day it rained and they were confined to the house. Tempers were a little frayed and the children who, down on the beach, were picturesque and self-contained, were now asking for cornflakes, or to be amused, or to play games. Almost an English nursery scene. She washed her hair but it turned out so bushy that she had to cover it with a head scarf, until such time as she could go to the hairdresser's in the late evening. Paula said it was ridiculous going to a hairdresser just as it was ridiculous wearing make-up in the sun, and she thought they might bicker. So she went for a bicycle ride, up and down the dusty road, disturbing here and there the puddles, making a bit of a splash and giving herself some salutary lectures about cheerfulness. She could not expect the others to share her grief, to know that at night she had dreamt of an adult head, his, pushing through her vagina, had dreamt of his voice, had dreamt of his stance, was dreaming minutely of him.

She was wheeling the bicycle into a shed when she laid eyes on him, soft brown hair falling over one side of his face, dark brown eyes, the long nose and the beard. She knew of course that it was not him. She looked again. It was, it wasn't. She called for Paula to come down, and together they stooped to see him, then Paula exclaimed, said she couldn't believe it, got up on tiptoe to look again over the acacia hedge and found that he was looking back at them. He smiled. They were shameless and curious, like very young girls.

It was not him, but his spitting image. She held on to Paula's wrist.

'My God, you're shaking,' Paula said.

'I'll die if he's called Rod, Roderigo . . .,' she said.

They went towards him on the pretext that they thought he had been calling to them or that he needed some assistance.

The moment she heard that he too was called Rod she was in a dither. She would direct all her fantasy onto him. She would replace the other. She imagined him courting her. She thought of wild schemes, midnight trysts, a ladder, a rope, a dash, meeting him in the woods, just one wild rendezvous. She saw him undress her, undo the sash of her new wrap-around skirt, she saw him lay her gently on the ground, she felt the pine needles, his weight on her, his hair across her mouth, she saw his hands and how she would steer them where she wanted, and how they would not speak, simply congress. They met two or three times and his interest was mounting. Each morning she lay on the mattress by the beach and in her mind plotted it. No love here, no tenderness, no considerateness, just separate and mutual self-interest. Afterwards, she would be free, even heartless. She saw them side by side, the two identical men, in chains, each one silently awaiting her and she saw herself choose this new one, the younger one, in order to punish the one she loved. She would lose a whole night's sleep, a night given up to love, to lips, to hair, to nails, to clawing, to bites, to bruises and to the expiation of love.

It could not have been simpler. Each and every house guest was out. Some had gone by boat to see Lord Byron's Grotto and somewhat whimsically she had sent Byron her errant wishes. Some had gone to shop for marble, a few had gone to the beach as usual, and nobody was due back until shortly before dinner. She was sitting in a basket chair, under the olive tree, having a spin to regale mind and body when he stood on the opposite side of the hedge and watched her. Taking utter delight in being watched, she drew her legs up under her lap and smiled but without acknowledging him. He eased his way through a hole in the hedge, touched the basket chair to try and slow it down while she for her part moved it at a greater dizzier speed so that she saw him vaguely and distantly, in a way she would see him when they met in private. They went inside for a drink.

Inside everything was coolness, the polished tiles, the loose lawn chair covers, and the blue glasses laid out on the tray with a cloth over them. Even the bees buzzed softly. She made a cocktail of rum and lemon, then felt a finger on her wrist, him telling her in garbled English that her veins were like rivers. She looked at him, appraised him and it was as if she was mimicking every sweet gesture that had gone before. They sat together, they linked arms, they touched glasses, their lips smacked. It would be all right.

'Make a wish,' one of the younger girls said to her at dinner because a eucalyptus leaf had fallen off a tree, directly onto her plate. They were eating out of doors. She had been making a wish ever since they sat down which was that she would be able to slip away quietly and keep her date with him. He had done a drawing of their two houses, the side road, then the main road where there was the discotheque where they were to meet. She was preparing to feign a migraine. She would be excusing herself soon, while they were still all sitting down, and the maids still busy serving, and the housekeeper upstairs turning back the beds for the night. She would go through the drawing room, down the hall and to the kitchen, out by the door that led to the garden and through a little lich gate to the world. She felt like a nun. She had to refuse food, yet longed to taste the lovely juicy bits of orange-coloured melon, longed for it to slide down her throat. Now and then she opened her mouth unconsciously as if to partake of someone's piece of raw ham. She had to make do with the odd grain of sea-salt which she knew to be a good remedy to quell hunger. By the time she got to the discotheque she would not be hungry and probably they would slip out before they had finished their first drink. She wore satin underclothes and could see already what a novelty they would be, these old-fashioned lace drawers bought off a stall in England. The talk was about this and that, headaches, exercise, the over-crowding of the world. Not one of the men did she fancy. She had seen them in all guises, in their bathing trunks, in their terry robes, in shorts, in sports jackets, and now immaculately dressed in dark suits, pinstripe shirts and beautiful cuff-links. They had no mystery and they emitted no sparks.

Her excusing of herself was not nearly so straightforward. For one thing she hesitated twice and then when she announced a migraine gusts of excessive and unexpected sympathy were showered on her. She had no idea it was a condition which could wreak such reaction. She must lie down, she must have a tisane, she must have a cold compress, she must be nursed through it. Already she saw him in the discotheque deciding she was not coming and settling for someone else, ironically someone not unlike her. As she left the table two of the women came with her, to make matters worse they occupied a chair and an armchair in her bedroom and it was useless protesting about their dinners which she insisted were getting cold. Natur-ally they talked. They looked at her make-up, one tried her hair dryer, they fiddled while she pretended to be going to sleep. She had to do a little imitation snore before they tiptoed away telling each other sagely that she had nodded off.

The next ordeal was getting up and repairing her face in the dark, then finding her shawl, then opening the door without allowing it to creak. She realised that she was lucky to be in a house with a second staircase which was just outside her bed-room. As she went down the steps she saw the garden so temptingly lit and the nightingales sang as if to serenade her. She went barefoot over the loose chippings and thought of the agony to the soles of her feet that would soon be compensated for with the reverse. Except that he might have fled. Once she was out of hearing she put on her high-heeled shoes and ran up the little road and along the main road to the discotheque that was called Five Lanterns.

*   *   *

She was lying on the beach and, by now fond of the sun, almost lapping it up. The children were pestering her to play with them again. They were pulling her hair, throwing things at her, saying 'Ssh' just before they squirted her with their air guns. She had bought them chocolate, broken it up into minute pieces, to make it last longer, provided a little breakfast party with lemonade drunk from a doll's tea set. She had told them all sorts of risqué stories and was told risqué stories back; several centred on the lavatory or their underclothes. Now she wanted to doze. She had gone without a night's sleep, and she wanted to float. Because she was happier they were all clamouring for her attention, and she was being asked if this piece of jewellery, or that buckle were absolutely right, or if that fat man ate too much or was the victim of a glandular plot. Then her heart gave a little shudder as she saw him, the new Rod, stalking towards their stretch of the beach. He was wearing long blue shorts and was naked to the waist. He was looking for her.

'He's following you,' Paula said.

She smiled and said, 'Possibly', but it was of no consequence. Each time he skirted the area he came that much closer, and already she had rehearsed what she must say to him, that probably she was going to Florence, next day, that she was meeting friends. It had happened, and fizzled out in the night, in the woods, under trees, witnessed by a ridiculous stray dog that kept sniffing at their bare over-excited bodies. Finito. At dawn they had sallied home, hand in hand and were not a perch out of the wood before he wanted her again, and had her robustly on the roadside, using a broken motor-cycle as a prop. He could hardly swallow with excitement. He made noises as if swallowing milk or juice, but by then she simply wanted to lie between her own sheets, to stretch her limbs and say that she had succeeded in what she had set out to do.

He walked across to where she and Paula were sitting, cross-legged, on their haunches, doing their fitness exercise. A little cut on his hand gave him the opening. He asked if either of them had a plaster. Paula took one out of the big straw basket, where there were also scissors, cotton and needle, mints, eau de cologne, various medicines and little lavender sachets.

'You do it,' Paula said to her slyly, and picking up his scratched hand, she remembered the man in the woods of the night before, and she decided how ruthless life can be. Under his breath he told her she was lovely, bella, buona, and asked when she would be alone. She shrugged, and simply pointed to all the people and even at that moment the children were doing 'This little piggy went to market' to her toes. Watching him walk away, it was the very same as if the two men were interchangeable, the same hair, the same stoop, so that if either of them were to exhibit their sweaters, the two would have a curvature in the back as if filled out by a hump. And yet it had failed.

'So it's not looks,' she thought, and clenched her back teeth, in order to mettle herself.

They were in a restaurant, Paula, Paula's husband Ned, the house guests and some friends who had come down from their holdings in the mountains to partake of some cosmopolitan life. The roof was of vine leaves but no breeze stirred and the evening was uncannily hot and tense. There would be a storm. People's orders were being passed along, hot plates, cold plates, plates with different mounds of pasta, and her own plate with about three dozen pale-pink shells, some of which had a little fish in the centre, and some had none. They were like jewels. Eating them would take a long time and she would enjoy it, and inhale the night, the pre-storm night, the warm air, the scent of the oleander flower beyond; she would dip the dry bread into the sharp white wine, and be thankful that grapes, and flowers, and sun and beautiful shellfish were all being poured into her, to make her better. Jocasta was preening herself and telling everyone that the *only* way to live was to sleep all morning, to swim in the afternoon, to pat the horses at six, to go to India in the winter, and to wear stones and metals that were conducive to one's birth sign. No one listened.

'Shut up, Jocasta,' her boyfriend said, and in pique she took out a velvet-lined ring box, touched it with the back of her forefinger, and said it reminded her of the horsey's slippery nose. The box had contained a ring, a pretty ring she said, a pretty emerald; then she expounded vulgarly on the properties of her horsey especially his wet snout. Her boyfriend, Serge, was drunk. Occasionally she would pat him under the chin and he would gaze at her through his glasses, and behind that through a whirlpool of drunkenness, and tell her not to be so stupid, tell her to shut up. All the while he was fiddling with knife and fork, making a racket between those hitting his glass or the wrought iron of the candle sconce.

Julia asked him about his mother, and he said his mother was a drunk like him. Julia suggested he eat. With his knife, he hacked down the bits of lamb, the peppers and the onions off his skewer and they fell hurriedly onto his plate and laughing he handed the plate to a perplexed young waiter. Then taking the skewer he looked at it, ran his finger down the length of it to remove the excess oils, threw it at Jocasta and just missed one of her great self-loved almond eyes. But it grazed her temple all the same. Suddenly she was mute, like a lamb, meek and whimpering while he was leaning across the table saying, 'Sorry,' and others were offering handkerchiefs, and Paula was asking the waiter for disinfectant and Ned was pouring everyone wine in order to blot out the incident. People at other tables who stared were being assured by him that it was all a joke.

In the general commotion a fierce dismay about life engulfed Julia. So this is what people did to one another, once they had slept together, had their fill and tired of one another. The law of life – hideous. It was as if all the meals, all the wine bottles, all the empty carafes, all the cold hors d'œuvres, all the pink linen serviettes, all the laid tables, all the silver pegs to keep the table-cloths down, all the red noses, all the menus, all the head waiters, all the lesser waiters, all the lonely cloakroom attendants, all the yellow cloakroom tickets, all the capes, cardigans and crushed velvet jackets were all sham. She pressed her hands to her temples to try and organise her thoughts. Why in God's name had she and the real Rod separated, why had they not cultivated the little human garden that was theirs? Why had they let each other go astray? The long waterproof plaster gave

Jocasta a jaunty look, and all it needed now was a beret on her head to complement the slant. Someone asked Serge for the skewer as a souvenir. He was so drunk he was unable to see it and began to grope with his hand.

The holiday continued. She gave herself up to each moment, each sensation, the sun, thunder, storm, meals. She ate fish avidly, devoured it, in order for her brain to be enriched with phosphorus, in order for her disposition to be altered. She would burn the past away, and watch it hiss and disappear in the brightest and yellowest of phosphorescent lights. Her eating shellfish was by now a feature, using no knife or fork, but tearing into it with fingers, nails, lips, teeth and gums, sucking each shred of flesh, each speck of roe, also the juices that lingered in the crevices of the shells, and then without any reference to finger bowl or to their exclamations she would pick up another and suck with even greater determination. In between she would eat some sardines, devour them, head, tail, backbone and all, and then she would take a few rings of fried octopus, before returning to her favourites, the pink and white prawns, with the wily-toothed shells. They photographed her doing this day after day, and it even got so that she asked permission to help in the kitchen with cleaning them, before they were consigned to the pans of boiling salted water. The smell of shellfish got under her nails, into her hair, onto her scalp, in her ear lobes, and the flavour, though still delicious, was so much part of her taste buds that she could eat now without eating.

It was like a black cat or a spectre that was just in the act of disappearing around a corner. He was going and she was letting him go. All sorts of memories still suggested themselves – but she stamped on them like someone stamping on a worm. The mental impact of her foot crushing him away gave her fleeting satisfaction. There was a new moon the night she formally took her leave of him, said a last goodbye, and went upstairs to execute it. They had a vow, that if either ever wanted to break the friendship, to prevent all possibility of its ever being viable again, they were to return each other's talismans. The one from

him to her was a dun rounded stone, and the one from her to
him was a black swan's feather. She looked at the stone for the
last time, let it roll in the palm of her hand, played with it, and
remembered how he used to play with it, and her, together;
and how once it had got lost inside her, this little ball of smooth-
ened atlantic sandstone. Before long she would receive the
feather and that would be that. He would assume she had found
someone new. She washed it in soapy water to remove all
traces of her person. She polished it on her satin skirt. She used
a box that there had been a marble egg in, and wrapped it with
extreme care, choosing silver sellotape to adhere it. There was no
delay about posting because one of the guests was going back
to England the following morning, and would post it to the
office where he called each week for his 'post restante' mail.
He would know what it was before opening it, he would know
by the shape of the box and he would open it with under-
standable dread. He too was sentimental and it was he who had
suggested parting gifts so that they might have some relic of
each other.

Aperitifs, digestifs, oil, sweets, wool. Each hoarding offered a
different thing, and then again the same set of things, as they
drove towards a mountain to visit friends. The landscape was
radically different; and more dramatic. Horseshoes of wooded
mountain enclosed steep private bays, and everywhere the
bright red earth exuded energy while the olive groves seemed
bathed in silver and propelled by a sweet wind. Twice they
almost had an accident, going around serpentine bends, and all
the time there was a nervous exchange of hooters. The houses
were a sandy yellow and most of the shutters had clothes
spread out to dry. It was not yet siesta time. Wedges of marble
up on the mountains were sometimes like flecks and sometimes
as spacious as castles. There was an area so marbled it seemed
as if the whole plain was under fresh snow. The driver, Maria,
also an interpreter, was telling Julia how they quarried the
marble, how it was done with sand and water, along with the
agency of great steel ropes that rotated. She described it well,
how the lumps of marble snapped off from the mountain face,

how if it was too huge they cut it, then despatched it to the various factories, where it was again cut, then chiselled and polished, where it took the form of a statue, or a horse or a naked woman or an ashtray. Julia was trying to be interested but she could feel him invading her thoughts, like a ghost creeping back into her. One minute she was all right, free, and the next minute as they had to slow down abruptly and as she heard the handlebars of a bike graze along their mudguard, he was part and parcel of her again, a living being, a life, to whom she was saying 'Don't go.'

She saw herself go home, within a few days, go in the door, pick up the mail, and she saw the room, and the garden with the chrysanthemums just starting, and in a flash she inhaled autumn damp, saw burning leaves, beautiful puffs of smoke; smoke, like thoughts wandering here, there, and everywhere; big bonfires, little bonfires, mellow fruitfulness. An indescribable melancholy possessed her. It was at once sorrowful and nourishing. It was not that she wanted to eschew fate, it was simply that she wanted to be the container of it and of all that must yet happen to her. She saw him as she had once seen him in a green cloak, which he wore to please her, and being slightly unaccustomed to it, his cigarette was held a little awkwardly, and the memory of the floods of future memory that were yet to be, stabbed her and she began to cry.

'What is to cry in Italian?' she asked.

'You mean to wipe?' Maria asked.

'I mean *weep*,' Julia said.

'Piangere,' Maria said.

'Piangere.' They both said it.

She stared ahead at the poplars, like guardsmen along the mountainside, and then higher up at the wooded peaks, that in their own dusk were like beings breathing with life and impregnation. She would never forget him, she did not want to forget him, he could be part of her, and this invisible presence would be inside her like a watch, ticking and hidden, a source of new faithful, imperishable energy.

Clara 🌿

I have taken up an appointment here. It is purely temporary and I thank the heavens for that as I would not want to be here indefinitely. It is a dreadful place. Excuse me for disheartening you but when I get up in the morning I look out on a seedy town comprising shops and shopfronts, public houses with their porter barrels outside, a school bus, a defunct market house, all having the greyness of old toughened cobweb. I have a tertible longing then, to crawl back into bed and cover my head with a bolster which I believe is damp within. Yes a longing to withdraw. Still I get up. I shall only be here until December, December the fifteenth. Ah, how joyous my Christmas is going to be! I might even go abroad to catch a bit of winter sunshine.

I've been to a lot of places and have got used to my own company. I've spent months in the desert and experienced both the searing wind and the scalding heat. Confined to the company of men for months on end but I got used to it. You could say I am aloof. People seem to be afraid of me. Perhaps it's my appearance – it's grey and grave. I have a beard. I like cats. If I weren't an engineer I expect I would have been a missioner. I always wanted to explore. Not for pleasure but to see the world and evaluate differences in things and in people. But nothing gets inside me, at least nothing that I can remember. I am like a man who lives in a corridor and who intends to slide into another one, to disappear. I want to go to Africa and hopefully I will. These things seem to arise of their own accord.

As far as the locals were concerned there was the crude oil that arrived by boat and there were these vats and tanks and pipes and valves, and God knows what. In some mysterious way the stuff was put in at one end and came out through the other in a refined state. But they knew nothing about the procedure, about pressure, about filling, about temperatures, or the danger involved. In fact they seemed to expect the thing to work of its own accord the way a foetus does. So I have to train three people. They are well-meaning fellows but innocents as regards machinery. They talk to it or bang it as if it were a beast and then they forget to put in a stopper or their assistants forget, or they do not pay attention to some detail so that not a day passes without some little crisis. We have had three major accidents.

Yes I have contemplated Monte Carlo in the winter, the villas with balconies and an empty expanse of beach, maybe a promenade. Guests whom I imagine to be reserved and fastidious, seeking quiet enjoyment rather than the hectic summer stuff. So it was.

Like a child I marked off the days on the calendar, marked them thoroughly, so that there was a blue-black x on the days just past, the very same as if they never existed. In a sense they did not. It has been work, enclosure in the factory, as if one was living inside a big vat and subject to the acrid smell of smouldering sulphur. It was an unreal place. The human beings looked very small. I worried constantly about their carelessness. They laughed at me and called me old man's beard even though I am just forty. I did the paperwork in my bedroom each night, the damp and cold offset by a paraffin heater with a scorched yellow cellophane door. From time to time I opened it and the flame shuddered. My landlady brought me cocoa around eleven and tried to linger. She is a large buxom woman who must have been a beauty once. She reminds me of one of those overblown velvet roses that women used to wear on the hips of their dance skirts. Her eyes are the softest green. In fact they are like greengages and as big as that. She wears a lot of perfume and the house is redolent with the smell of that and the smell of porter. The perfume is eau de cologne. I saw the bottle on the kitchen shelf beside her knitting and her prayer book.

*   *   *

Were I to tell you the history of most of the local people you
would think it exaggeration that so much human misery and
bungle could be compressed into one place. But truly there is
misery and ructions in most of the houses – the married men
quarrel, both they and the bachelors drink nightly and then
stumble home to their steamy beds. The wives rant and exclaim
and the many spinsters are like little wishbones so easy is it to
bend or deflect them in their course. A lot of people talk to themselves. Only the children on their way to and from school show
any kind of heartiness. They lag behind, they play tricks
on each other, they let chestnuts loose from a string and donk
whoever happens to be passing and sometimes they shed their
knitted gloves or their pixie caps and throw them into rainwater
or the market scales. Being a stranger I heard most of their life
stories and when the novelty had worn off I was tempted to send
for a hearing aid and pretend that I was deaf.

The nights were bleak. One can sit and do drawings, and
work out figures, and worry about profit and loss for so long
but there does come a moment when you stop and then you rub
your eyes and lean back in your chair and somehow you expect
a cat or a woman or something to smile up at you and if they
should, your toil does not seem in vain. My rented room was
over a public house. It is run solely by Mrs Rogers and until
the small hours there were men down there drinking, murmuring and occasionally shouting.

Such were my impressions, and such was the manner in which
I would have described them. I expect I was dormant then. Emotion had not flown through my being. December! I used to see
it written up in every sort of colour, like a digit twinkling on and
off, luring me to it. No longer so. The change is on. I expect it
commenced the night I was lying on the horsehair sofa reading
about petty crime in the weekly newspaper when I heard shouting and commotion. I thought that perhaps Mrs Rogers was in
peril and reluctantly I went down. There in the doorway she
was positively haranguing a couple who were doing their utmost to escape. How she grappled with them, how she cursed
and ranted. She was witch-like in her augustness. They would
live in perpetual gloom, and rancour. The wife wore a striped

fur coat and the husband was portly and had a bronzed moustache.

'Tinkers wouldn't do it.'

'Your mother will not lie in her grave until right is done.'

These were the words I caught. They got into the car and drove at such a speed that it was a mercy that there was neither dog nor christian on the street as there would have been a fatality.

Mrs Rogers closed the public house, put the crowbar along the door, dimmed the lights and implored me to sit with her until her tremulations had passed. She poured me a brandy and gave herself a hefty port. I did not want to hear the story as I gathered from the few sentences I heard that it was about property, that someone was diddling someone else, and that she had strong opinions about the matter. They are peculiar about money. They are generous to the point of blackmail and if you refuse a drink from them you are a heathen. But about property they are grasping and mediaeval and stubborn. People fighting over boundaries, dead people's wills disputed, two elderly men taking an axe to each other over the course of a little running stream. It's all in the papers. Sitting there with the fire nearly out and a scarf over the lamp to soften the glow, I felt impatient and knew I would not get back to bed till all hours. Yet I liked her. Fat, alone, and in many ways selfless.

She had chilblains, she was childless. She often gave tea and cake to her customers without charging. All of a sudden she shook me. She asked did I believe in the other world, in the spirit world.

'Not really,' I said.

'You know there's someone watching,' she said, and added that sometimes they just tap on the shoulder. 'Sometimes those not long gone,' she said and she drew the tweed cardigan around her body as if she had just been tapped on the shoulder unknownst to me.

'I'm glad you're here, Jack,' she said. 'I feel you were sent.'

My name is Jan, but they all call me Jack. Just another piece of perversity.

*　　　*　　　*

My chief delight was a walk. Only then could I be really detached and forget the factory. I tried to identify trees, wild flowers, the many birds. I carried my binoculars to focus on the hawks high up in the heavens. Then did I feel clean and unbothered. Every Sunday I took my walk. Down by the canal where there were a pair of winter swans in their half-collapsed nests brooding, or maybe plotting. Or I went towards the mountains, up a thin rocky road that developed into a track and as I got nearer to them the mountains were less dusky because close at hand the heather was somewhat scruffy and the roots showed.

There would be the odd couple walking, or there would be a man with a gun and ferret. Often in the evening I would hear the snipe, then the curlew and for some reason the sounds struck me as the epitome of melancholy and I would hurry back to my lodgings. I was getting quite fond of Mrs Rogers and I had only to admire a brooch or a jug of flowers on the hall table to be given a big plate of scones for tea. She used to say I was mad on walking and it was she who gave me the black-thorn stick.

One Sunday I stood at a gateway which I had often passed by before. There was a rough chain on the gates but since the hasp was broken one could easily pass through. There were two avenues leading from it. A new one that had been steam-rollered and an old one, untrodden, with red-leaved trees on either side. They looked like maples. The scene was quite be-witching so I slipped through the gates and walked along. It was a soft day and I walked and breathed in the air with the very same relish as if I were breathing an elixir into me. I thought what a lovely peaceful country tableau – the chapel spire, the chimney smoke, and the winter branches a bright red as if the blood of life was being transfused into them. In a way winter is the real spring, the time when the inner thing happens, the resurge of nature. I was proud of the way my feet seemed to be springing over the soft velvet-like grass. The high teas had not yet destroyed my constitution. I said to myself that it would be a walk I would always cherish. Little did I know.

I had not come prepared for rain, but rain it did, just as I came to a bend in the avenue and I had to run for cover to a

little thicket of hawthorn trees and I had to crouch in there.
They say they are unlucky. It was like being in an ark and bone
dry. The dry earth beneath was strewn with twigs, squashed
berries and faded blossom. Suddenly as I crawled forward I
came to a little clearing and a big house came into view. So
suddenly that I thought I was looking at a picture. It was a two-
storey house built of the most beautiful golden burnished stone.
The hall door was white and the downstairs front window curved
out into a bay. I kept going closer and closer as if drawn towards it until by now I was out of the thicket and not far from
the paling wire that surrounded the front garden. It seemed to
be composed of motley things – fruit trees that grew any old
way, clumps of devil's pokers and pampas grass that was feathery
and wild. The grass was very high and yellow. It was aftergrass.
The place seemed untouched, unlived in, it seemed unreal. For
some reason I felt that I was looking at a photograph and yet
I could see that the stone was dampened from the rain, that
the many chimney pots were a jaunty red, and that the creeper
was like black thread stitched to the stone wall, with a few
glorious sumptuous red autumn leaves that had survived. I even
thought something might stir, that there might be some movement inside the house, a figure might appear, the faded blind
might just be raised, or the white hall door opened. Of course
nothing happened.

Presently two huge sheepdogs came bounding towards me.
I thought they might snap, but no, they fawned over me, vying
with each other for my affections and as I touched and stroked
them I heard myself asking them their names, who fed them,
who was their master; the usual questions. When the rain stopped
the sky was the most heartening colour, a colour in which gold
and silver were dominant and I tell you I felt like someone who
was being sucked into a beautiful dream. I felt peaceful all over
and in no way forlorn, having the dogs for company while in
the back of my mind was the dim realisation that I would never
see that house again but that I would always remember it. Then
just as I was taking my fill of it, I saw the thing. In the upstairs
window the face of a woman, a very white face pressed itself
to the pane and when the dogs saw it they yapped like mad, and

ran towards it with the fiendishness of wolves. I tell you I ran
in the opposite direction because it was not normal nor was the
way they yapped and my whole body went crêpe with fright.
I had retraced the length of the avenue in minutes and found
myself gasping as I stood at the iron gates and looked back at
both avenues, fearfully, and thought of the innocence with
which I had trespassed. Whose house was it and who had lived
there.

'You didn't go as far as "Tintrim",' Mrs Rogers said when I
told her.

I had described the place, the green iron double gates, the
stile, and the two avenues.

'Holy B,' she said and looked up to heaven and then she said
it was the grace of God no-one saw me, as I might be shot. It
was one of the few topics on which she did not want to expound.
It was probably for that reason that I did not mention the face.
Also I was ashamed of myself and thought I was getting like
those very people, that I was seeing things.

As Mrs Rogers would be the first to agree, when sorrows come
they come not in single file but in battalions. The next day I had
an accident. I was unslept and therefore contrary with everyone,
also wanting to be in several places at the same time. I fell. I
was hurrying across a catwalk shouting at some of the boys to
lower the pressure and I knew I was about to fall and could not
stop it. It was quite a drop. It is an odd thing that shame more
than terror was what I felt as I hurtled through the air onto the
floor. At any rate I landed on my side and was convinced that
every bone in my body was broken. There were various calls
and shouts for help and I remember them coming towards me
in a bevy and by now indeed my head was spinning and I heard
words disjointed, the way one hears when one has had ether.
Stretcher, pulse, breathing, ribs, Jesus, these sort of words. I
think they thought I was dead because I had passed out. I was
unaware of most of the drama that went on around me but they
got the stretcher, hefted me onto it and for some reason I thought
I was in China on a rickshaw and the faces and the pipes all
looked to be very steamed up. I raved. I raved only about work

which is a good thing. They hawked me through the town and they said Mrs Rogers almost fainted when they brought me in the pub door. Then she revived sufficiently to give me brandy and to fetch from her own bedroom the rose silk-covered eiderdown. They called the doctor. In fact it was from him that I began to unveil some of the mystery of the house but that was later. He was somewhat in his cups when he came and it was not till midnight. I had other callers. I was brought fudge, holy water and some scapulars. These kindnesses were brought by women and I don't know who was the more embarrassed, they or me, when they stood at the end of the bed not quite looking at me, but seeming to absorb things. Out of an instinctive shyness I drew the covers nearer to me and indeed must have looked like a hawk peering out at them saying thank you.

The doctor arrived unannounced. I was in my bed, disgruntled with pain when a big stout figure comes through the bedroom door, raises his arm as if in anger and says, 'Where is the retired Black and Tan?'

I think I was supposed to be amused.

'There he is,' he says, and he strode towards me, then bent over me and touched my head playfully, so playfully, the very same as if I were a young person or a puppy dog. Had he been soberer the gesture might have been lighter but as it was, I felt I was the subject of a grip more than a friendly touch. He said he had just gone in home and was sitting down to his dinner and that the message was just given to him by a schoolchild through the opened window. I apologised.

'All in the day,' he said and felt for the sprained shoulder. He smiled. He said it was funny how many people wrenched it in exactly the same place, and how adept he was at clicking it back into shape. He said the body was like putty really, and one could do what one liked with it. Then he took off his overcoat, his tweed jacket and began to roll up his sleeves.

'Right,' he said.

Before I could ask a question my pyjama top was ripped off and he was at the far end of the bed in a horizontal position and his foot was pressing through the injured shoulder with the utmost determination.

'Feck it,' he said because I had done exactly the wrong thing in trying to resist. He explained to me that I was to do nothing whatsoever but allow his booted foot to press down on me and readjust the little sprain and be as right as rain.

'Got that,' he said. I have to say he was a good-humoured man but being so fortified with whiskey or porter or whatever it was he was much more ebullient than I, and I was also squeamish about his damp shoe. But I obeyed. I lay there like some paralysed invalid waiting to hear my own shoulder click back into place, and God knows it might have but some primaeval resistance welled up in me and far from lying limp and fallow I began to resist with renewed might. Before I could control the situation I realised he was knocked off the bed, was upon the floor in a tumble and rearing to box with me. The rest is muddled as these squabbles are. What I gather happened was that he thought we had engaged in a fight about tactics whereas I was responding to some dumb reflex by resisting his push, whereupon he put both boots to both shoulders whereupon I found this unsporting as well as unmedical, reached with my good shoulder, hit him, knocked him to the floor and unbelievably gave him a sprained ankle.

The furore brought Mrs Rogers in, and she at once started to abuse us both and assumed that we were both drunk and had launched into the foolish sally of politics. A hungry drunken doctor with a sprained ankle on the linoleum floor, myself with a broken shoulder and a woman telling us that we should be ashamed of ourselves. He and I were at once allies, and I found myself becoming spokesman for us and no matter what I said he backed it up with 'Sound, sound.' His ankle was swelling up at a fantastic rate and soon the midwife-cum-dispensary nurse from three doors down was summoned to bandage it. He and she discussed work, calls and it seems the latest disaster. A baby had been born blind up the country. Soon they were sparring. She accused him of not being in the dispensary when he should be, and he said sagely how could he be in two goddam places at the same time.

Blessedly there was a rattle of glasses as Mrs Rogers came through the door with a brass tray and some of the necessary.

He blessed her ceremoniously and her hands shook badly as she handed each of us a lethal amount of whiskey. Her manner was some way between sympathy and bossiness. The drink lessened the pain and I felt that maybe I was settling in, that maybe I would not get out of there. It is true I felt it then. I felt myself slipping. I felt lazy and soporific and in some way hopeless, though the hopelessness was helped by the drink, by their story-telling and the weird eventlessness of life.

The doctor talked way into the night after the women had gone to their slumbers. He became sentimental. He recalled the first day he had come to that village on a push bicycle, remembered how he had walked up the hill, stood at the top and proudly said to himself that he was going to be doctor to the whole community. He had ideals then. 'Twenty years, Mick,' he kept saying. In that twenty years he had been responsible for conceiving six children, had built a two-storey house in the town, had been twice in danger of being struck off the register and had seen things that would turn you to stone, Mick. Thank God he spared me details of surgical operations. His eyes had tears in them. It might have been drink but I think it was a mixture of drink and that onrush of memory that can overtake us when we realise our life is a failure, and we meet a sympathetic listener, who is also a stranger. He could talk to no-one.

'I sing dumb,' he said.

His wife barged from morning till night, his beautiful daughter was a kleptomaniac and had stolen cosmetics from the chemist, his eldest son who was in a most expensive boarding school could not put two and two together. A dunce. As for his professional status the country people would just as soon have the vet. Most of his bills were unpaid. Madness and misery were rampant. Intrigue was behind every hedge.

'The skeletons in the cupboards, Mick,' he said, and drew his head back, opened his mouth, and in speechlessness conjured up a drama in every home. Religion he insisted was the opiate of the people. But as he said, 'Mum is the word, mum is the word, Mick.'

I wondered if I was not being taught some kind of code. Then it came out. A pup of a fellow was trying to steal his post, a younger doctor. He had written to the local authorities and reported him and was only waiting for the opportunity to catch him out in something really incriminating. I learnt that this doctor owned 'Tintrim' but lived in a bungalow forty miles to the west where he had a private practice and the care of a convent. 'Tintrim' was the house where I walked to.

'Biding his time till he ousts yours truly,' the doctor said. 'No go,' he said, 'no go,' and the terrible thought occurred to me that if he had to do midwifery at that moment it would be disaster for him. 'Tintrim' he said was a cursed house. Always mortgaged, always the poor mouth until the factory came along and bought sixty acres of the land. A woman had lived there with her only daughter and had died there. The husband had had some sort of tragic death and by sign language I was to divine that he had hanged himself from an apple tree. The daughter had a screw loose. The son and his wife were waiting to inhabit the place.

'Murky,' he said.

'In what way?' I said, thinking that maybe there was murder involved.

'People will stop at nothing,' he said and I thought how moral and how exemplary we are once we tackle the vices of others. As he was telling me this he was waving an empty glass and forcing me in my enfeebled condition to break rules, that is to steal downstairs, to get the key of the bar from above the lintel, to get in and bring him a nightcap, and a pint of porter as a chaser. I did all of that. I said how I'd walked to 'Tintrim' and how it cast a strange sort of spell over me.

'If I was you I'd go elsewhere,' he said, and reeled off names of other woods where there were other houses or ruins of houses. He did not have to tell me that there were more burned ruins there than any place else in the world.

'Big plums, sugar plums,' he said and recalled the mother's generosity and how she would have a basket in the vestibule to hand to him as he left. It would be full of things like gooseberries or a slab of cake or a plucked fowl. He said her first name. It was Lena. 'A lady . . . a chip off the old block,' he said. I got the feeling that maybe he had loved her. Maybe once on the way out he had just kissed her throat or something like that. Anyhow he laughed aloud to himself as he contemplated the smoky amber drink that was going to bring him further and further away from the dastardly cares that were now wearing him down.

When he decided to leave I had to get out of bed and help him up. It was not easy because his deepest inclination was to lie down and have me undo his tie, take off his boots and cover him with the rose eiderdown. I managed to drag him up but I was unable to get him down the stairs in silence. He raved on about those sugar plums. He said did I ever hear that one about one fine day in the middle of the night when two dead men got up to fight, with two blind men looking on, two cripples looking for the priest and two dummies shouting hurry on! I forgot about my shoulder and walked with him in my pyjamas up the cobbled street towards his own house. It was one of those lovely hushed winter nights with only a dog or two about, the stars teeming and bright, a silence reigning over all things when no car is going to crank or no cock is going to crow, when two men are just seen to stagger home and joke about heads which on the morrow will be no joking matter.

On Sundays there were certain rituals. The landlady would be up very early and would light a fire in the parlour and later her sister and a flock of children would come, and there would be boiled potatoes and boiled mutton for lunch. Often by the time they arrived the fire would have gone out and Mrs Rogers would scold herself for having forgotten it and we would be put to task to light it again. Mrs Rogers swore by paraffin oil for lighting a fire and her sister swore by white sugar and between them once they got such a roaring fire going that the lace runner over the mantelpeice caught fire. Mrs Rogers ripped it off and quelled the flames with her bare hands while at the same time she lamented the lovely little threads and flowers that had got burnt away. It was the crochet work of a man in Australia. She put it to soak and was already conjecturing aloud as to who could mend it.

'I have my roast now for Monday,' her sister would say and

then go on to explain that a joint was under the meat safe, safe
from flies, safe from appetites. She enjoined her children to eat
up though they did not have to be encouraged. That was one
ritual.

The other was that a few regulars called at the side door directly after second Mass, were admitted to the parlour and partook
of drink illegally while Mrs Rogers somewhat randomly kept
an eye out for the guards. The conversation was pretty slack,
each waiting for the other to tell something of interest and when
something was told the hearers would evince disbelief and say
'Get on with you,' and almost accuse the teller of fabrication so
that he would have to tell it again, and stress the moribund
parts, until he had his group enthralled. I seemed to remember
stories of a stillborn calf, of galvanised spray that did not turn
out to be rust-proof and of some lower-class woman whose arm
was now in a sling because her husband had taken the carving
knife to her. The exclamations, the disbelief, the 'go on with
you', and the final succumb jar in my head as does everything
that has happened to me here.

As it was getting nearer my return to my own country I believe that I was more forbearing than at first. At any rate I was
drinking with them, I was buying rounds of drinks and I was
sitting down to mutton that was so greasy that the alcohol got
soaked up by it and later I was having detestable red and green
jelly in order to be polite. Instead of flopping onto my bed as
I would have liked, I would get my walking stick and my ga-
loshes and have a ramble. On the last Sunday of which I speak I
had planned to go to the house. Somehow I felt that I had to, that
there was some kind of onus on me. I was even thinking what
it might look like, and if the dogs were likely to be there.

As it happened I was not able to go. The whole routine had
changed that Sunday. There was no fire lit, there was no Auntie
Josephine coming. Mrs Rogers was home from first Mass and
was frying my breakfast on the little stove. I could see at a
glance that she was agitated because there were wandering
patches of red on her neck. And though attending to a fried
egg, she would pick up her felt hat, remove the big pearl hat-pin

and skewer the poor hat in another place. The hackney car had let her down. She was to go to the hospital and instead the villain had gone to Dublin with a party who were attending a hurling match. She ranted about its being a 'material' age and how no-one had any honour any more and how what would her little friend think and she hated to let someone down. Naturally I had to offer to take her. I had bought an old Peugeot during my stay and it was on its last legs.

'Will it go that far?' she said.

'How far,' I said, nettled.

'Fifteen or twenty miles,' she said, and added that irritating thing that they do to confound matters, 'as the crow flies.'

'It should do,' I said.

It was to St Mary's she said, as if I was familiar with the place. I took it to be the county hospital but after we had set out I learned that it was a mental hospital and a decided reluctance seeped up in me. Lunatics do not have a fascination for me. On the contrary. I had to go once as a child and got overwrought there. She sensed my resentment and said how modern it all was, and said that the padded cell was a mere curiosity now. Would I like to see the padded cell? No thank you. She joked about things and fell to telling me of her early days in America and how once walking home with her intended, he pointed to a house of ill-repute and asked her if she wouldn't like to go there.

'The cheek,' she said, and I took it that they had never married. Often she would nudge me by way of thanking me for bringing her. Then she said how she was going to miss me and that if I wished she would get me a turkey before going away. She said if they were not drawn they could hang for weeks and I could think of her on Christmas day. She then asked what kind of stuffing was favoured in my part of the world and I remembered the actual taste of the wonderful chestnut one my housekeeper used to do. She said, 'You're making my mouth water,' and made me stop. Contrary to her prognostication she was not car-sick and all in all the drive was very pleasant, as on her advice we took back roads, and it was lovely to see the hedges and the bare winter trees and the birds wheeling and

circling about. The silvered air too was full of the noise of rushing water from the ditches and water seemed to hang like
crystals from the trees. Beyond the brackened country were
beautiful blue mountains, ranges of them like skies. It was
hunting country and she tried to rack her brain to remember
if there was a hunt that day, then she listed the people who
followed the hounds, the toffs, then the farmers, then the shop-
keepers, then the hucksters. In fact she was like one of those
wound-up birds whose chatter had to go its course before it
commences its repertoire again.

Soon we were in the town and my memory is of pebble-dash
bungalows in dreary rotation on either side, a black-looking
church spire in the distance and flocks of people either coming
or going from their devotions. It was the month of the holy
souls. Quite suddenly she was a bundle of nerves, opening and
closing the amber clasp of her handbag, taking out a flapjack,
dabbing powder on to little avail and saying daft disconnected
things about the scenery, the bungalows, and so forth.

'Do you know, Jack, I'm afraid,' she said as we drove up the
tree-lined new drive, observing the five-miles-per-hour traffic
notice. As we turned a corner and my eye was full of yew trees
I let out an involuntary cry because in the upstairs middle
window I saw a face, that of a young girl, just as I had seen
before at 'Tintrim', and when I looked again it was gone.

'Nothing to be afraid of,' I said, but she had sensed my
flounder.

'It's their stares,' she said and asked if I had ever been to such
a place. I lied and said no because I was unfit to talk. I was shaking and had that terrible sensation of a repetition, of having
been in that driveway before, the witnesser of those yew trees,
as someone on the brink.

There were only two other cars parked outside and she said,
not without hope, that maybe it was past visiting hours and
she would not get in. I had forgotten to ask whom she was
going to see.

'Clara,' she said with the same assumption as she had said
St Mary's.

In she went, through the first open door, and then I saw her ring a bell and she was admitted through a second door with a stained-glass panel. I decided that I was getting badly affected by the place and that it was a good thing that I really was leaving because my imagination was getting heady. I got out of the car for air, lit a cigarette and was leaning against the back mudguard when she hurried down the steps and called to me, 'Jack, will you come, will you come.'

I thought maybe somebody had tried to accost her, to which she said it was jollier if two of us went in. To coax me she handed me one of the packages she was carrying and said I could give it as a gift. I believe it was a pot of homemade jam.

We went up a stone stairs and smelt Jeyes Fluid, and behind that smell, inherent in the very bones of the place was the smell of cabbage. We passed windowed wards with thick tweed curtains drawn and then a big refectory with its table quite bare. Not even a salt-cellar or a bowl of flowers on it, just the knots in the wood and stains. Over the fireplace the big imposing photograph of Our Lord Jesus Christ with the ringleted hair, and a bleeding heart so red I thought it was moving. But of course by now I was seeing things. Then we were admitted by a nurse to a littler room where the few visitors sat with the patients and the patients looked up at us. The first face I saw was yellow and pinched, almost a jaundiced face, that of an old woman who was laughing as she ate a bar of chocolate and smeared it everywhere. I saw another woman with a metal curling pin in the top of her head to make it wavy. It was a dismal place with the saints everywhere around the walls and a tray of tea things on a side table.

I saw Clara and I tell you I had to hold on to the back of a dining chair to give myself some semblance of steadiness. She was like a little torch – pale faced, golden, fairy-like. These words are not improper. She was sucking a little gold cross, the very picture of youngness, and wrongedness. I felt when I saw her that it was as if some terrible mistake had happened. She had no business there. Then I thought how deceived we are by looks and for all I knew she was a dangerous unbridled creature. Mrs Rogers said hello, and how well Clara was looking, and how I was the foreign gentleman who'd broken his own shoulder and the doctor's ankles and how we were late because the hackney driver did a bunk and scooted and how we'd brought damson jam, Mackintosh toffees, a marble cake that was still warm. Thereupon she opened the lid of the tin so that Clara could smell the cake that soon she would be cutting.

'Say thank you, Clara,' the nurse said, and the face that look-ed up and looked about us would wring a reaction from a stone. It was beautiful but aghast. It was an oval face and the eyes were the blackest I'd ever seen, black as if wet. The skin was soft and sleek like a kid glove and the colouring brought to my mind those descriptions in rose catalogues – soft, salmon-pink opening to a paler pink, scented, matt. She had a white throat carried by a long beautiful branching neck. Had she tried to cut it? One thinks, one sees, and one is lost. She would not say a word.

'Say thank you, Clara.'

'How are you, Clara?'

'Say hello to the foreign gentleman, Clara ... He's called Mr Herema.'

She looked at me as if she really saw me through and through. There was, I seem to think, clairvoyance as well as pity in her look but I did not care, because she had charmed me as only silence can. There they were urging her to speak, and there was I saying to myself how she spoke from such reaches of silence and how in a way I hoped she would never speak. And her smile. Nothing coquettish about it, just as if her innermost being was telling her that all was well, and that there *was* occasion to smile.

Chiefly to get them from pestering her I took out my notebook to do her a little drawing. I drew her an artichoke. Why it? God would be a better consultant on the matter. Perhaps it was to do with not being able to speak. I drew it carefully, had each leaf a little opened so that she could see into it and see its fuzzy centre which I did in light blue pencil. The more they coaxed her, the more she would smile, not as a gambit but probably to disarm us. Once she parted her lips and Mrs Rogers let out a gasp and said 'Tis coming now,' and we all waited agog for words to issue out of her as if a gold streamer was going to come from her mouth, but nothing did.

Being them, they alternated between coaxing and abusing and in the end I knew she would not budge when she put the little gold cross back into her mouth and began to suck on it persistently. The saddest thing was that one knew from the eyes that there were things she wanted to say, badly say. I also had an unpleasant feeling that if she did speak she might not be able to shape her words properly, and that they would tumble out in an unseemly disconnected mess. I wondered what she had done. Tried to take her own life or tried to take someone else's? I handed her the drawing and she took it and looked at it with the utmost gratification.

To distract them I asked about visiting hours and if there were any regulations about sending books or journals and it is maybe because of this that she thought I was taking an interest in her and that hours after we had left she uttered my name in a whisper. I had suggested that since it was near Christmas they might dress up and put on a little pantomime. They were ribald at that and one of the old ladies just leapt up into the air and did a crazy yippee. I said that maybe Clara could recite and obviously, saying these things I had got through to her. Or else she was sick of being silent. Anyhow she spoke.

The news of this soon spread to the village and thence to the factory. The boys were joking and codding about it. They said was I baby-snatching. They gave me such lascivious looks that you would think, to use one of their own expressions, that I'd brought the girl up the mountains. At any rate I was pleased and thought that what luck because now Clara would be able to recite a poem and so I selected one for her. It was from an old school book that I found in the house, a book that had belonged to Mrs Rogers' niece. The poem was called 'Fontenoy'. It was about soldiers in Europe on the eve of battle sweetly recalling their own acres. It was the reversal of my situation because I was still aching for my own country. It was a fiery poem with lines like:

> *All night long we dream of you*
> *And waking think we're there*
> *Vain dream and fooling waking*
> *We never shall see Clare.*

I called on her a few days later and brought the book. I put it down to chance. I was on that road on the way back from seeing someone off at the airport, and I thought that I might as well call. But why had I bought a cream cake and why was I idiotically going up the steps holding a white box with Dainty Dairy written on it? That is a matter for conjecture.

She was thrilled to see me. She ran from her basketwork and smiled as if she were hugging me. It took time to free me from the cake box and then she opened it and danced about. There was a different nurse on duty and the whole atmosphere seemed more relaxed. She was called Kathleen but begged me to call her Kay and was bursting to tell me her own life story, which was grim. Her husband had broken a coffee table the previous Saturday and she wasn't speaking to him.

'Serves him right,' she said and went on to explain how he had the cheek to ask her out for a drink the night before to make up.

'Care for a B and B, darling,' he said to her and Clara was going 'sssh' because she wanted to read out the poem I'd brought, as she said to have a 'rehearsal'. She was so excited that she got fanciful and put on a ridiculous accent, which was touching. We cut the cake with my penknife and pieces were passed around to some of the inmates. How they loved it, how they swallowed it with such an amount of relish, and were already speculating about a second helping. All it needed was for streamers and a bit of Jack Frost to be on the window, for it to be Christmas Day. There was Clara reciting, and the others eating and the nurse pretending that she'd call another nurse but you could see she had no intention of doing it.

'Home rule,' she said and explained that the matron had gone to a wedding. I thought it would be only seconds before they started dancing and lighting matches and getting obstreperous. She read my mind. She called me out to the landing for a matter of urgency. The whispering was so secretive that even I could not understand it. Soon I did. She was in charge of Clara and if I liked I could take the two of them for a little drive, just a half mile down the road and back, for a bit of a diversion.

The preparations downstairs! Clara buttoning up her coat. Clara looking for a headscarf. The nurse retrieving her handbag from behind a bag of turf. Then having to put on make-up and brush her lashes with mascara. All to go into the woods! It was an old wood, full of all kinds of trees, healthy and diseased ones, evergreen and bare, an old wood where some boughs had fallen down and had taken root again in the ground. Everything was rampant and the towering branches jostled for space. Clara became so animated. She ran up to trees and was prattling to them. She was like a little encyclopaedia. Sweet chestnut was not a native, but was introduced from Roman times and was good cover for snipe and good coppice. The timber could be used for coffins.

'Huh,' Kay said to that, and lit a cigarette. I had to hold several matches for her and I had an uneasy feeling that she was going to make me a proposition. She said that she liked men but had no time at all for women. Clara more or less ignored us so busy was she, admiring the holly trees and spouting the Latin names of plants.

'For the love of Mike, will you dry up,' Kathleen said and Clara, whose spirits were unquenchable, rattled on about rhododendrons, poplars, mountain ash and the magic attached to each one, and Kathleen decided to ignore her and divulge her own full story, her children, the illnesses they had had, her hire purchase furniture, and how she would be in England in twenty-four hours if she met the right man.

We were walking along, with her prattling, and me listening, and suddenly she said, 'Jesus and Mary.' Clara was not there. Kathleen called her name, made a mouthpiece with her two hands and called imperatively.

'Would she do that?' I said, feeling totally idiotic at having brought them out at all.

'She'd do anything,' she said.

'Is she violent?' I said.

'She ate a poisonous weed, had to be pumped,' Kathleen said and I could see now that she was shaken, as her cheeks were scarlet and she made little absurd runs in various directions. I thought how simple it would be and how natural therefore for a lunatic to try and escape. It was the first time I thought of Clara as a lunatic. Kathleen and I chose different paths and made an arrangement to shout if and when we found her. If. I rebuked myself for this new kind of behaviour of mine, for this laissez-faire. My mind ran on to the consequences, Kathleen being blamed, my idiotic attempts at telling people that I had taken them out in all harmlessness. And Clara – she would be captured and punished. I dreaded that.

It was a devilish place to search, because not only did the woods provide ample cover and various kinds of camouflage but beyond was a huge area of unused bog with the ripened bracken dense, and high as my waist, while underfoot lurked a swamp into which one was very likely to be sucked. Combing my way through the fern I bumped into Kathleen and she hissed like a weasel, so vexed was she at our folly. There was a lake to the left of the bog and we both looked towards it with a similar foreboding. There were browning water-lily leaves on its surface and the edges were fringed with bulrushes. Could one drown in it, was the question neither of us asked. It looked still, eerily so, as did the whole bog. It was nothing other than a great vacated bronzed world where nature lorded but human life was nil. The main road was about two miles off, and Kathleen suggested we go in separate directions and aim for the chapel beyond. One could just see the spire, a mere shaft in the distance.

Kathleen's hair and face were all askew and in between ejaculations to her maker she said she would be struck off as a nurse. She took the path nearest the lake and I went into the thick of the bog, wading my way before me. I still did not believe that Clara was gone. In fact I kept thinking that I would meet her, like a warrior wading to me. These ferns were too high for her, almost cheek-high and by now her suede shoes and her feet would be wringing. I had noticed her shoes simply because they looked so shabby. They were purple and in places the suede had worn thin. I came on an old still – there was a U-pipe of steel, a galvanised pan and bottles hidden underground. I expect someone made home brew there and realised that Mrs Rogers and her affiliates were not responsible for the entire inebriation of the parish. Bending down to examine it I looked directly along my eyeline and there lying inert in the fern was Clara. It was like seeing someone in a cradle.

'You will catch pneumonia,' was what I said and I said it gruffly. She did not move. I asked her what she thought she was doing.

'Nothing,' she said.

I said did she realise the panic she had caused. My relief at finding her had merely succeeded in rousing my anger, the way it does. She stood up, wobbled somewhat, then brushed the back of her coat which was wet and looked at me with the beseeching look of a spaniel who has done wrong.

'It was only fun,' she said, and in reply I just snorted and started to walk back in search of Kathleen. She tagged behind. Presently she hummed a song and no doubt this was her way of wanting to talk. As we entered the woods I began hollering Kathleen's name and I was annoyed at the clarity of my own echo, annoyed under those circumstances that is.

'You have good lungs, Jack,' she said.

'I am not Jack,' I said, and I realised that I wanted badly to scold her, even biff her so as to get rid of my huff.

The suede shoes were like sods of turf so wet were they, and it was on these I commented, as I looked down at them scornfully.

'I'm only young,' she said, and she was wiping her face, her smudged face, with a big wet leaf and she wiped every bit of it and then took a second leaf as if to rinse it. Kathleen answered my holler and we walked on in silence. I expected we would all meet at the car. The woods were full of odd noises, noises all the more pertinent because of our solemnness. There was the dripping of water, and a soft thud as something fell to the ground, and the scurry of things – hares or rabbits – in the undergrowth. Of course I wanted to forgive her but it would have been precipitate. I would have lost face. She was now by my side and we came to a very old oak tree that had made certain of its own space. It was not hemmed in, it stood there, wide, stately, unencumbered like a tree inhabiting its own world.

'Look, look, mistletoe,' she said and broke a sprig off and suddenly twirled it in the air, and kissed me. It was her – over-animated, tomboyish – trying to ask forgiveness. Yet instantly she was ashamed of what she had done. Her face was an image of shame and her eyes were on the verge of overflowing. She threw the mistletoe to the ground. I picked another piece and put it in her buttonhole. Then I kissed her to give some complexion to the event and it was all quite different. It was not a playful kiss at all. The outer skin of her lips clung to mine a second longer than was appropriate. Then as I drew back from her, baffled by the raciness of my own blood she took hold of my coat sleeve and nestled in it. I held her. That was all. No-one had held her for a long time. She was like a breakable. That was all. That is all.

'It's not wrong,' she said.

'It's not wrong,' I said, and then so discreetly, so winningly, she swore me to secrecy. I asked if in fact she intended to run away.

'Where would I go?'

The reply was gravity itself. Then she nodded her head in the direction of the road to say we had better head there and get over the scolding that was imminent. We walked quickly. Sometimes she ran. By not asking me to be her saviour she had in fact rallied all my support.

There was the expected tirade from Kathleen. How Clara was a bold girl, had no feelings for anyone else, no consideration, how Clara would not get sponge cake for her tea, how Clara would be reported to the Matron and so on. She did not believe a word of it. We walked, all three of us hand in hand down a path and though her palm was very still in mine it was potent with meaning. In the car peace was restored. Clara sat in the back and I could feel her presence behind me, touching me, yet not touching me, I could feel the energy flowing out of her onto me, the energy, the fiendish energy of the invisible. She took the opportunity to give voice to the things in this world that did not bore her. Woods didn't, walking didn't, Christmas didn't, satin shoes didn't, visitors didn't, outings didn't. Yet she became downcast as we motored up the drive.

'He'll come again, he'll bring loot,' Kathleen said. They were so sure of me. To them I was some kind of benevolent uncle. Clara ran in. There is something about a person's back that can arrest and hurt one's whole being. I felt all her desperation in her run. I thought of her in ten years, slow like the others, a somnambulist, finished. Kathleen sat in the car and was exorcised about Clara's plight, said it was wrong to have her locked in there with old fogeys, made to take tranquillisers and to have every letter she wrote seized. Clara wrote to strangers as future pen-pals and also she wrote looking for employment. She wanted to be either a lady's companion or an understudy to a lady on the stage. I wished I had not heard that. It was somehow too rending. She did not want to go back to 'Tintrim' as it was haunted. That I believed.

'She's no more mad then I am,' Kathleen said, and stubbed a half-cigarette before getting out.

'So why is she here?' I said.

'Ask her brother, dear.'

It was the sarcasm of the word 'dear' that struck me as fishy.

'He certified her, didn't he, gave a cock and bull story about how she tried to strangle his wife . . . if anyone tried to strangle his wife it's him . . . arguing from morning till night . . . she won't answer the door . . . keeps the telephone under her nightgown . . . they're the ones that's mad.'

'Can't anyone help her?' I said.

'Divil a one,' she said, and in the hum-drumness of her tone was a conviction that no-one would help her either, that she would go on being a part-time nurse, go on being subject to a man who broke coffee tables when he was drunk, that she would go on.

It was a few days before the trouble started. I do not know if the nurse blathered or if Clara's high spirits became too much for joyless people. At any rate I got a letter to my lodgings. It looked ominous. The back of the manilla envelope was blotched with uneven crusts of violet sealing wax. The message was short and to the point: 'Keep away from her, Puck.' I thought of taking it to the Sergeant but Mrs Rogers advised against that. She said, 'Lie low, lie low, Jack.'

When I got to the factory I felt decidedly ill at ease. The Manager cut me dead. A few of the workmen nudged and one had the audacity to say that I looked like a man who had just deposited a million. There was nothing but commotion that day and two lots of machinery broke down. During a tea break the Manager and I went to his office. It was the first time I saw his sulky side. He said it was a simply bloody thing and that all I must do is not meddle. The factory were buying the rest of 'Tintrim' land and when that deal was safely done, Clara could be let out of the asylum and live in the gate lodge. It was the first time that he was ruthless with me. I can hardly believe that I used to sit the odd time with him and his wife, be showered with praise, with food, and a litany saying how indispensable I am. I tried to reason with him to say that Clara could sell the land as easily as her brother who was anyhow stealing it from her, but he said to stop fecking, to stop fecking about. She was under age and that land might double or treble in the next twelve months and anyhow he had made a deal with her brother involving timber and things, a deal that was to everyone's satisfaction. First he was buying every tree on the place at a cut and then the land at the auction price. I guessed it without having to be told.

'Holy Roman Catholic thieves united,' I said.

'I'll give you a piece of advice, Jack,' he said, but before he could verbalise it I told him what to do with it, using his own much-used rustic vernacular.

Towards the end of the day, the night shift had just come on and I was getting my coat to leave. I heard my name being called and in the dusk beyond the doorway I saw a figure wearing a cap back to front. Out of courtesy he took it off as he entered. He was a stocky fellow with hair so white he could have been an albino. For a minute I thought it was Clara's brother.

'They are wise to you,' he said in a droll voice, and instantly he began to grin. I thought that maybe he was an idiot and had just come to look at me or to make a joke. He said did I know the lonely mountains. I said what was the inference there.

'You'll be pulp,' he said and it was then that I saw his face, pock-marked. Chicken pox, or scars – it could be either.

'You do not believe in the immortality of the soul?' I said.

I was marshalling all the irony I could.

'We do a good skull job . . .' he said.

Had he been one of my trainees I could have reasoned with him, this lout looking for adventure. 'Get lost,' I said rather unaffectedly. He didn't budge. He had been holding a cigarette in the crook of his hand and now he puffed on it as he looked at me, and as it seemed to me conjectured on how he would beat me up. I learned later that he had done time in jail for an offence, and that he was living with a woman in a caravan in some woods. He was the local hooligan. I learnt this from the publican. 'Tis an odd thing to find oneself a stranger in a strange macabre situation and know that for no reason except a trick of fate one is going to fight a dirty battle. All for Clara. Her influence was deepening in me. I had a large whiskey to which I did not add water and I asked the publican to join me. Then I put it to him if there was an honest man in the town.

'It all depends,' he said.

They have that maddening way of making you feel that they are villains but that on a whim they might reform. I sounded him out about the local doctor, about Clara's brother, and even about Clara herself. He said the doctors would fight to the hilt and he was on the side of the local fellow if only for the fact that he'd come into a pub like any farmer and drink a pint. The other fellow, Clara's brother would only go to cocktail bars with his missus. By such idiotic prejudice I was going to have to rally friends. But I would, I would. He would go into the kitchen, eat part of his tea and come out again chewing. He was eating raw onions and bread. He was a bachelor. I asked about Clara herself.

'A cracked little lady,' was how he described her.

He then told a story of how when she was little, his mother, God rest her, had sent Clara to buy a postage stamp, and Clara had adhered the postage stamp to her thumb and sallied down the street whence the stamp blew away. 'It blew away like that,' Clara had said to an irate woman who scolded her. For some reason it completely melted my heart. He went on to describe her mother as a fine woman, praised her for making her own jam, for having the best Rhode Island Reds in the countryside, and for being a marvellous cook. Mother and daughter were bosom friends. Clara never went away to school and he pronounced that as foolish since she had a good brain box. Before Christmas they used to give card parties and raffle a turkey and a goose. My heart was lifted by his description of blazing fires in the three downstairs rooms, of the oak dining table laid with white cloth, lovely glasses, and groaning with the Christmas fare that the two of them had prepared for weeks.

'I used to gorge,' he said and went back for another bit of his soda bread.

'She's in St Mary's,' I said.

'She won't have much clicking there,' he said and true to some juvenile instinct in him slicked back his hair. When I came out onto the street it was pelting and I drew the collar of my coat up both to shelter myself and so as not to be seen. There was no doubt in my mind about what I must do.

It was Sunday again. I had conferred with the three people who were likely to help me but it all had to be very hush-hush. Mrs Rogers lit candles in the chapel and promised to give her support. She even hinted that the parish priest might be on our side. That seemed like the best fortification we could have.

As I drove along I tried not to think too earnestly of what lay ahead. The crows that perched on the telegraph wires would suddenly fly off in a cluster and I felt them guiding my mission there. The hayricks were covered over with black plastic and various sheepdogs had a craze for chasing motor cars.

If anything, the town her brother lives in is more morose than ours. It is a seaside town but these places without crowds and sunshine and coloured balls and candy floss are wastelands indeed. They are like bare stages awaiting the performers. I did not see the sea as I drove into town, it being hidden behind a high grass bank, but I did catch its bracing iodine smell and this I inhaled for strength. I passed the convent where Clara's brother was the medical consultant and then I drove slowly past pebble-dash bungalows until I came to his one with 'Geata Bawn' on the gate. White gate. There was nothing white about this mission of mine, there was darkness, there was doubt and there was the furtiveness of me about to pose as a patient with a serious heart condition. During the week I had phoned frequently but I had failed to make contact with him, just as I had failed to see Clara. The two times I had called at the hospital I was told that she could see no-one as she was having treatment. The word sent a shiver through me because I feared that they were tampering with her brain. Only for the temporary nurse becoming my ally I might have suspected the worst. She sneaked a letter out from Clara. It was short, it had none of the musings of youth. It said it trusted me. It said that there were people in the world who were against her having fresh air. The sentence that struck me most was the one that said, 'There is no need to be afraid. God is good to us, Jack.'

The nurse's husband was there the second evening I called, and upon hearing the saga took a big machine gun from out of a creaking chest. He said if we wanted an ambush we could have it on the spot. 'The Big Willie,' he called the gun, and his wife remonstrated with him not to be such a bombast. I promised him a greyhound to keep his mouth shut.

Going into her brother's driveway I cannot say that I felt composed. There was the much-vaunted evidence of his wife's good gardening, a fine display of chrysanthemums, roses cut right down, and the shrubs blazing with berries or vivid leaves. I took stock of these things the way one does when in a pickle. His wife opened the door furious and without even looking at me said, 'No calls on Sunday.' I recognised her as the woman Mrs Rogers had evicted although she looked coarser without benefit of powder or paint. In fact she looked wild. Her hair was piled in a white towel and I presume she had just washed it. She was about to retreat when I lifted a weak gloved hand and I was almost ashamed of my own ability to sway her. I said that I could hardly breathe and my voice was appropriately faint. I saw her look at me and take some sort of stock of me and wonder aloud if she could get me some tablets. I said that if I could see the doctor for five minutes that I would be forever indebted and I made clear that I expected his fee to be double on a Sunday. She hummed and she hawed, and eventually, somewhat grudgingly, she conducted me into his surgery. It was spotless. There was a swivel chair, a leather-top desk and a photo of them at a dress dance with a government minister and his wife. There was also a glass case full of medicines and blue jars with Latin labels on them. These I noticed the most. He came in somewhat huffily and said it was his wife's good nature that had engineered this. He had a low voice and there was a compunction about him. He wore a fawn cardigan which he was hurriedly buttoning. He asked me formally what the trouble was and guessed my identity before I even spoke.

'You swine,' he said but his voice was trembling.

I said I was not going to apologise as I thought the matter too grave for that and I reminded him of the telephone calls that I had made to him in the week and of the urgent telegram to which he had not replied. He ground his teeth in useless anger. I shall never forget the coldness both of him and of the room. It smelt of anaesthetic and you would not infer that patients had sat there morning after morning spilling out their woes. He saw that I was not intimidated and immediately said that no one was as sorry as he for his sister's condition, and that of course only he and the matron knew the full extent of it. He tapped his own head to denote how mad Clara was. I was horrified by such effrontery but said to him that Clara seemed recovered now. I decided to win him over.

'You should not have visited her, you should not have brought her off the premises,' he said, and as if I needed the information he guaranteed that it would not happen again.

'She's under strict security,' he said.

'Surely you wouldn't deprive her of a visit,' I said and tried a smile, to mollify him.

'She is in my care now,' he said softly, too softly, and added that he knew what was best for her, what overwrought her, what brought on her dementia, and so forth. I longed to know that if in the week she had become silent again or had given in to some terrible outburst.

'I am boss,' he said . . . 'I am the doctor,' and he pointed to his framed degree on the wall. All I saw was the number of letters after his name.

'I could marry her,' I said.

Not even to myself had I made that kind of statement. I was engaged once but it was cancelled due to a piece of destiny. Since then I enjoyed the monastic life.

'Tell that to the Marines,' he said.

I was wrong to blurt it out when I had so many other cards up my sleeve but my dislike of him was too intense to expect prudence.

'She is below the age of consent,' he snarled.

'Not for long,' I said, fuelling his anger.

'Do you think we'd let you?' he said and dared to criticise my religion, my profession and my race, three things about which he had not an iota.

'I could report you to the Medical Council,' I said and was hasty enough to mention the local doctor whom he was trying to depose. He just sneered. The local doctor was small fry compared with his sister, a huge house and lands worth over a hundred thousand pounds.

'I can have her insensate in under five minutes,' he said, and he nodded to the cabinet in which the dark blue jars stood in a row, their true properties concealed to me. I had read of evil, I had even met a bit of it, but I felt that I smelt it now the very same as if one was smelling a rotted carcass. What's more I believed he would do it. He would alter her thoughts or twist them or take them away, as he found fit. I was more shaken than I have ever been.

'Just try anything on,' he said, and as he said it, I felt by suggestion that my own mind was being a little invaded, that I was losing grip. Indeed I was, because I saw Clara for a moment totally disfigured as she ran onto a trampoline and screamed and begged to get away. One cannot hear a suggestion of threat without oneself becoming affected by it. I was holding my spectacles and oh my God I found that my anger had crushed them. The pieces were like shreds of ice inside the soft suede case. He saw it too. I felt the torrent of language and violence that was ready to come out of me. I knew that I could kill him in minutes and yet some small voice said 'Wait, caution, Clara.'

I said in pity's name to let her free, and that he could have
the place lock, stock and barrel. I said that I would educate
her, send her to a university in France, I even promised not to
see her if that was what worried him. He softened. He said he
could not do a thing as his hands were tied. He mimed a man
who was in fetters. I realised that he meant his wife who had
indeed looked ferocious as she admitted me. I appealed to him.
I was aware of how I raised and lowered my voice to have
effect on him. I spoke of his soul, the blot on his soul for ever.
I spoke of human life as being an individual, sole gift, and said
that at bottom I believed he cared for her. That touched him.
I even spouted Shakespeare, the quality of mercy is not strained
... and, oh dear reader, he joined me in the recitation of it as if
we were comrades. I said if he committed her to a lifelong
sentence his life would be pitched into hell.

'A hell – what do you think it is now?' he said, and out of the
depth of some terrible hidden dungeon, he spoke like some
small child who has lost its reason. 'And what is it now?' he
said, on the very verge of tears, and it was as if Satan struck,
because his wife pushed the door in and asked him in the name
of heavens what he was doing standing there blubbering, *what*
were those tears in his eyes.

Naturally she guessed who I was and instantly began to
scream and give orders to have me out of there, while at the
same moment she had clutched me so that I was not able to
move without chucking her to one side. A crazed woman
tugged at my collar while a lather of curses issued from her
tongue. I thought ridiculously that that was why I had never
married. The words that came out were of such fluency and
such malice that I do not know where she found them, but
they must have always been in her awaiting their expression. She
tore at my beard. I may be exaggerating but her will to harm
me was something other than hate, it was desire gone very wrong,
it was desire that was choking and thwarting her. I realised
how jealous she was of Clara, and of me, of life, of happiness
just as I realised how unhappy she was. In her everything had
gone inside and was caged there; her soul had become a carnival
of madness. Were it not for Clara I would have gone straight

to the airport, without even collecting my belongings. While trying to harm me she was asking him what he had said, to repeat every word he had said. Locks of wet hair hung over her face giving her a more berserk look.

'Nothing, darling,' he said.

The darling was cravenous indeed.

'Answer,' she said, and it was as if a leash dangled from her fat wrist, whereas in fact ivory elephants were what fell.

'What have you told him?' she asked.

I winked at him because I believed I had won him over. I had touched his conscience. In fact I thought he was about to tell the truth, to tell her what he was intending to do which was to free Clara. Instead of that he said that she was to have no misgivings. I saw that he was going to yield to her, out of fear perhaps, or to avoid a scene or maybe because of something much deeper. I recall the glance between them and a flinch in his expression that said he would do anything rather than allow her rage to run loose. He assured her that in answer to my threats he had not budged an inch and that he and she had no notion of being intimidated. Shame. Shame. I would have gone to the gallows there and then if I thought it would convert him.

'We'll have you run over,' she said, and launched into a rhapsody about how they would do it, about the slate quarry where they would dump my body and the flocks of crows that would peck my eyes out. I knew that I was in the very thick of unreason and I counselled myself to get quietly but quickly out.

'Darling,' he said, as he dragged her away from me and though I dearly wanted to strike her I slipped through the open doorway. In the hall as I groped for my hat I could tell from the sound of her shrieking that he was holding her down, that she was trying to break loose and such a scene they'd often lived before.

I drove out of there at a wizard speed, flaking some of the peddle-dash from their pier, and in no doubt as to which direction I should take. It is all quite clear. I know what I must do. I will stop at nothing. I will find allies. The nurse is on my side. We will not be sundered. I will not be brought to the slate quarry. The crows will not drink my blood. I will fight. I will win. My heart is all agog. It seems to me we might succeed . . . Pray for us if you will.

Mrs Reinhardt ❦

Mrs Reinhardt had her routes worked out. Blue ink for the main roads, red when she would want to turn off. A system, and a vow. She must enjoy herself, she must rest, she must recuperate, she must put on weight, and perhaps blossom the merest bit. She must get over it. After all, the world was a green, a sunny and enchanting place. The hay was being gathered, the spotted cows so sleek they looked like Dalmatians and their movements so lazy in the meadows that they could be somnambulists. The men and women working in the fields seemed to be devoid of fret or haste. It was June in Brittany, just before the throngs of visitors arrived, and the roads were relatively clear. The weather was blustery but as she drove along, the occasional patches of sunlight illuminated the trees, the lush grass and the marshes. Seeds and pollen on the surface of the marshes were a bright mustard yellow. Bits of flowering broom divided the roadside, and at intervals an emergency telephone kiosk in bright orange caught her attention. She did not like that. She did not like emergency and she did not like the telephone. To be avoided.

While driving, Mrs Reinhardt was occupied and her heart was relatively normal. One would not know that recently she had been through so much and that presently much more was to follow. A lull. Observe the roadside, the daisies in the fields, the red and the pink poppies, and the lupins so dozy like the cows; observe the road signs and think if necessary of the English dead in the last war whose spectres floated somewhere in these environments, the English dead of whom some photograph, some relic or some crushed thought was felt at that moment in some English semi-detached home. Think of food, think of shellfish, think of the French for blueberries, think of anything, so long as the mind keeps itself occupied.

It promised to be a beautiful hotel. She had seen photos of it, a dovecote on the edge of a lake, the very essence of stillness, beauty, sequesteredness. A place to re-meet the god of peace. On either side of the road the pines were young and spindly but the cows were pendulous, their udders shockingly large and full. It occurred to her that it was still morning and that they had been only recently milked so what would they feel like at sundown! What a nuisance that it was those cow's udders that brought the forbidden thought to her mind. Once in their country cottage, a cow had got caught in the barbed wire fence and both she and Mr Reinhardt had a time of it trying to get help, and then trying to release the creature causing a commotion among the cow community. Afterwards they had drunk champagne intending to celebrate something. Or was it to hide something? Mr Reinhardt had said that they must not grow apart and yet had quarrelled with her about the Common Market and removed her glasses while she was sitting up in bed reading a story of Flaubert. The beginning of the end as she now knew, as she then knew, or did she, or do we, or is there such a thing, or is it another beginning to another ending and on and on.

'Damnation,' Mrs Reinhardt said, and speeded just as she came to where there were a variety of signs with thick arrows and names in navy blue. She had lost her bearings. She took a right and realised at once that she had gone to the east town rather than the main town. So much for distraction. Let him go. The worst was already over. She could see the town cathedral as she glanced behind, and already was looking for a way in which to turn right.

The worst was over, the worst being when the other woman, the girl really, was allowed to wear Mrs Reinhardt's nightdress and necklace. For fun. 'She is young,' he had said. It seemed she was, this rival or rather this replacement. So young that she shouted out of car windows at other motorists, that she carried a big bright umbrella, that she ate chips or cough lozenges on the way to one of these expensive restaurants where Mr Reinhardt took her. All in all she was gamine.

Mrs Reinhardt drove around a walled city and swore at a system of signs that did not carry the name of the mill town she was looking for. There were other things, like a clock, and a bakery and a few strollers and when she pulled into the tree-lined square there was a young man naked to the waist in front of an easel, obviously sketching the cathedral. She spread the map over her knees and opened the door to get a puff of air. He looked at her. She smiled at him. She had to smile at someone. All of a sudden she had an irrational wish to have a son, a son who was with her now, to comfort her, to give her confidence, to take her part. Of course she had a son but he was grown up and had gone to America and knew none of this and must not know any of this.

She need never have gone into that cathedral town but as she said herself, she had seen it, she had seen the young man painting, she had given a little smile and he had smiled back and that was something.

For the rest of the journey she remained alert, she saw trees, gabled houses, a few windmills, she saw dandelions, she passed little towns, she saw washing on the line and she knew that she was going in the right direction.

Her arrival was blessed with magic. Trees, the sound of running water, flowers, wild flowers, and a sense of being in a place that it would take time to know, take time to discover. To make it even more mysterious the apartments were stone chalets scattered at a distance throughout the grounds. It was a complex really but one in which nature dominated. She went down some steps to where it said 'Reception' and, having introduced herself, was asked at once to hurry so as to be served lunch. Finding the dining room was an expedition in itself – up steps, down more steps, and then into a little outer salon where there were round tables covered with lace cloths and on each table a vase of wild flowers. She bent down and smelt some pansies. A pure sweet silken smell, like the texture of childhood. She felt grateful. Her husband was paying for all this and what a pity that like her he was not now going down more steps, past a satin screen, to a table laid for two by an open window, to the accompaniment of running water.

She had a half bottle of champagne, duck pâté and a flat white grilled fish on a bed of thin strips of boiled leek. The hollandaise sauce was perfect and yellower than usual because they had added mustard. She was alone except for the serving girl and an older couple at a table a few yards away. She could not hear what they said. The man was drinking Calvados. The serving girl had a pretty face and brown curly hair tied back with a ribbon. One curl had been brought onto her forehead for effect. She radiated innocence and a dream. Mrs Reinhardt did not look at her for long but thought she has probably never been to Paris, never even been to Nantes but she hopes to go and will go one day. That story was in her eyes, in the curls of her hair, in everything she did. That thirst.

After lunch Mrs Reinhardt was escorted to her chalet. It was down a dusty road with ferns and dock on either side. Wild roses of the palest pink tumbled over the arch of the door and when she stood in her bedroom and looked through one of the narrow turret windows it was these roses and grassland that she saw, while from the other side she could hear the rush of the water and the two images reminded her of herself and of everybody else that she had known. One was green and hushed and quiet and one was torrential. Did they have to conflict with each other? She undressed, she unpacked, she opened the little refrigerator to see what delights were there. There was beer and champagne and miniatures of whisky and Vichy water and red cordial. It was like being a child again and looking into one's little toy house.

She had a little weep. For what did Mrs Reinhardt weep – for beauty, for ugliness, for herself, for her son in America, for Mr Reinhardt who had lost his reason. So badly did Mr Reinhardt love this new girl, Rita, that he had made her take him to meet all her friends so that he could ask them how Rita looked at sixteen, and seventeen, what Rita wore, what Rita was like as a débutante, and why Rita stopped going to art school and then he had made notes of these things. Made an utter fool of himself. Yes she cried for that, and as she cried it seemed to her the tears were like the strata of this earth, had many levels and many layers, and that those layers differed and that now she was crying for more than one thing at the same time, that her tears were all mixed up. She was also crying about age, about two grey ribs in her pubic hair, crying for not having tried harder on certain occasions as when Mr Reinhardt came home expecting excitement or repose and getting instead a typical story about the non-arrival of the gas man. She had let herself be drawn into the weary and hypnotising whirl of domesticity. With her the magazines had to be neat, the dust had to be dusted, all her perfectionism had got thrown into that instead of something larger, or instead of Mr Reinhardt. Where do we go wrong? Is not that what guardian angels are meant to do, to lead us back by the hand?

She cried too because of the night she had thrown a platter at him, and he sat there catatonic, and said that he knew he was wrecking her life and his, but that he could not stop it, said maybe it was madness or the male menopause or anything she wanted to call it, but that it was, what it was, what it was. He had even appealed to her. He told her a story, he told her that very day when he had gone to an auction to buy some pictures for the gallery, he had brought Rita with him and as they drove along the motorway he had hoped that they would crash, so terrible for him was his predicament, and so impossible for him was it to be parted from this girl whom he admitted had made him delirious, but Happy, but Happy, as he kept insisting.

It was this helplessness of human beings that made her cry most of all and when long after, which is to say at sunset, Mrs Reinhardt had dried her eyes, and had put on her oyster dress and her Chinese necklace she was still repeating to herself this matter of helplessness. At the same time she was reminding herself that there lay ahead a life, adventure, that she had not finished, she had merely changed direction and the new road was unknown to her.

She sat down to dinner. She was at a different table. This time she looked out on a lake that was a tableau of prettiness – trees on either side, overhanging branches, green leaves with silver undersides and a fallen bough where ducks perched. The residents were mostly elderly except for one woman with orange hair and studded sunglasses. This woman scanned a magazine throughout the dinner and did not address a word to her escort.

Mrs Reinhardt would look at the view, have a sip of wine, chew a crust of the bread that was so aerated it was like communion wafer. Suddenly she looked to one side and there in a tank with bubbles of water within were several lobsters. They were so beautiful that at first she thought they were mannequin lobsters, ornaments. Their shells had beautiful blue tints, the blue of lapus lazuli, and though their movements had at first unnerved her she began to engross herself in their motion and to forget what was going on around her. They moved beautifully and to such purpose. They moved to touch each other, at least some did, and others waited, were the recipients so to speak of this reach, this touch. Their movements had all the grandeur of speech without the folly. But there was no mistaking their intention.

So caught up was she in this that she did not hear the pretty girl call her out to the phone and in fact she had to be touched on the bare arm which of course made her jump. Naturally she went out somewhat flustered, missed her step and turned, but did not wrench her ankle. It was her weak ankle, the one she always fell on. Going into the little booth she mettled herself. Perhaps he was contrite or drunk, or else there had been an accident, or else their son was getting married. At any rate it was crucial. She said her 'hello' calmly but pertly. She repeated it. It was a strange voice altogether, a man asking for Rachel. She said who is Rachel. There were a few moments of heated irritation and then complete disappointment as Mrs Reinhardt made her way back to her table trembling. Stupid girl to have called her! Only the lobsters saved the occasion.

Now she gave them her full attention. Now, she forgot the mistake of the phone and observed the drama that was going on. A great long lobster seemed to be lord of the tank. His claws were covered with black elastic bands but that did not prevent him from proudly stalking through the water, having frontal battles with some, but chiefly trying to arouse another: a sleeping lobster who was obviously his heart's desire. His appeals to her were mesmerising. He would tickle her with his antennae, he would put claws over her, then edge a claw under her so that he levered her up a fraction and then he would leave her be for an instant only to return with a stronger, with a more telling assault. Of course there were moments when he had to desist, to ward off others who were coming in her region and this he did with the same determination, facing them with eyes that were vicious yet immobile as beads. He would lunge through the water and drive them back or drive them elsewhere and then he would return as if to his love and to his oracle.

There were secondary movements in the tank of course but it was at the main drama Mrs Reinhardt looked. She presumed it was a him and gave him the name of Napoleon. At times so great was his sexual plight that he would lower a long antenna under his rear and touch the little dun bibs of membrane and obviously excite himself so that he could start afresh on his sleeping lady. Because he was in no doubt but that she would succumb. Mrs Reinhardt christened her The Japanese Lady, because of her languor, her refusal to be roused, by him, or by any of them, and Mrs Reinhardt thought oh what a sight it will be when she does rise up and give herself to his embraces, oh what a wedding that will be! Mrs Reinhardt also thought that it was very likely that they would only be in this tank for a short number of hours and that in those hours they must act the play of their lives. Looking at them, with her hands pressed together, she hoped the way children hope for a happy ending to this courtship.

She had to leave the dining room while it was still going on, but in some way she felt with the lights out, and visitors gone, the protagonists safe in their tank, secured by air bubbles, would secretly find each other. She had drunk a little too much, and she swayed slightly as she went down the dusty road to her chalet. She felt elated. She had seen something that moved her. She had seen instinct, she had seen the grope and she had seen the will that refuses to be refused. She had seen tenderness.

In her bedroom she put the necklace into the heart-shaped wicker box and hid it under the bolster of the second bed. She had robbed her husband of it – this beautiful choker of jade. It had been his mother's. It was worth ten thousand pounds. It was her going-away present. She had extracted it from him. Before closing it in the box she bit on the beads as if they were fruits.

'If you give me the necklace I will go away.'

That was what she had said and she knew that in some corner she was thereby murdering his heart. It was his family necklace and it was the one thing in which he believed his luck was invested. Also he was born under the sign of Cancer and if he clung, he clung. It was the thing they shared, and by taking it she was telling him that she was going away for ever, and that she was taking some of him, his talisman, relic of his mother, his relic of their life together. She had now become so involved with this piece of jewellery that when she wore it she touched her throat constantly to make sure that it was there, and when she took it off she kissed it, and at night she dreamed of it, and one night she dreamt that she had tucked it into her vagina for safety, and hidden it there. At other times she thought how she would go to the Casino and gamble it away, his luck and hers. There was a Casino nearby and on the Saturday there was to be a cycling tournament, and she thought that one night, maybe on the Saturday she would go out, and maybe she would gamble and maybe she would win. Soon she fell asleep.

On the third day Mrs Reinhardt decided she would go driving. She needed a change of scene. She needed sea air and crag. She needed invigoration. The little nest was cloying. The quack-quack of the ducks, the running water were all very well but they were beginning to echo her own craving and she did not like that. So after breakfast she read the seventeenth-century Nun's Prayer, the one which asked the Lord to release one from excessive speech, to make one thoughtful but not moody, to give one a few friends, and to keep one reasonably sweet. She thought of Rita. Rita's bright blue eyes, sapphire eyes and the little studs in her ears that matched. Rita was ungainly like a colt. Rita would be the kind of girl who could stay up all night, swim at dawn and then sleep like a baby all through the day even in an unshaded room. Youth.

Yet it so happened that Mrs Reinhardt had found an admirer. The Monsieur who owned the hotel had paid her more than passing attention. In fact she hardly had to turn a corner but he was there, and he would find some distraction to delay her for a moment, so as he could gaze upon her. First it was a hare running through the undergrowth, then it was his dog following some ducks, then it was the electricity van coming to mend the telephone cable. The dreaded telephone. She was pleased that it was out of order. She was also pleased that she was still attractive and there was no denying but that Mrs Reinhardt could bewitch people. It was when judging a young person's art exhibition that he met Rita. Rita's work was the worst, and realising this she had torn it up in a tantrum. He came home and told Mrs Reinhardt and said how sorry he had felt for her but how plucky she had been. It was February the twenty-second. The following day two things happened – he bought several silk shirts and he proposed they go to Paris for a weekend.

'If only I could turn the key on it and close the door and come back when I am an old woman, if only I could do that.' So Mrs Reinhardt said to herself as she drove away from the green nest, from the singing birds and the hovering midges, from the rich hollandaise sauces and the quilted bed, from the overwhelming comfort of it all. Indeed she thought she may have suffocated her husband in the very same way. For though Mrs Reinhardt was cold to others, distant in her relationships with men and women, this was not her true nature, this was something she had built up, a screen of reserve to shelter her fear. She was sentimental at home and used to do a million things for Mr Reinhardt to please him, and to pander to him. She used to warm his side of the bed while he was still undressing, or looking at a drawing he had just bought, or even pacing the room. The pacing had grown more acute. When she knitted his socks in cable stitch she always knitted a third sock in case one got torn, or ruined, while he was fishing or when he hunted in Scotland in August. She went just to be near him though she dreaded these forays. They were too public. House parties of people thrown in upon each other for a hectic and sociable week. The landscape and the grouse were the same wonderful colour – that of rusted metal. The shot birds often seemed to her that they had just lain down in jest so un-dead did they seem. Even the few drops of blood seemed unreal, theatrical. She loved the moors, the rusted colour of farm and brushwood. But the screeches of the dying hares and the dying stags pierced and then haunted her. They were so human. She cried one day up there on the crest of the mountain when those over-human sounds reached her. He saw it but walked on. It was a man's world, it was man's terrain, it was not the place for tears. She blew her nose and walked up. It was a good thing that the wind was so fierce and, also being busy at the hunt, the men were not searching faces for emotion. It was not like sitting down at dinner and flirting and making compliments.

She often thought that the real secret of their love was that she kept the inside of herself permanently warm for him like someone keeping an egg under a nest of straw. When she loved, she loved completely. As a young girl she was using a sewing machine one day and by accident put the needle through her index finger, but she did not call out to her parents who were in the other room, she waited until her mother came through. Upon seeing this casuality her mother let out a scream. Within an instant her father was by her side and with a jerk of the lever he lifted the thing out and gave her such a look, such a loving look. Mrs Reinhardt, was Tilly then, an only daughter, and full of trust. She believed that you loved your mother and father, that you loved your brother, that eventually you loved your husband and then most of all that you loved your children. Her parents had spoilt her, had brought her to the Ritz for birthdays, had left gold trinkets on her pillow on Christmas Eve, had comforted her when she wept. At twenty-one, they had had an expensive portrait done of her and hung it on the wall in a prominent position so that as guests entered they would say, 'Who is that? Who is that?' and a flurry of compliments would follow.

When she turned thirty, her husband had her portrait painted and it was in their sitting room, at that very moment, watching him and Rita, unless he had turned it around, or unless Rita had splashed housepaint over it. Rita was unruly it seemed. Rita's jealousy was more drastic than the occasional submarines of jealousy Mrs Reinhardt had experienced in their seventeen years of marriage – then it was over women, roughly her own age, women with poise, women with husbands, women with guile, women who made a career of straying but were back in their own homes by six o'clock. Being jealous of Rita was a more abstract thing – they had only met once and that was on the steps of a theatre. Rita had followed him there, ran up the steps, handed him a note and ran off again. Being jealous of Rita was being jealous of youth, of freedom and of spontaneity. Rita did not want marriage or an engagement ring. She wanted to go to Florence, she wanted to go to a ball, to go to the park on roller skates. Rita had a temper. Once at one of her father's soirées she threw twenty gold chairs out of the window. If they had had a daughter things might now be different. Or if their son lived at home, things might now be different. Four people might have sat down at a white table, under a red umbrella, looked out at a brown lake, whose colour was dunned by the overhanging trees and saplings. There might be four glasses, one with coca cola, one or maybe two with whiskey and hers with white wine and soda water. A young voice might say, 'What is that?' pointing to a misshapen straw basket on a wooden plinth in the middle of the lake and as she turned her attention to discern what it was, and as she decided that it was either a nest of swans or ducks the question would be repeated with a touch of impatience – 'Mam, what is that?' and Mrs Reinhardt might be answering. Oh my, yes, the family tableau smote her.

So transported back was she, to the hotel, and a united family, that Mrs Reinhardt was like a sleepwalker traversing the rocks that were covered with moss, and then the wet sand between the rocks. She was making her way towards the distant crags. On the sand there lay caps of seaweed so green, and so shaped like the back of a head that they were like theatrical wigs. She looked down at one, she bent to pore over its greenness and when she looked up, he was there. A man in his mid-twenties in a blue shirt with lips parted, seemed to be saying something pleasant to her, though perhaps it was only hello, or hi there. He had an American accent. Had they met in a cocktail bar or at an airport lounge, it is doubtful that they would have spoken but here the situation called for it. One or other had to express or confirm admiration for the sea, the boats, the white houses on the far side, the whiteness of the light, the vista; and then quite spontaneously he had to grip her wrist and said 'Look, look,' as a bird dived down into the water, swooped up again, re-dived until he came up with a fish.

'A predator,' Mrs Reinhardt said, his hand still on her wrist, casually. They argued about the bird, she said it was a gannet and he said it was some sort of hawk. She said sweetly that she knew more about wild life than he did. He conceded. He said if you came from Main Street, Iowa, you knew nothing, you were a hick. They laughed.

As they walked back along the shore he told her how he had been staying further up with friends and had decided to move on because one never discovers anything except when alone. He'd spend a night or two and then move on and eventually he would get to Turkey. He wasn't doing a grand tour or a gastronomic tour, he was just seeing the wild parts of Brittany and had found a hotel on the other side that was hidden from everybody. 'The savage side,' he said.

By the time she had agreed to have a crêpe with him they had exchanged those standard bits of information. He confessed that he didn't speak much French. She confessed that she'd taken a crammer course and was even thinking of spending three months in Paris to do a cookery course. When they went indoors she removed her headscarf and he was caught at once by the beauty of her brown pile of hair. Some hidden urge of vanity made her toss it, as they looked for a table.

'Tell me something,' he said, 'are you married or not?'

'Yes and no . . .' She had removed her wedding ring and put it in the small leather box that snapped when one shut it.

He found that intriguing. Quickly she explained that she had been but was about not to be. He reached out but did not touch her and she thought that there was something exquisite in that, that delicate indication of sympathy. He said quietly how he had missed out on marriage and on kids. She felt that he meant it. He said he had been a wild cat and whenever he had met a nice girl he had cheated on her, and lost her. He could never settle down.

'I'm bad news,' he said and laughed, and there was something so impish about him that Mrs Reinhardt was being won over.

On closer acquaintance she had to admit that his looks were indeed flawless. So perhaps his character was not as terrible as he had made out. She used to press him to tell her things, boyish things like his first holiday in Greece, or his first girl, or his first guitar and gradually she realised she was becoming interested in these things although in them there was nothing new. It was the warmth really and the way he delighted in telling her these things that made Mrs Reinhardt ask for more stories. She was like someone who has been on a voyage and upon return wants to hear everything that has happened on land. He told her that he had made a short film that he would love her to see. He would fly home for it that night if only he could! It was a film about motor-cycling and he had made it long before anyone else had made a film about it, or written a book about it. He told her some of the stories. Scenes at dusk in a deserted place when a man gets a puncture and says, 'What the hell does it matter . . .' as he sits down to take a smoke. She sensed a purity in him alongside everything else. He loved the desert, he loved the prairie but yes he had lived on women, and he had drank a lot and he had slept rough and he had smoked every kind of weed under the sun, and he wished he had known Aldous Huxley, that Aldous Huxley had been his dad.

'Still searching,' he said.

'It's the fashion now,' she said a little drily.

'Hey, let's get married,' he said, and they clapped hands and both pretended it was for real. Both acted a little play and it was the very same as if someone had come into the room and said, 'Do it for real kids.'

In jest, their cheeks met, in jest, their fingers interlocked, in jest, their knuckles mashed one another's and in jest they stood up, moved onto the small dance area and danced as closely as Siamese twins might to the music from the juke box. In jest, or perhaps not, Mrs Reinhardt felt through the beautiful folds of her oyster dress the press of his sexuality and round and round and round they danced, the two jesting betrothed people, who were far from home and who had got each other into such a spin of excitement. How thrilling it was and how rejuvenating to dance round and round and feel the strength and the need of this man pushing closer and closer to her while still keeping her reserve. On her face the most beautiful ecstatic smile. She was smiling for herself. He did slide his other hand in her buttock, but Mrs Reinhardt just shrugged it off. The moment the dancing stopped they parted.

Soon after they sat down she looked at her tiny wrist-watch, peered at it, and at once he flicked on his blue plastic lighter so that she could read the tiny black insect-like hands. Then he held the lighter in front of her face to admire her, to admire the eyes, the long nose, the sensual mouth, the necklace.

'Real,' he said, picking up the green beads that she herself had become so involved with and had been so intimate with.

'Think so,' she said and regretted it instantly.

After all the world did abound in thieves and rogues and ten thousand pounds was no joke to be carrying around. She had read of women such as she, who took up with men, younger men, or older men, only to be robbed, stripped of their possessions, bled. She curdled within and suddenly invented for herself a telephone call back at the hotel. When she excused herself he rose chivalrously, escorted her through the door, down the steps and across the gravel path to the car park. They did not kiss goodnight.

*　　　*　　　*

In the morning the world was clean and bright. There had been rain and everything got washed, the water mills, the ducks, the roses, the trees, the lupins and the little winding paths. The little winding paths of course were strewn with white, pink and pale blue blossom. The effect was as of seeing snow when she opened the windows, leaned out and broke a rose that was still damp and whose full smell had not been restored yet. Its smell was smothered by the smell of rain and that too was beautiful. And so were her bare breasts resting on the window ledge. And so was life, physical well-being, one's own body, roses, encounter, promise, the dance.

She drew back quickly when she saw that there Monsieur was down below, idly hammering a few nails into a wall. He seemed to be doing this to make a trellis for the roses but he was in no hurry as he looked in her direction. He had a knack of finding her no matter where she was. The night before as she drove back late he was in the car park to say that they had kept her a table for dinner. He had brought a spare menu in his pocket. The big black dog looked up too. Somehow her own whiteness and the milk-likeness of her breasts contrasted with the blackness of the dog and she saw them detached, yet grouped together in a very beautiful painting, opposites, one that was long and black with a snout, and one that was white and global like a lamp. She liked that picture and would add it to the pictures that she had seen during the years she sleepwalked. She sleepwalked no longer. Life was like that, you dreamed a lot, or you cried a lot, or you itched a lot, and then it disappeared and something else came in its place.

Mrs Reinhardt dawdled. She put on one dress then another, she lifted a plate ashtray and found a swarm of little ants underneath, she took sparkling mineral water from the refrigerator, drank it, took two of her iron tablets and by a process of association pulled her lower eyelid down to see if she was still anaemic. She realised something wonderful. For whatever number of minutes it had been, she had not given a thought to Mr Reinhardt and this was the beginning of recovery. That was how it happened, one forgot for two minutes and remembered for twenty. One forgot for three minutes and remembered for fifteen but as with a pendulum the states of remembering and the states of forgetting were gradually equalised and then one great day the pendulum had gone over and the states of forgetting had gained a victory.

What more did a woman want? Mrs Reinhardt danced around the room, leapt over her bed, threw a pillow in the air and felt as alive and gay as the day she got engaged and knew she would live happily ever after. What more did a woman want? She wanted this American although he might be a bounder. He might not. She would have him but in her own time and to suit her own requirements. She would not let him move into her hotel apartment because the privacy of it was sacred. In fact she was beginning to enjoy herself. Think of it, she could have coffee at noon instead of at nine thirty, she could eat an éclair, she could pluck her eyebrows, she could sing high notes and low notes, she could wander.

'Freedom!' Mrs Reinhardt told the lovely supple woman in the flowered dressing gown who smiled into the long mirror while the other Mrs Reinhardt told the lovely woman that the mirabelle she had drank the night before was still swishing through her brain.

After breakfast she walked in the woods. Crossing a little plaited bridge she took off her sandals and tiptoed so as not to disturb the sounds and activities of nature. It was the darkest wood she had ever entered. All the trees twined overhead so that it was a vault with layer upon layer of green. Ferns grew in wizard abundance and between the ferns other things strove to be seen while all about were the butterflies and the insects. Mushrooms and toadstools flourished at the base of every tree and she knelt down to smell them. She loved their dank smell. The air was pierced with birdsong of every note and every variety as the birds darted across the ground, or swooped up into the air. This fecundity of nature, this chorus of birds and the distant cooing of the doves from the dovecote thrilled her and presently something else quickened her desires. The low, suggestive, all-desiring whistle of a male reached her ears. She had almost walked over him. He could see her bare legs under her dress. She drew back.

He was lying down with his shirt open. He did not rise to greet her.

'You,' she said.

He put up his foot in salutation. She stood over him trying to decide whether his presence was a welcome or an intrusion.

'Amazing,' he said and held his hands out, acceding to the abundance of nature about him. He apologised for his presence but said that he had cycled over to see her just to say hello, he had brought her some croissants hot from the oven but that upon hearing she was sleeping he decided to have a ramble in the woods. He had fed the croissants to the birds. He used some French words to impress her and she laughed and soon her crossness was washed away. After all, they were not her woods, and he had not knocked on her bedroom door, and she would have been disappointed if he had cycled off without seeing her. She spread her dress like a cushion underneath her and sat folding her legs to the other side.

It was then they talked. They talked for a long time. They talked of courage, the different courage of men and women. The courage when a horse bolts, or the car in front of one just crashes, the gnawing courage of every day. She said men were never able to say 'finito'. 'Damn right,' he said and the jargon struck her as comic compared with the peace and majesty of the woods.

'You smell good,' he would sometimes say and that too belonged to another environment but for the most part he impressed her with his sincerity and with the way he took his time to say the thing he wanted to say. Before the week was out she would lead him to her bed. It would be dark and it would be unexpected, an invitation tossed at the very last minute as when someone takes a flower or a handkerchief and throws it into the bullring. She would be unabashed, as she had not been for years.

They stayed for about an hour, talking, and at times one or other would get up, walk or run towards the little bridge and pretend to take a photograph. Eventually they got up together and went to find his bicycle. He insisted that she cycle. After the first few wobbles she rode down the path and could hear him clapping. Then she got off, turned round and rode back towards him. He said that next time she would have to stay on the bicycle while turning around and she biffed him and said she had not ridden for years. Her face was flushed and bicycle oil had got on her skirt. For fun he sat her on the bar of the bicycle, put his leg across and they set off down the avenue at a dizzying speed, singing Daisy Daisy give me your answer do, I'm half crazy, all for the love of you . . .

He would not stop even though she swore that she was going to fall off any minute.

'You're OK . . .' he'd say as he turned the next corner. In a while she began to stop screaming and enjoyed the swoon in her stomach.

Mrs Reinhardt stood in the narrow shower, the disc of green soap held under one armpit when she saw a rose branch being waved into the room. As in a mirage the petals randomly fell. Which of them was it? Him or Monsieur? She was feeling decidedly amorous. He climbed in through the window and came directly to her. He did not speak. He gripped her roughly, his own clothing still on, and he was so busy taking possession of her that he did not realise that he was getting drenched. The shower was full on, yet neither of them bothered to turn it off. The zip of his trousers hurt her but he was mindless of that. The thing is he had desired her from the very first, and now he was pumping all his arrogance and all his cockatooing into her and she was taking it gladly, also gluttonously. She was recovering her pride as a woman, and much more as a desirable woman. It was this she had sorely missed in the last ten months. Yet she was surprised by herself, surprised by her savage need to get even with life, or was it to get healed? She leaned against the shower wall, wet and slippery all over and lolled so that every bit of her was partaking him. She did not worry about him, though he did seem in quite a frenzy both to prove himself and please her, and he kept uttering the vilest of words calling her sow and dog and bitch and so forth. She even thought that she might conceive so radical was it and the only other thought that came to her was of the lobsters and the lady lobster lying so still while all the others crawled over her.

When he came she refused to claim to be satisfied and with a few rough strokes insisted he fill her again and search for her every crevice. This all happened without speech except for the names he muttered as she squeezed from him the juices he did not have left to give. She was certainly getting her own back.

Afterwards she washed and as he lay on the bathroom floor out of breath she stepped over him and went to her room to rest. She felt like a queen and lying on her bed her whole body was like a ship decked out with beauty. A victory! She had locked the bedroom door. Let him wait, let him sweat. She would join him for dinner. She had told him so in French knowing it would doubly confound him. She went to sleep ordering herself pleasant dreams, coloured dreams, the colours of sunlight and of lightning, yellow sun and saffron lightning.

He kept the dinner appointment. Mrs Reinhardt saw him from a landing, down in the little salon where there were lace tablecloths and the vases of wild flowers. She remembered it from her first day. He was drinking a Pernod. It was almost dark down there except for the light from the table candles. It was a somewhat sombre place. The drawings on the wall were all of monks or ascetics and nailed to a cross of wood was a bird; it seemed to be a dead pheasant. He was wearing green, a green silk dinner jacket – had she not seen it somewhere? Yes, it had been on display in the little hotel showcase where they also sold jewellery and beachwear.

The moment she went to his table she perceived the change in him. The good-natured truant boy had given way to the slightly testy seducer and he did not move a chair or a muscle as she sat down. He called to Michele, the girl with the curly hair, to bring another Pernod, in fact to bring two. Mrs Reinhardt thought that it was just a ruse and that he was proving to her what a man of the world he was. She said she had slept well.

'Where's your loot,' he said, looking at her neck. She had left it in her room and was wearing pearls instead. She did not answer but merely held up the paperback book to show that she had been reading.

'You read that?' he said. It was D. H. Lawrence. 'I haven't read that stuff since I was twelve.'

He was drunk. It augured badly. She wondered if she should dismiss him there and then but as on previous occasions when things got very bad Mrs Reinhardt became very stupid, became inept. He gave the waitress a wink and gripped her left hand where she was wearing a bracelet.

She moved off as languidly as always.

'You're a doll,' he said.

'She doesn't speak English,' Mrs Reinhardt said.

'She speaks my kind of English,' he said.

It was thus in a state of anger, pique and agitation that they went in to dinner. As he studied the four menus he decided on the costliest one and said it was a damn good thing that she was a rich bitch.

'Rich bitch,' he said and laughed.

She let it pass. He said how about taking him to Pamplona for the bullfights and then went into a rhapsody about past fights and past bullfighters.

'Oh, you read it in Ernest Hemingway,' she said, unable to resist a sting.

'Oh, we've got a hot and cold lady,' he said as he held the big wine list in front of him. The lobster tank was gapingly empty. There were only three lobsters in there and those lay absolutely still. Perhaps they were shocked from the raid and were lying low, not making a stir so as not to be seen. She was on the verge of tears. He ordered a unique bottle of wine. It meant the girl getting Monsieur, who then had to get his key and go to the cellar and ceremoniously bring it back and show the label and open it and decant it and wait. The waitress had changed clothes because she was going to the cycle tournament. Her black pina-fore was changed for a blue dress with colours in the box pleats. She looked idyllic. Ready for showers of kisses and admiration.

'How would you like me to fuck you?' he said to her as she watched Monsieur pouring the wine.

'You have gone too far,' Mrs Reinhardt said, and perhaps fearing that she might make a scene he leaned over to her and said, 'Don't worry, I'll keep you.'

She excused herself, more for the waitress, than for him and hurried out. Never in all her life was Mrs Reinhardt so angry. She sat on the hammock in the garden and asked the stars and the lovely hexagonal lamps and the sleeping ducks to please succour her in this nightmare. She thought of the bill, and the ludicrous jacket, as she realised, also on her bill, and she cried like a very angry child who was unable to tell anyone what had happened. Her disgrace was extreme. She swung back and forth in the hammock cursing and swearing, then praying for patience. The important thing was never to have to see him again. She was shivering and in a state of shock by the time she went to her room. She really went to put on a cardigan and to order a sandwich or soup. There he was in her dressing gown. He had quit dinner he said, being as she so rudely walked out. He too was about to order a sandwich. The fridge door was open and as she entered he clicked it closed. Obviously he had drunk different things and she could see that he was wild. He was not giving this up, this luxury, this laissez-faire. He rose up and staggered.

'Round one,' he said and caught her.

'Get out of here,' she said.

'Not me, I'm for the licks.'

Mrs Reinhardt knew with complete conviction that she was about to be the witness to and participant in the most sordid kind of embroilment. Alacrity took hold of her and she thought, coax him, seem mature, laugh, divert him. But seeing the craze in his eyes, instinct made her resort to stronger measures and the scream she let out was astounding even to her own ears. It was no more than seconds until Monsieur was in the room grappling with him.

She realised that he had been watching all along and that he had been prepared for this in a way that she was not. Monsieur was telling him in French to get dressed and to get lost. It had some elements of farce.

'OK, OK,' he was saying. 'Just let me get dressed, just let me get out of this asshole.' She was glad of the language barrier. Then an ugly thing happened, the moment Monsieur let go of him he used a dirty trick. He picked up the empty champagne bottle and wielded it at his opponent's head. Suddenly the two of them were in a clinch and Mrs Reinhardt searched in her mind to know what was best to do. She picked up a chair but her action was like someone in slow motion, because while they were forcing each other onto the ground she was holding the chair and not doing anything with it. It was the breaking bottle she dreaded most of all. By then her hand had been on the emergency bell and as they both fell to the floor the assistant chef came in with a knife. He must have dashed from the kitchen. These two men were of course able to master the situation and when he got up he was shaking his head like a boxer who has been badly punched. He said he always hated frogs.

Monsieur suggested that she leave and go over to Reception and wait there. As she left the room he gave her his jacket. Walking down the little road her body shook like jelly. The jacket kept slipping off. She was conscious of just having escaped indescribable horror. Horror such as one reads of. She realised how sheltered her life had been but this was no help. What she really wanted was to sit with someone and talk about anything. The hotel lounge was propriety itself. Another young girl, also with a rose in her hair, was slowly preparing a tray of drinks. A party of Dutch people sat in a corner, the dog snapped at some flies and from the other room the strains of music as there was a wedding in progress. Mrs Reinhardt sat in a deep leather chair and let all those pleasant things lap over her. She could hear speeches and clapping and then the sweet and lovely strains of the accordion and though she could not explain to herself why, these sounds made her feel enormously safe, made her feel as if perhaps she was getting married and she realised that that was the nice aftermath of shock. She reckoned that by now they would have got rid of him, and wondered foolishly if he would have to hitch-hike to his own hotel.

The principal excitement next morning was the birth of seven baby ducks. The little creatures had been plunged into the brown rushing water while a delighted audience looked on. Other ducks sat curled up on stones, sulking perhaps since they were so ignored in favour of a proud mother and these little daft naked creatures. The doves too fanned their tails in utter annoyance while everyone looked towards the water and away from them. She sat and sipped coffee.

Monsieur sat a little away from her dividing his admiration between her and the baby ducks. He flaked bread between his hands then opened the sliding door and pitched it out. Then he would look at her and smile. Speech was beyond him. He had fallen in love with her, or was infatuated, or was pretending to be infatuated. One of these things. Maybe he was just salvaging her pride. Yet the look was genuinely soft, even adoring. His swallow was affected, his cheeks were as red as the red poppies, and he did little things like wind his watch or rearrange the tops of his socks all for her benefit.

Once he put his hand on her shoulder to alert her to some new minutiae of the ducks' behaviour and he pressed achingly on her flesh.

'If Madame were to find out!' she thought and shuddered at the prospect of any further unpleasantness. She did not ask about the bounder but she did ask later for a glance at her bill and there indeed was the veston, the gentleman's veston for sixteen hundred francs. After breakfast she sat out on the lawn and observed the behaviour of the other ducks. They passed their time very amiably she thought, they doze a lot, then scratch or clean themselves, then re-doze, then have a little waddle and perhaps stretch themselves but she doubted that a duck walked more than a furlong throughout its whole life.

Then on beautiful crested hotel notepaper she wrote to her son. She deliberately wrote a blithe letter, a letter about ducks, trees and nature. Two glasses with the sucked crescent of an orange in each one were laid in an alcove in the wall and she described this to him and thought that soon she would be indulgent and order a champagne cocktail. She did not say. 'Your father and I have separated.' She would say it later when the pain was not quite so acute, and when it did not matter so much. When would that be? Mrs Reinhardt looked down at the cushion she was sitting on, and saw that it was a hundred per cent Fibranne, and as far as she was concerned that was the only thing in the world she could be absolutely sure of.

*   *   *

Going back to her room before lunch she decided to put on a georgette dress and her beads. She owed it to Monsieur. She ought to look nice even if she could not smile. She ought to pretend to and by pretending she might become that person. All the burning thoughts and all the recent wounds might just lie low in her and she could appear to be as calm and unperturbed as a summer lake with its water-lily leaves and its starry flowers. Beneath the surface the carp that no-one would cast down for. Monsieur's tenderness meant a lot to her, it meant she was still a person to whom another person bestowed attention, even love.

'Poor lobsters,' she thought and remembered those beseeching moves. When she opened the heart-shaped box in which the beads were hidden Mrs Reinhardt let out a shriek. Gone. Gone. Her talisman, her life insurance, her last link with her husband Harold gone. Their one chance of being reunited. Gone. She ran back the road to the Reception. She was wild. Madame was most annoyed at being told that such a valuable thing had been so carelessly left lying around. As for theft she did not want to hear of such a thing. It was a vulgarity, was for a different kind of premises altogether, not for her beautiful three-star establishment. She ran a perfect place which was her pride and joy and which was a bower against the outside world. How dare it, the outside world, come into her province? Monsieur's face dissolved in deeper and deeper shades of red and a most wretched expression. He did not say a word. Madame said of course it was the visitor, the American gentleman, and there was no knowing what else he had taken. As far as Madame was concerned the dregs of the earth had come into her nest and though it was a small movement it was a telling one, when she picked up a vase of flowers, put them down in another place, and put them down so that the water splashed out of them and stained the account she was preparing. This led to greater vexation. It was a moment of utter terseness and poor Monsieur could help neither of them. He pulled the dog's ear.

Mrs Reinhardt must ring her husband. She had to. There in full view of them, while Madame scratched figures onto the page and Monsieur pulled the dog's ear, Mrs Reinhardt said to her husband Harold in England that her beads had been stolen, that his beads had been stolen, that their beads had been stolen, and she began to cry. He was no help at all. He asked if they could be traced and she said she doubted it.

'A case of hit and run,' she said, hoping he would know what she meant. Perhaps he did because his next remark was that she seemed to be having an eventful time. She said she was in a bad way and she prayed to God that he would say 'come home'. He didn't. He said he would get in touch with the insurance people.

'Oh fuck the insurance people,' Mrs Reinhardt said and slammed the phone down. Monsieur turned away. She walked out the door. There was not a friend in the world.

Mrs Reinhardt experienced one of those spells that can unsettle one for ever. The world became black. A blackness permeated her heart. It was like rats scraping at her brain. It was pitiless. Phrases such as 'how are you', or 'I love you', or 'dear one', were mockery incarnate. The few faces of the strange people around her assumed the masks of animals. The world she stood up in, and was about to fall down in, was green and pretty but in a second it would be replaced by a bottomless pit into which Mrs Reinhardt was about to fall for eternity. She fainted.

They must have attended to her because when she came to, her court shoes were removed, the buttons of her blouse were undone and there was a warm cup of tisane on a stool beside her.

A presence had just vanished. Or a ghost. Had just slipped away. She thought it was a woman and perhaps it was her mother anointing her with ashes and she thought it was Ash Wednesday. 'Because I do not hope to live again,' she said but fortunately no-one seemed to understand. She sat up, sipped the hot tea, apologised about the necklace and about the scene she had made. She was uncertain how far she had gone. King Lear's touching of the robe of Cordelia sprung to mind and she asked God if the dead could in fact live again, if she could witness the miracle that the three apostles witnessed when they came and saw the stone rolled away from Christ's grave.

'Come back,' she whispered and it was as if she was taking her own hand and leading herself back to life. The one that led was her present self and the one that was being led was a small child who loved God, loved her parents, loved her husband, loved the trees, and the countryside, and had never wanted anything to change. Her two selves stood in the middle, teetering. These were extreme moments for Mrs Reinhardt and had she succumbed to them she would have strayed indeed. She asked for water. The tumbler she was holding went soft beneath her grip and the frightened child in her felt a memory as of shedding flesh, but the woman in her smiled and assured everyone that the crisis had passed which indeed it had. She lay back for a while and listened to the running water as it dashed and re-dashed against the jet-black millstone, and she resolved that by afternoon she would go away and bid goodbye to this episode that had had in it enchantment, revenge, shame, and the tenderness from Monsieur.

As she drove away, he came from behind the tree-house bearing a small bunch of fresh pansies. They were multi-coloured but the two predominant colours were yellow and maroon. They smelt like young skin and had that same delicacy. Mrs Reinhardt loved him and valued the moment. It was like an assuage. She smiled into his face, their eyes met, for him too it was a moment of real happiness, fleeting but real, a moment of good.

The new hotel was on a harbour and for the second time in four days she walked over boulders that were caked with moss. At her feet the bright crops of seaweed that again looked like theatre wigs but this time she saw who was before and behind her. She was fully in control. What maddened her was that women did as she did all the time and that their pride was not stripped from them, nor their jewellery. Or perhaps they kept it a secret. One had to be so cunning, so concealed.

Looking out along the bay at the boats, the masts, and the occasional double sails, she realised that now indeed her new life had begun, a life of adjustment and change. Life with a question mark. Your ideal of human life is? she asked herself. The answer was none. It had always been her husband, their relationship, his art gallery, their cottage in the country, and plans. One thing above all others came to her mind and it was the thousands of flower petals under the hall carpet which she had put there for pressing. Those pressed flowers were the moments of their life and what would happen to them – they would lie there for years or else they would be swept away. She could see them there, thousands of sweet bright petals, mementoes of their hours. Before her walk she had been reading Ruskin, reading of the necessary connection between beauty and morality, but it had not touched her. She wanted someone to love. As far as she was concerned Ruskin's theories were fine sermons but that is not what the heart wants. She must go home soon, and get a job. She must try. Mrs Reinhardt ran, got out of breath, stood to look at the harbour, re-ran and by an effort of will managed to extricate herself from the rather melancholy state she was in.

During dinner the head waiter would come, between each of the beautiful courses, and ask how she liked them. One was a fish terrine, its colours summery, white, pink, green, the colours of nature. She would love to learn how to make it. Then she had dressed crab, and even the broken-off claws had been dusted with flour and baked for a moment so that the effect was the same as of smelling warm bread. Everything was right and everything was bright. The little potted plant on the table was a bright cherry pink, robins darted in and out of the dark trees and the ornamental plates in a glass cupboard had patterns of flowers and trelliswork.

'A gentleman to see you,' the younger waiter said.

Mrs Reinhardt froze, the bounder was back. Like a woman ready for battle she put down her squashed napkin and stalked out of the room. She had to turn a corner to enter the main hall and there sitting on one of the high-backed Spanish-type chairs was her husband, Mr Reinhardt. He stood up at once and they shook hands formally like an attorney and his client at an auspicious meeting. 'He has come to sue me,' she thought, 'because of the necklace.' She did not say why have you come? He looked tired. Mrs Reinhardt flinched when she heard that he had taken a private plane. He had been to the other hotel and had motored over. He refused a drink and would not look at her.

He was mulling over his attack. She was convinced that she was about to be shot when he put his hand in his pocket and drew the thing out. She did not mind being shot but thought irrationally of the mess on the beautiful Spanish furniture.

'They found it,' he said as he produced the necklace and laid it on the table between them. It lay like a snake as in a painting, coiled in order to strike. Yet the sight of it filled her with tears and she blubbered out about the bounder, and how she had met him and how he had used her and suddenly she realised that she was telling him something that he had no inkling of.

'The maid took them,' he said and she saw the little maid with the brown curly hair dressed for the tournament and now she could have plucked her tongue out, for having divulged the tale of the bounder.

'Was she sacked?' she asked.

He did not know. He thought not.

'Fine place they have,' he said, referring to the lake and the windmills.

'This also is lovely,' she said and went on to talk about the view from the dining room, and the light which was so searing, so white, so unavoidable. Just like their predicament. In a minute he would get up and go. If only she had not told him about the bounder. If only she had let him say why he had come. She had closed the last door.

'How have you been?' he said.

'Well,' she said, but the nerve in her lower jaw would not keep still and without intending it and without in any way wanting it to happen Mrs Reinhardt burst into tears, much to the astonishment of the young waiter who was waiting to take an order, as he thought, for a drink.

'He tried to blackmail me,' she said and then immediately denied it.

Her husband was looking at her very quietly and she was not sure if there was any sympathy left in him. She thought, 'If he walks out now it will be catastrophic,' and again she thought of the few lobsters who were left in the tank and who were motionless with grief.

'There is us and there is people like him,' Mr Reinhardt said, and though she had not told the whole story he sensed the gravity of it. He said that if she did not mind he would stay and that since he was hungry and since it was late might they not go in to dinner. She looked at him and her eyes were probably drenched.

'Us and people like him!' she said.

Mr Reinhardt nodded.

'And Rita?' Mrs Reinhardt said.

He waited. He looked about. He was by no means at ease.

'She is one of us,' he said and then qualified it. 'Or she could be, if she meets the right man.'

His expression warned Mrs Reinhardt to pry no further. She linked him as they went in to dinner.

The wind rustled through the chimney and some soot fell on a bouquet of flowers. She saw that. She heard that. She squeezed his arm. They sat opposite. When the wind roars, when the iron catches rattle, when the very window panes seem to shiver, then wind and sea combine, then dogs begin to howl and the oncoming storm has a whiff of the supernatural. What does one do, what then does a Mrs Reinhardt do? One reaches out to the face that is opposite, that one loves, that one hates, that one fears, that one has been betrayed by, that one half knows, that one longs to touch and and be reunited with, at least for the duration of a windy night. And by morning who knows? Who knows anything anyhow.